Heart of Glass

A-List novels by Zoey Dean:

THE A-LIST

GIRLS ON FILM

BLONDE AMBITION

TALL COOL ONE

BACK IN BLACK

SOME LIKE IT HOT

AMERICAN BEAUTY

HEART OF GLASS

Heart of Glass

An A-List Novel

by
Zoey Dean

 LITTLE, BROWN AND COMPANY
New York ᛫ Boston

Little, Brown and Company

Hachette Book Group USA
237 Park Avenue, New York, NY 10017
Visit our Web site at www.lb-teens.com

First Edition: April 2007

The characters and events in this book are fictitious. Any similarity to real
persons, living or dead, is coincidental and not intended by the author.

ALLOYENTERTAINMENT   Produced by Alloy Entertainment
                      151 West 26th Street, New York, NY 10001

ISBN-10: 0-316-01096-0
ISBN-13: 978-0-316-01096-2

10 9 8 7 6 5 4 3 2

CWO

Printed in the United States of America

When people say, "She's got everything,"
I've got one answer: I haven't had tomorrow.

—Elizabeth Taylor

Get the Flipping Cuffs, Okay?

"*Calculate This!*'" Anna Percy read the title page of the script she was holding. "'A zany comedy about a socially inept loner who invents a gorgeous female robotic math wizard.'"

"Write, 'Defines a new low in the art of screenwriting, suitable only for fireplace kindling,' and move on," her friend Sam Sharpe advised.

Anna and Sam were sprawled on a pale blue couch. To their left, a wall of floor-to-ceiling windows offered a stunning view of white sand beach and softly rolling waves, while the living room itself had been decorated in sea foam and cerulean, as if to bring the ocean itself into the living spaces. Between them on the floor was a huge pile of movie scripts. It was their job to read them all.

"That doesn't really seem fair," Anna mused, her back to the windows. "I mean, we're getting paid to write our evaluation. By your father."

Their original plan for the summer had been to work as interns on Sam's father's film, *Ben-Hur,* a remake of the classic. But when they'd realized that would mean commuting an hour each way to Palmdale to arrive in time for the shooting (which started promptly every morning at 6 A.M.), they'd politely decided to be script readers for Jackson's production company, Action Jackson Productions.

"Look, we just graduated from high school and we're young and ambitious, so whatever. Reading scripts is just something to do for the summer. And you never know: maybe I'll find the right one that will launch my professional directing career. Who needs film school?" Sam scoffed. She swung her feet up onto the couch and stretched out.

Anna knew that Sam wanted to be a director. Not a popcorn, *Snakes on a Plane*–type director, either. A serious director. In fact, Sam had directed a number of student films that were really good. Not only that, her father was America's Most Beloved Action Hero, Jackson Sharpe, which meant she had both industry access and financial backing should she ever find her Perfect Script. Sam Sharpe was well connected.

Before Anna moved from New York to Beverly Hills this past January to live with her father and finish school at Beverly Hills High School, the film industry was the furthest thing from her mind. She had zero interest in celebrities and red carpet premieres, but living in California and being Sam's friend meant that the industry—everyone in Los Angeles called the film and TV business "the industry"—was the expensive and designer water in which she swam.

But no matter. In the fall, she'd be going to Yale, with the intent of studying serious literature. For the next two months, until she headed to New Haven, she could do pretty much whatever she wanted to do. Unfortunately, she hadn't yet figured out exactly what that was.

Sam reached for her iBook and read aloud as she typed in her evaluation of the script she'd just finished.

"*'Burnt Toast* by Norman Shnorman. Logline: A former bikini model moves to Wyoming, becomes a cook, and falls for the sheriff's quirky, intellectual son. Recommendation: Use script to line bottom of birdcage, then ban Norman Shnorman from film industry for life.'"

"That's kind of harsh, Sam. You didn't even read the whole thing."

"Read ten pages and skimmed the next ninety-seven, which, trust me, is more than Norman deserves." Sam stretched and rubbed the back of her neck. "You don't seem to understand how this town works, Anna. Every geek boy who goes to film school writes a screenplay the day after he graduates. And what do they write about? Themselves and their geek-boy fantasies."

"Well, if other geek boys grow up to run studios and direct movies, then the scripts might be right up their alley," Anna pointed out, flipping over the title page to *Calculate This!* and skimming the first page. "It says here the brooding loner has 'dashing good looks.'"

"That's called geek-boy wishful thinking." Sam pushed her laptop aside. "So sad, but probably true.

And all the more reason that I'm going to be a ground-breaking director. Fuck the geek-boy Hollywood network." She seemed to shift gears as she rose and tugged Anna up from the plush sofa. "We've been at this for hours. Let's ask the cook to fire up some fettuccini Alfredo with shaved truffles—or chili burgers, depending on whether you're in the mood—then walk up the beach, watch the fireworks, and celebrate truth, justice, and the American way. But let's change into something ridiculously hot now so that we don't have to do it before we go meet Eduardo and Caine at House of Blues. Have you seen my flip-flops?"

It still felt strange to Anna when someone said Caine Manning's name as if there were an Anna-and-Caine—as in, a couple. Probably because she'd spent her entire time in Los Angeles as an on-again, off-again part of Anna-and-Ben, as in, Anna and Ben Birnbaum. A couple. Ben Birnbaum. Her first love. Her only love. Her—

No. She wasn't going to get caught in that trap. That was then, this was now.

She caught sight of her reflection in the antique, gold-plated mirror that hung over a thick mahogany bookcase filled with movie scripts in the corner of the room and eyed herself quizzically. Straight blond hair, no makeup, broken-in faded Levi's and her favorite battered green Calvin Klein T-shirt. She liked what she saw, though she knew she was more New York City chic than Los Angeles lollipop.

"Where the hell did I put those flip-flops?" Sam dropped to her knees to look under the couch.

"Probably wherever you last put them."

Anna smiled. On paper, she and Sam Sharpe were the oddest of friends. Sam was spoiled, popular, and dramatic—her grandparents had been strictly working-class Lakewood until Jackson Sharpe found his affinity for the movie camera twenty years earlier, and the money came rolling in. Anna's family, on the other hand, had been privileged since the Gilded Age. Sam read scripts. Anna read books. Sam was temperamental. Anna had been raised to be even-tempered. They didn't have a great deal in common. Yet they'd found common ground. What Anna liked best about Sam—other than the fact that she was really smart—was that she had a huge heart and was fiercely loyal to her friends. Even those friends whom Anna would prefer to have relocate—preferably far, far away.

Besides, she reminded herself, she'd come to Los Angeles to shake up her life. Having a great friend like Sam who was steeped in the culture—the peculiar and specific culture—that was twenty-first-century Hollywood was definitely a step outside of Anna's usual literate, well-bred box. And that, she had decided long ago, was a very good thing.

She'd made other friends in Los Angeles, too. Guy friends. There was Ben Birnbaum, son of Hollywood's most prominent plastic surgeon to the stars, and a great guy, who unfortunately had a penchant for secrets. And there was Caine Manning, currently of Anna-and-Caine, who was actually a little bit older and who worked for Anna's father at the latter's investment company. Anna and Ben had been off and on for six months. Anna and Caine had been on for just a few weeks. She was still getting used to it.

While Sam continued hunting for her shoes, Anna walked out through the open sliding glass doors, onto the back deck, and gazed out at the pristine sands of Malibu beach.

"Fourth of July back in New York was never like this," she called back to Sam. She felt a grin spread across her face.

"How would you know? You never spent the Fourth of July in Manhattan!" *Sam might have a point,* Anna mused, as she tried to recall if she ever *had* been in New York City for this holiday.

Sam stepped out onto the redwood deck with two Stoli vodka–spiked all-natural lemonades, her favorite cocktail du jour. She handed one of the tall, frosted glasses to Anna and lifted her own high in the air. Anna saw that she was still barefoot.

"Fuck my flip-flops, I'll find them later. Here's to America, here's to us and our comfortable lives that we've done nothing to earn, and here's to some insane fun later on tonight with our alarmingly good-looking boyfriends. And here's to Marty Martinsen never coming home."

"I'll second . . . well . . . most of that." Anna clinked

glasses with her friend and then sipped her drink. "Honestly, I wouldn't mind hanging here for the rest of the summer."

"Can you think of a better place to watch fireworks? You know we've got invitations to three different Fourth of July parties—including the cast party of *Hermosa Beach* and the CAA bash on the *Queen Mary*, by the by. But nothing could top this."

For the past week, they'd been house-sitting at a magnificent Malibu beach estate spread owned by Marty Martinsen, president of Transnational Pictures. Sam's father had made many movies with Transnational, and Marty had become one of Jackson Sharpe's only trusted friends in a town where a trusted friend was pretty much an oxymoron. Whenever he was leaving town, he'd call Jackson and offer his house to him for his use and pleasure. They both knew the offer was moot, because Jackson could afford to pay cash for any beachfront estate that he wanted, whether it was in Malibu or Bali, or on the dark side of the moon.

This time, though, when Marty called to say he'd be vacationing in Malta for two weeks, Sam had jumped at the opportunity to house-sit. Then she'd invited Anna to house-sit with her. Anna had quickly accepted. Going to Marty Martinsen's estate with Sam was pretty much a guaranteed good time with her favorite Beverly Hills female friend. The place was more like a private beachfront hotel than a house. It came with a cook, a caretaker, and a maid, all of whom remained on the job even when Marty was out of town. The ultramodern structure had two-story-high glass windows that faced the ocean, and a modern, eclectic interior right out of *In Style* magazine.

The past week with Sam had been utterly relaxing and totally fun. Every morning they would sleep late, lounge on the sun-drenched terrace eating blueberry pancakes and reading fashion mags, and then take a long beach walk. After that, they'd settle down for the summer job Sam had snagged for them. Their chief responsibility was to write coverage—synopses and their considered personal opinions—on the dozens of screenplays that were sent to Action Jackson Productions offices on the Transnational lot every single day.

When Anna had protested that that she had no experience reading or evaluating screenplays, Sam had laughed. Hollywood, she explained, was all smoke and mirrors. No one had experience until they got started.

"That sunset is a total waste, unless you've got naked guys serving you. If they're here, I can't see them from this angle," came a feminine voice behind them.

Anna shut her eyes briefly, the better to prepare herself for the onslaught that was Cammie Sheppard. Cammie and Sam had been best friends forever, which meant that if Anna wanted to hang out with loyal Sam, she had to put up with the anything-but-loyal Cammie. When Anna thought about which friends of Sam she had to tolerate, Cammie was right at the top of the list. Living proof that there was no correlation between outer and inner beauty, Cammie was the kind of girl whose arrival at parties caused anyone with a pulse to stop talking midsentence and stare.

This was no hyperbole; Anna had watched the Cammie Effect in action more than once. With lush, shoulder-length strawberry blond curls and an even more lush, curvaceous body, she oozed so much sex appeal, she made Scarlett Johansson look like Ugly Betty.

"Hey, Sam. How goes it, Gwynnie?" Cammie asked, plucking Sam's drink from her hand and taking a sip.

Anna did a mental eye roll. The "Gwynnie" reference was Cammie's way of saying that Anna looked like Gwyneth Paltrow, pre-marriage and pre-babies (Cammie always clarified). Anna herself did not see the resemblance, except for hair color, height, and—maybe—build.

Cammie, who never left the house without looking perfect, was well dressed for the evening's activities—watching the fireworks that would be launched from a barge a half mile out to sea (a private show paid for by the hundred or so homeowners on this stretch of beach) and then some serious clubbing at House of Blues on Sunset Boulevard. She wore a white-and-blue Chloé spaghetti-strap slip dress, mile-high baby blue Jimmy Choos, and a delicate ruby, sapphire, and diamond pendant. How very patriotic.

Anna glanced down at her own T-shirt, faded jeans, and black Reef flip-flops and felt like a lost wren to Cammie's confident peacock.

"Who let you in?" Sam asked. She leaned against the railing and held her face up to catch the setting sun.

"Gertrude, Sue, Madeline, Lisette—whatever the house-keeper's name is." Cammie lifted the curls from her neck. "I adore coming to Malibu. It reeks of sex. Except in that direction." She pointed in the direction of a blocky beach-front mansion to the south. "Do you know who your neighbor is? Or should I say, Marty's neighbor?"

Sam shrugged.

"Gibson Wills. My father's WLE—Worst Living Enemy."

"Everyone in this town is your father's worst living enemy, Cammie," Sam pointed out. "Unless he's your father's NBF—New Best Friend."

Back when she lived in New York, this interchange would have left Anna utterly baffled. Now, she under-stood the code. Cammie's dad was Clark Sheppard, a founder of Apex Talent and notoriously the worst son-of-a-bitch agent in Hollywood despite his many deals and successes. Anna knew this firsthand, since—God help her—she'd briefly worked for Clark as an intern. That experience had ended when Cammie had plotted a complicated, and successful, scheme to drive Anna out. Amazingly, Anna also knew who Gibson Wills was, since Gibson was almost as big an international action movie star as Jackson Sharpe. Or at least he had been a decade earlier.

"Gibson sued my father over some deal. Who knows, who cares?" Cammie went on. "And he lost. He claims that was the beginning of the end of his career as a movie star. That's probably the truth. Last I heard, he was doing TV commercials in Japan for anti-aging face cream." She'd taken Sam's drink and proceeded to drain half of it. "The man is a joke. He hasn't spoken to my father in years but sends him petrified rabbit pellets in a Godiva chocolate box every Christmas. Hey, want to go check out his manse? It's probably hideous. Gibson has zero taste. Seriously. My father says he has people dress him."

All this "my father this" and "my father that" was curious to Anna, because she was pretty sure Cammie did not get along with Mr. Sheppard at all.

"Who's coming with?" Cammie asked. She looked at her nails. "God. I need a manicure."

Sam shook her head. "Not me. I have to go tell Marlene—that's her name, by the way—that we'll want dinner out here on the deck. "And I have to find something—anything!—for my feet. Maybe I'll go raid Mrs. Martinsen's closet. Just kidding. Don't be too long, okay?"

"Let her know we want champagne. I'm dying of thirst." Cammie headed for the narrow, weather-beaten wooden staircase that led down to the beach. "What time do the fireworks start, anyway?"

"We've got forty-five minutes, so we can eat while we watch."

"Know what, Sam? Screw food. Get the bubbly—we can eat at the club. They actually have a decent kitchen. But I've got my dad's car and driver, so we can drink all we want. Let's go, Anna—want to come with and check out Gibson's monstrosity?"

Anna was shocked that Cammie was inviting her; usually the two of them barely held onto civility. Yet being Cammie's enemy was exhausting, not to mention an utter waste of time. If, for some unknown reason, this was Cammie's version of an olive branch, she was inclined to accept it.

"Sure, why not?" Anna told her.

They moved toward the staircase together. Five minutes later, while Sam was prowling barefoot around Marty's French-style kitchen in search of the Taittinger's, she and Cammie had kicked off their own footwear and started down the magnificent and largely deserted beach that was Malibu's greatest and most famous asset. Gibson's estate was a few hundred yards to the south of Marty's—the very next one over.

Cammie stopped, put her hands on her hips, and took in their surroundings. Anna did the same.

"This place is so beautiful." Anna knew she was stating the obvious.

"It is, I agree."

"My mind goes round and round about the whole class thing all the time. It did in New York, and it does here. How it might just be fundamentally wrong for the few to have so much when the many have so little. Not that it's such a revelation, I know."

"Well, that's because it *is* . . . how did you put it? Fundamentally wrong," Cammie asserted, pushing some curls off her face.

Anna was surprised at Cammie's reaction. She'd always

thought of the girl as having the conscience of a—she hated to say it, but it was a perfect simile—mascara wand. And then she realized. "Adam's starting to rub off on you, Cammie."

Adam Flood was a good friend of Anna's; in fact, she'd briefly dated him, though even then her heart had belonged to Ben. Adam was far from being a Beverly Hills rich kid who took everything for granted. Instead, he was a Michigan native and one of the most decent human beings whom Anna had met north of the 10 and west of the 101—an excellent student, the starting point guard on the BHHS basketball team, and one of the few people Anna knew out here whose mother and father were still married to each other. When Adam and Cammie had hooked up toward the end of the winter, Anna had been sure it was the oddest pairing in human history and destined to end quickly. But it hadn't.

"I'm working on making him more shallow," Cammie deadpanned. "All that Adam Flood goodness is hard to take."

They kept walking until they were about two hundred yards from Gibson's mansion. From the beach, it appeared low-slung and boxy, with a wider area to the rear lined with rectangular windows, and an incongruent New England–style widow's walk along the roof.

Cammie rubbed her chin. "It's mega-ugly. Notice that the house has a fat ass, just like Gibson. What a hoot. Wait till I tell my dad."

"It sounds like you and your dad are getting along better these days," Anna ventured.

"Oh, believe me, Anna, I know my father is a sphincter. But he's an effective sphincter. He doesn't let anyone take advantage of him. In fact—"

"Stop right there, you two!"

An angry male voice bellowed over the loudspeakers on Gibson's deck. It was so sudden and so loud that Anna literally jumped. Immediately, two blinding spotlights were fixed on her and Cammie.

"What the fuck?" Cammie exclaimed.

Anna felt a shiver of fear. "Who is it?"

"It's Gibson!"

"You're on my property! Identify yourselves!" the crabby voice boomed out over the sand.

Cammie cupped her hands and shouted up toward the house. "Turn off the spotlights!"

Anna winced. Not a good way to win friends and influence people.

"Identify yourselves!"

"I'm Cammie Sheppard, daughter of your nearest and dearest friend, Clark. Now turn off the goddamn spotlight! You're blinding us!"

There was silence, but the perfect circle of white light remained on them.

"What an asshole," Cammie mumbled. "Let's just keep walking—screw him."

"HOLD IT, DAUGHTER OF THE JACKASS OF

THE WESTERN WORLD!" The voice was twice as loud now. Anne literally had to cover her ears.

Cammie whirled, irate. "You're the jackass! Stop screaming at us!"

"Don't egg him on, Cammie," Anna urged worriedly. "Let's just get out of here and go back to Marty's house."

"DON'T MOVE! DO NOT MAKE ANY SUDDEN MOVEMENTS!"

Annie exchanged looks with Cammie. "Is he serious?"

Clearly, Cammie wasn't any more certain than she was, so they both just stood there. Not more than two minutes passed before they saw Gibson Wills himself charging down the stone steps at the back of his house, flanked by two uniformed Malibu police officers. His face, pulled so tight his skin was practically translucent under the spotlights, was alight with glee. As he approached them, Anna could see he wore black jeans and a simple white sweatshirt.

"I'm having my annual Fourth of July party for the municipal employees of Malibu," Gibson told them, and then motioned to the two cops. "Thank God these two officers of the law arrived early. Gentlemen, these two young women are clearly trespassing on my property. Do your duty and arrest them."

Cammie made a face of disbelief. "You can't possibly be serious, Gibson."

"Mr. Wills," Gibson corrected.

"Gibson," Cammie said again, in a move that Anna knew would infuriate him. It was like Cammie couldn't resist.

"Do it," Gibson ordered the cops.

The shorter of the two policemen, who had the perfectly white Chiclet teeth of a twentysomething guy who had hoped to become a movie star before giving up and joining the men in blue, unclipped a set of handcuffs from his belt and strode over to Cammie and Anna, who hadn't moved since Gibson's voice had first boomed out over the loudspeaker, and ordered them to hold their ground. "Ladies, happy Fourth of July. You are both under arrest. You have the right to remain silent. Anything you say can and will be used against you in a court of—"

"We know, we know," Cammie declared, tossing her strawberry blond mane disdainfully. "We watch *CSI*. In fact, my father packages all three *CSI*s. Just get the flipping cuffs, okay?"

The First Felon I Ever Dated

Cammie and her lawyer—a no-nonsense woman with aggressively short jet-black hair and a bone-thin physique, and wearing a magnificently tailored black Armani skirt-and-jacket combination—stepped into the brightly lit, windowless conference room where Anna and her own lawyer sat waiting at a long black conference table. "Carol Farrell," Cammie's attorney introduced herself quickly, and nodded in Cammie's direction. "Sit." She pointed to the cheap leatherette seat next to Anna.

"Hello, Carol." Anna's attorney was Richard Lodge, courtly, portly, and white-haired. "Nice to see you again."

"Can we can the chitchat and move this thing along?" Cammie asked them both, as she fell dramatically into the black pleather seat next to Anna. "I'm meeting Sam for facials and an ayurveda massage at A La Mer in an hour. I really don't have a lot of time."

"That's why I'm here," Carol declared, as she leafed through some papers in her black briefcase. "To get you out of here. This is the most ridiculous case I've ever heard of. Come on, Richard, we're going to talk with the DA and get this thing dismissed."

Richard smiled and retrieved his own briefcase. "I couldn't agree more, Carol. Anna, relax. This shouldn't take very long."

The two lawyers departed.

"She's a bitch," Cammie announced. "I love that in an attorney." She took out a nail file and went to work on her left hand, despite the fact that she was allegedly on her way to a manicure.

Meanwhile, Anna's hands were sweating and she felt a little sick to her stomach. She'd hardly slept at all the night before, visions of herself in cold, unforgiving handcuffs and behind bars seared into her brain.

Perhaps they would have gotten off with a warning if Cammie hadn't insisted that Gibson and the cops who had arrested them were all "total idiots." Lesson one: Cops don't like to be called idiots. Go figure. In fact, the police had threatened to add the additional charge of resisting arrest as they loaded both girls into their black-and-white police cruiser. At the Malibu police station, they were dumped into a spartan, fluorescent-lit holding cell with a couple of fiftyish drunk women and three stunning young women from an escort service who tried to recruit Anna and Cammie with promises of "five hundred on a bad night, seven-fifty on a good one."

Cammie took one of their business cards just for fun.

After an excruciating hour of mostly terse silence, they were issued a citation for misdemeanor trespassing and told to return to the courthouse the next morning at ten for their arraignment. Would they need court-appointed attorneys?

Cammie had laughed at that one.

Free to go, they'd immediately called Sam, but it turned out that Sam had already heard the news of their arrest and was outside in the waiting area. Sam and Cammie had continued with their evening excursion to the House of Blues, but Anna had called Caine to bow out of their clubbing plans. Caine had understood and said he'd phone her in the morning. Then she'd driven back to her father's place in Beverly Hills, never letting her Lexus get anywhere near the speed limit.

What was strange, and somewhat reassuring, was her father's reaction. Jonathan Percy had been remarkably calm about the whole affair when Anna had recounted the story. After assuring Anna that it was highly unlikely that she'd be doing hard time at Vacaville for trespassing, he'd called Mr. Lodge, one of the lawyers he kept on retainer, and instructed him to meet Anna the next morning at the DA's office. "Don't worry, Anna," Jonathan had insisted. "It's going to be fine."

"Have you ever been arrested, Dad?" she'd asked, after she'd gotten herself a bottle of Fiji water from her father's fridge.

"No. Though I came close when I was at Yale. A bunch of us went streaking down Main Street in New

Haven the night before the homecoming game and got hauled in, but they let us go when they saw we'd written *Harvard Sucks* in black magic marker on our asses. You don't have to worry—you were trespassing. It's not like armed robbery."

That was easy for him to say, Anna had surmised. She'd tossed and turned all night, had barely eaten any breakfast, and had carefully chosen clothes that she thought would make a good impression on a judge, were she to end up before one—a conservative knee-length navy skirt, a white blouse, and kitten-heeled navy sandals, topped off with her grandmother's pearls.

"You're not worried about this at all?" Anna couldn't help asking. She actually had a book in her Fendi bag— the paperback of *Everything Is Illuminated*—but hadn't been able to do anything but watch Cammie give herself a manicure.

"Please," Cammie scoffed. She'd been reapplying rose lip salve. "This is some asshole's vendetta, not an arrest." Cammie found some gum in her Louis Vuitton hobo bag and curled the stick into her mouth without offering any to Anna. "He called my father right afterward. To gloat."

"Was your father upset?"

"Only that I didn't have a gun to put Gibson out of his misery. What a pathetic loser. He thought he could show my dad and me how powerful he was. Trespassing. You gotta be kidding." She gave Anna a cool once-over. "You're dressed like a girl with no bodily functions. Does Ben really get off on that prim-and-proper shit?"

"Ben and I aren't exactly together anymore," Anna admitted cautiously. It had been a couple of weeks since Anna had told Ben that she needed time to think about their relationship—such as it was—and then had turned down Ben's graduation-night invitation in favor of an evening with Caine at a jazz club. The night had been fun. Really fun, in fact. There really didn't seem to be any point to hiding this from Cammie. In fact, Cammie probably knew already.

"Really."

Anna heard the interest in Cammie's voice. Well, maybe she didn't know. But Ben and Cammie had once been Ben-and-Cammie. He was, in fact, the only guy who had ever dumped Cammie Sheppard. Anna knew that part of Cammie wanted Ben back, if only to prove that she could win him over so that she could be the one to drop him. Anna knew she shouldn't care, but she did. Even the mere thought of Cammie with Ben added an extra knot to her already-nervous stomach.

"Yes, really."

"So what prompted you to—"

The door opened, and the two high-powered attorneys walked back in, trailed by a movie-star-handsome man clad in an impeccable charcoal-colored Giorgio Baroni suit, crisp white shirt, and a red patterned tie. Anna automatically stood.

Cammie didn't. Instead, she yawned.

The man in the Baroni suit held out his hand to them anyway. "Anna Percy? Camilla Sheppard? I'm Andrew Levitan, the DA who's been assigned to your case. I'm sorry, but we've got a bit of a situation here."

"Andrew—I hope you don't mind that I call you Andrew—having the pregnancy test come back positive is a 'situation' to be terribly sorry about," Cammie declared. She still held her nail file in one hand. "This is just two cute girls walking over some has-been's semi-private sandbox. So do the right thing. Make the charges go away, I can go for my facial, and you people can go do . . . whatever it is you do."

"Have a seat, Anna." Andrew motioned politely to the chairs at the conference table. "I'm confident we can work all this out to both of your satisfaction."

Anna sat; Levitan and the lawyers did too. When Mr. Lodge flashed her the world's quickest thumbs-up, Anna felt a bit of relief. Maybe this was going to work out after all. Maybe the DA would drop the charges—

"I'm afraid I can't drop the charges," Levitan told them. "I got the order from high up. This is one of those things where the complainant—Gibson—can make a lot of noise. But I do think your lawyers and I have worked a way out of this. If you girls are willing, I'd like to put you into a brief community service program. If you complete the program successfully, we can get this case dismissed in the interest of justice."

Cammie leaned toward the handsome young DA, putting her impressive cleavage—the best that money could buy—on serious display. "Andrew—that's your name, right? I choose what—or who—I do. 'Community service' isn't on my list."

Andrew smiled gently. "This won't be anything like graffiti removal on the 405 freeway. You can thank your lawyers' powers of persuasion that I've got something else in mind."

"I'll do it whatever it is," Anna insisted, and fixed her eyes on Levitan. This was no time to put up with Cammie's snarky behavior. If she wanted a police record, that was her problem. Cammie could go to trial for all Anna cared.

"Actually, I think when you both hear what I have to say, you're going to be thanking me. You're not ordinary defendants. You're not going to do ordinary community service." Levitan leaned in close to them and smoothed his red power tie. "And the best part is, nobody is even going to know you're doing it."

"Joe's Clams?" Anna asked, as Caine pulled his electric blue Ford F-150 pickup truck into the half-full parking lot. "We're going to Joe's Clams for dinner?"

Caine laughed. "Best seafood in the Marina, in my humble opinion. You got a problem with that?"

Anna hesitated. "No . . . it's fine."

"My brilliant powers of observation tell me you've been here before," Caine teased as he turned off the engine. "Let me guess. You've been here with what's-his-name?"

"Ben," Anna filled in. "Good guess. Yes. His father's yacht is docked near here. But it's really fine. The food is great. Especially the crab cakes."

"His father's yacht. Huh. My father didn't have a yacht. He didn't even have a rowboat." Caine bounded out of the pickup, flashed around to Anna's side, and helped her step down to the pavement. Just as she had the first time she'd seen him, when he'd been sent by her father to rescue her after a fender-bender in a slightly dicey section of town, Anna was struck by how unlikely a young investment banker this guy was. His arms were covered in intricate tattoos, and he wore his dark choco-late hair short and spiky. There was stubble on his chin and a gold hoop in each ear. The only clue as to the nature of his work was the white button-down Brooks Brothers shirt he wore rolled up to his elbows, along with conservative woolen trousers and black cowboy boots. "He did have a canoe once. Great for fly-fishing."

"I didn't mean anything by that." Caine had told her a little about his modest upbringing in the Pacific Northwest.

Caine laughed and nudged his shoulder into hers. "Don't sweat it. Hey, did I mention you're the first felon I've ever dated? It's kinda hot."

Anna laughed. Caine was six years older than her, and possessed a maturity and ease that she found refreshing. Plus, as far as Anna could tell, he was scrupulously honest, which was more than she could say for Ben. When she'd gotten tired of Ben hiding the truth from her—the latest time had been during the week before graduation, when it turned out that an old girlfriend of Ben's from Princeton was basically stalking him—Caine had been right there.

Yes, Ben had done his best to apologize, and Anna had found herself falling under his familiar spell. But she had resisted, and since graduation, she and Caine had seen each other quite a bit.

Still, walking into Joe's Clams made her think about Ben. Their very first night together, when he'd abandoned her on the pier, and the only landmark she'd been able to remember was this clam shack. God, she'd been through so much with him. . . .

Anna pushed those thoughts aside as Caine ushered her to a corner table and ordered two Anchor Steams and a basket of fried oysters for them to share. The place was exactly as Anna had remembered, with a nautical theme, its warped wooden floor covered in peanut shells.

When the beers arrived, Caine lifted his bottle to Anna. "To my favorite felon."

"Hopefully not for long."

"So what's the deal on the community service, again? I wasn't really tracking in the middle of that traffic jam."

Anna grinned. "The DA offered us this amazing deal—he basically said we should never have been arrested or charged, but now that it had happened, he had to follow through with something. Anyway, there's this foundation he knows called New Visions, which does benefit work for at-risk girls and teens. They're doing a charity fashion show in a couple of weeks at the Los Angeles County Museum of Art. Some sort of big fund-raiser. Cammie and I are supposed to help plan it."

"Trust Anna Percy to get 'community service' planning a charity fashion show."

"I know!" Anna exclaimed. She took a swallow of the beer—it was ice cold and delicious. "I mean, that's the kind of thing I might want to work on anyway. It actually sounds like fun."

"There's this song my grandmother used to sing— something about how the rich get richer and the poor get poorer," Caine commented, as he opened a package of crackers and ate one of them.

"You didn't grow up rich. You told me last week your father runs a garage in Oregon. And yet you went into investment banking. Which means that if you follow in *my* father's footsteps—"

"I'll eventually be joining the leisure class, playing golf in those nasty-ass pastel pants, and—God forbid, don't tell my father—voting Republican. Man, my life is gonna suck."

Anna laughed and whacked his arm. "I don't think you have to change your essential self just because you make money."

"And how would you know that, exactly, Anna Percy, since you've always been overprivileged?" Caine took another pull on his Anchor Steam.

Anna didn't like to think that her worldview was colored by her family's status, but how could it not be? She and Ben had talked about that once, she recalled. Ben felt that the more money his plastic surgeon hero of a father made, the more shallow and avaricious he became, and he wanted to be nothing like his dad. Of course, one of the things Ben didn't talk about was what exactly he wanted to do with his life. Yet didn't Ben take the luxuries in his life for granted? He'd taken her out on the yacht that very first night, and—

"Yo, Anna, where'd you go?" Caine asked.

Anna flushed and leaned forward. "Sorry."

"Thinking about him, no doubt."

"It's just that he was my first real . . . my only—"

It felt too awkward to say out loud.

"Got it," Caine replied quickly; it was clear from the look on his face that he really did.

"Is there anyone in your past like that?" Anna asked. If they were talking about Ben, it was only fair for her to hear something about Caine's past. He hadn't volunteered much. "Or is that too personal a question?"

"No, it's okay. There actually was someone, back at Stanford. A girl named Bernadette. We were snowboarding buddies." Caine's voice got soft. "Funny. I haven't thought about her in a long time."

"What happened? How long were you together?"

"We met senior year at Stanford. She was a serious boarder. Loved the deep stuff. Back country." He hesitated. "You sure you want to hear this?"

Anna nodded. "Please. Go on."

"She went to Switzerland for spring break and hooked up with a guy on their Olympic snowboard squad. Never came back to school. Don't know what she's doing now. Know how she broke up with me? E-mail."

Anna gulped. "That had to hurt."

"It did." He took another long pull on his beer. "I didn't plan to fall in love with her, but I did."

"Well, maybe love isn't something you *can* plan."

Caine studied Anna's face intently. "In some ways, she reminds me of you."

"How so?" She heard her own voice, faintly nervous.

He smiled and looked her straight in the eyes. "She was blond like you, but it's not just the blond hair. More like . . . something in her soul. I always had the sense that she was watching herself. Like you."

Anna was amazed that he knew this about her.

"I *do* do that. And frankly, it's exhausting."

"No kidding. I think you took that whole 'lead an examined life' thing you learn in philosophy a little too seriously," Caine teased.

"You know what? I agree with you. That's why I have decided this summer to simply have fun. That makes sense, doesn't it?"

"Works for me," he agreed. "And if the cops come to slip the handcuffs on you again—"

"What?" Anna raised her eyebrows.

Caine grinned. "I have some fur-lined ones we could try instead."

Body by Bohdi

S am was beyond irritated when Marty Martinsen
called from his private jet to say that he'd just
entered American airspace, and that he'd flown in
from Malta due to a budget crisis on the set of *Ben-
Hur*. She knew it was Marty's way of telling her to
vacate the Malibu beach house immediately. Sam really
liked his place, and, more importantly, she'd liked
being twenty miles north and west of the stepmother
from hell, aka Poppy Sinclair Sharpe, mother of the
month-old stepsister she hadn't anticipated ever having, Ruby Hummingbird Sinclair Sharpe.

Why did people go insane over babies? Their appeal
in general was utterly lost on Sam—although from time
to time, she did find herself having warm feelings
toward Ruby Hummingbird. Then she remembered
who the baby's mother was. The best she could usually
muster was studied diffidence.

Evidently America's Most Beloved Action Hero, aka
her father, didn't share her indifference. Whenever he was
around his new daughter, he turned into a doting, cooing

wack job. He claimed to want to prioritize his family over his career—that's what he'd told *Entertainment Weekly,* too. This particular day, he'd even planned to leave things in the hands of his assistant director and director of photography and take the day off for "family time."

However, Jackson had been called an hour ago and had learned via speakerphone that there was an emergency on set: his redheaded starlet, Amelia Rodgers—playing the lead hooker in a Roman brothel—had just had an ugly on-set fight with the cinematographer, who up until forty-eight hours ago had also been her boyfriend. Now Amelia had locked herself inside her trailer and refused to come out.

Poppy hadn't taken the news that her husband was abandoning the ship of his estate on this day reserved for the family very well. But he still got in the production helicopter when it arrived to take him to Palmdale.

Well, at least Sam's boyfriend, Eduardo, was—

"*Hola, amiga. ¿Cómo estás ahora?*"

Eduardo. He'd come up behind her, lifted her hair, and kissed the back of her neck. Instantly, Sam's pissiness with her father and the at-best-two-digit-IQ, dyed-red-headed bimbo he now called his wife melted away. She leaned her head back so that Eduardo could reach her lips. She kissed him upside down, then turned around so he could kiss her right side up.

That this incredible, sweet, smart, and beyond-hot guy was crazed for her never failed to amaze Sam. Eduardo Muñoz was five-ten, with smooth copper skin stretched over taut muscles. His close-cropped hair was dark, his eyes even darker. In Lucky jeans and a plain blue tennis shirt, he had an ease in his own skin, self-contentment in a land where "look at me!" neediness tended to ooze from peoples' pores. In addition to the looks thing, Eduardo was also well read, insightful, and trilingual. Born and raised in Peru, a student of international relations in Paris, he spoke English and French as easily as his native Spanish. He could, Sam was certain, get a million girls who were thinner and prettier than she was. Yet for some unfathomable reason, the gods had smiled upon her, Sam Sharpe, a pear-shaped, far-from-perfect-looking girl who lived in a place where looking less than perfect was considered a moral affront on par with cruelty to animals.

Maybe it was worse than cruelty to animals.

"What was that for?" Sam asked, smiling at Eduardo.

"Do I need a reason?"

"Definitely not." She inhaled deeply, then took a long sip of her Inca cola, a soft drink Eduardo had introduced to her when they'd gone to Peru right after Sam's high school graduation. "Whatever you're cooking smells heavenly."

They were near the stove in the new outdoor kitchen that Poppy had installed just outside the sliding glass doors from the main kitchen. Decked out in the various shades of red that had dominated the estate since Jackson had married Poppy, the outdoor kitchen featured a cooking console with both barbecue and gas ranges, a long mahogany table shielded from the California sun by twin freestanding umbrellas, a separate bar, and a refrigerator.

"Comida criolla." Eduardo used the name for traditional Peruvian dishes that Sam had learned to love during her week in Peru. *"Papas rellenas*, to start."

"Potatoes filled with shredded meat," Sam translated. Her mouth was already watering. Normally, if she was around a cute guy, she hid her appetite, and she'd been on more diets in her life than she could count. Atkins, Weight Watchers, the Zone, the Ultra-Zone . . . she was an expert on diets. Eduardo, however, encouraged her to eat.

As a surprise graduation present, Eduardo had flown Sam to his home country, where his father was a high-placed government official and his family owned substantial gold mining interests. Down there, Sam had found that many of the girls were actually round and pleasingly plump. Here in La La Land, they would have been considered morbidly obese. This had been culturally eye-opening for her, and the realization was both wonderful and terrible. Wonderful, because sometimes, when shopping with *über*-babe Cammie or naturally thin Anna or her diminutive friend Dee Young at their favorite boutiques on Rodeo Drive or Melrose Avenue, Sam felt like one of the new white rhinos at the Los Angeles Zoo. It also felt terrible, because Sam had been so indoctrinated with a skinny-is-beautiful message that even when she looked at the girls in Peru, all she could imagine was how they'd suffer if they ever came to California.

"What time is your friend supposed to be here?" Sam asked.

Eduardo glanced at his silver Rolex watch. "Any time now. And she's not really a friend—she's been recommended by our cultural attaché at the consulate. She's supposed to be a brilliant designer. This'll be done in five minutes." He stirred the *papas rellenas*. Sam couldn't believe that he could make cooking look so sexy.

"Mees Sharpe?"

Sam turned toward the glass doors. One of the Russian maids that her father favored, a statuesque blond named Svetlana, with chipped-ice cheekbones, hair to her ass, and a master's degree in Russian literature from Moscow State University, was standing in the doorway to the patio.

"Your guest," Svetlana announced in her thick, dramatic accent, gesturing to a slender woman with skin the color of honey. Her raven hair was parted in the center and fell past her shoulders. She couldn't have been older than twenty-five. She wore a wide, colorful skirt that grazed her knees, an off-the-shoulder black T-shirt, and an intricate turquoise necklace.

"I have put rack of clothing from her in screening room," Svetlana added.

"Thanks," Sam replied. The Russian woman bobbed her head gracefully and exited.

"Hello, I am Gisella Santa Maria." The young woman crossed to Sam and extended a thin arm. Her English

was only moderately accented. "It's a pleasure to meet
you. I'm very grateful that you'd even think of me."

Sam had to look up—a lot—to make eye contact
with the designer, who was much taller than Eduardo,
even in flat sandals. She was graceful, gorgeous, and
accomplished, but Sam breathed a bit easier now. She
couldn't see Eduardo falling for a woman who was
taller than he was.

She hoped that wasn't wishful thinking.

"*Hola, Gisella, estoy muy contento que estás aquí con
nosotros,*" Eduardo fired off, then kissed her on both
cheeks. "*Y estoy contento también que le conocerás a mi
novia Sam.*"

"What'd you say?" Sam had been working on her
Spanish in her free time and had actually improved a lot
during her week in Peru. But those words from Eduardo
were too much, too fast.

"I'll translate," Gisella interjected, "if Eduardo
doesn't mind. He said he's really glad that I'm here
today with you, and especially that I'm having a chance
to meet his girlfriend. I think your man is besotted."

Sam felt an involuntary smile spread over her face.

"And we're ready to eat," Eduardo announced with a
flourish.

Gisella stepped toward the stove and sniffed the air.
"*Papas rellenas?* It smells like home."

"It tastes like home," Eduardo assured her, then
filled the three brown earthenware plates at the wood
table, opened a bottle of red wine, and poured three full

glasses. "The wine's from Chile. Don't tell anyone. Sam, why don't you fill Gisella in on your friends' project?"

"There's this foundation called New Visions that helps at-risk girls here in Los Angeles. You know, low-income, busted families, that kind of thing. New Visions is putting on a charity fashion show at the county art museum. My two best friends are helping to organize it. I volunteered to help them out a little."

Sam took a bite of the *comida criolla* and closed her eyes to savor the flavors—meat, potatoes, and onion dominated her palate.

"It's very nice of Sam to do this," Eduardo added. "That's why you're here, Gisella."

"I'm grateful," Gisella told her.

Sam wasn't about to disabuse either of them of this notion. The truth was, though, that she felt mildly guilty about what had happened to her friends. After all, Anna and Cammie had been in Malibu to hang out with her, and if they hadn't been in Malibu, they wouldn't have been arrested in the first place. Besides, even though she knew it was ridiculous, the idea of Anna and Cammie working together on a project without her made her feel left out. So when Eduardo had mentioned there was a Peruvian designer in Los Angeles who was looking to have her clothing seen by a larger audience, Sam had magnanimously invited her to bring over some samples.

The three of them talked and ate for a while—was everyone from Peru as charming as these two? They hadn't

met each other before, so Eduardo and Gisella played the
Peruvian equivalent of Hollywood geography, figuring out
who they knew in common. It turned out they'd been at
the same wedding in Cuzco a few years ago, which they
remembered because the groom had gotten drunk and hit
on the bride's mother. It also turned out that Gisella was a
staunch opponent of the political party of which Eduardo's
father was a leader. Eduardo got a good laugh out of that.
Sam was reasonably sure it wasn't a flirtatious laugh.

Or was it?

Shit. Why did she have to be so insecure?

"Who are the models going to be for this fashion
show, Sam?" Gisella asked, after she washed down some
of the savory roast potato with the biting wine. "Have
they been chosen?"

"PacCoast Models." Sam named a hot new agency on
Sunset Boulevard that had splintered off from Storm, the
London agency that she'd heard was now representing
Kate Moss. "It was going to be Major Models, but when
my friends told me about the show, I made the call to
PacCoast on their behalf. The organizers were thrilled."
What the hell. She wanted Gisella to appreciate the kind
of clout she had.

"Then it will be great fun to see their models in your
fashions," Eduardo said, smiling at Gisella.

Sam studied his face. What did that smile mean, exactly?

"Well, the organizers will have to see if your designs
are good enough first," Sam said coolly. "Evidently there's
some committee that votes on it." Really, Gisella needed

to be very clear about who the power player was in this situation—and also that said power player was attached to the tasty Peruvian morsel sitting across from her.

"I brought my samples with me and gave them to the housekeeper." Gisella gestured inside. "Can we go and see them?"

Sam was interested—she had an idea of what to expect. But before she could reply, Poppy appeared in the outdoor kitchen. Of medium height, with large, natural breasts, she'd just had her hair colored red and cut gamine short, which made her giant turquoise eyes look even bigger and brighter, and she was wearing yoga workout clothes. Poppy had regained her figure through daily yoga with her personal trainer and was really in excellent post-baby shape. Seeing Poppy post-partum fat, out of shape, and out of breath would have cheered Sam immensely. But unfortunately that state had lasted for like a nanosecond.

"Omigod, Sam! What did you cook out here? *It smells like meat.*" Her face went nearly as pale as her billowy white yogawear. "There is to be no meat in this household. *No meat!*"

"Since when did we go meatless?" Sam asked. She deliberately stabbed her fork into a large hunk of Eduardo's savory chicken and brought it ostentatiously to her mouth.

"Carnivore!" Poppy gasped, placing her hands over her heart as if just listening to Sam was giving her palpitations.

"You went away to Malibu for more than a week, Sam." Poppy stated. "During that time, our household shifted to vegetarian. Preferably raw, whole foods in their natural state. Nothing that has a heart, everything from the earth. Meat is very toxic. Ruby Hummingbird needs to grow up in a home free of all toxins. She's extremely sensitive."

Sam swallowed a bite of the roast chicken and forked up another extra-large piece. "No, seriously. People have been eating meat for tens of thousands of years. Don't you think that if it was really toxic, the human race would have died out by now?"

"Look at the state of the world! Of course I believe it," Poppy insisted, chin jutting forward. "I've done a great deal of reading." She regarded Gisella. "Hello. I'm Poppy Sharpe."

"I'm Gisella." The Peruvian girl nodded. "Nice to meet you, Poppy."

Poppy smiled, and then turned back to Sam. "I will now have to have the meat toxins *explunged* from this kitchen, Sam," Poppy fumed. "Because of *you*."

Sam tried to hide her smile. Did Poppy just say *explunged*?

"Excuse me? What's going on? I'm smelling some bad karma in here."

A tall and very buff guy drifted up behind Poppy, wearing identical yoga workout clothes, except his were sky blue instead of snow white. He looked to be in his late twenties and had long, straight chestnut brown hair parted in the middle, piercing blue eyes, and a Fu Manchu moustache.

"Easy on the rhetoric," he cautioned Poppy, in a voice as soft and calm as a spring shower. "What a baby learns before it can speak will stay with it for life. This is the time for imprinting positive patterns that can last a lifetime."

"You are so right, Bodhi. This is the stepdaughter I was telling you about. She really, really needs your help." Poppy pointed right at her, and the guy gave Sam a serious up-down, up-down, and the slightest disapproving shake of the head at what he saw.

"I'm Bodhi Gilad. From Body by Bodhi. I'm sure you've heard of me. I was in *Inner Fitness* magazine last month. I could help you get into the best shape of your life, Sam. If you're willing do the work."

"I think Sam is perfect exactly as she is," Eduardo opined. As if to prove his point, he snaked an arm around one of her shoulders. Sam was thrilled.

"And I would defer to the expert, were I you. First the mind must be healed," Bodhi explained. "Then the body will follow."

Poppy looked at him with something approaching reverence. "That is so true," she said softly.

"It all comes from the spiritual core. Your spirit, mind, and body must be united."

"Uh-huh," Sam chirped, amused. It was so much easier to take Poppy and Bodhi with Eduardo's arm around her shoulder "Bodhi, how much do people pay you for those scintillating tarot card health bulletins?"

"Why must you always trash what you don't understand, Sam? Bodhi just happens to be the deepest, most brilliant man I have ever met in my life. And you should see him in shavasana position. It's a thing of beauty." Her relentless stepmother gazed up at him, her eyes shining.

Sam looked from Poppy to Bodhi and back to Poppy again. She knew that look. She'd seen it on starfuckers so many times before.

Holy shit. Was Poppy *doing* him? Was the Pop-Tart cheating on *her* father?

No. Jackson could put up with a lot. Poppy wasn't the sharpest piece of cutlery in the drawer. But her father was smart. He knew that about her when he married her, apparently. Yet if there was one thing that Jackson Sharpe demanded—from his coworkers, from his family, from his fans—it was loyalty. He had taken a long time to remarry after divorcing Sam's own mother. Even with his own penchant for dalliances on his movie sets, a cheating spouse would crush him. Then it would anger him. Then—well, who knew what he'd do?

Suddenly, Poppy seemed to get flustered, as if remembering just who her audience was. "Well, when your father gets home, I plan to put him on Bodhi's plan for healing and health, too. Or should I say, *if* your father gets back home."

Bodhi shook his hair out of his eyes. "When a couple's yin and yang lacks unity, it's a spirit-killer."

"I know," Poppy said sadly. "But he's always busy, always on the set—"

The yoga instructor nodded knowingly. "Jackson wants the Oscar. He craves the Oscar, the recognition from his peers. So temporal. So fleeting. So foolish. Who won the Best Actor Oscar in 1988, for example? No one re—"

Sam held up a hand to cut him off. "Dustin Hoffman. *Rain Man*. Freaking brilliant performance."

"He ought to want something else more than a statue," Poppy sniffed. "Come on, Bodhi, let's go back to the studio and work some more."

She led him back through the open doorway. This time, Sam watched her yoga teacher closely. Yes. No doubt about it. Bodhi's gaze followed her ass with something less than an honorable spiritual glint in his eyes. *Much* less.

That was all the confirmation that Sam needed. Either Poppy was doing the guy, the guy was doing Poppy, or they were pretty damn close to one, the other, or both.

Her father would shit Twinkie-pops if he found out. What a fantastic development.

That Old Ojai Magic

Dee Young could hear the roar of the crowd through the monitor in Evolution's dressing room in the bowels of the Staples Center, the huge basketball arena in downtown Los Angeles. Her father had produced their first album, and the guys in the band had an almost blind faith in his musical judgment. Tonight, they had "arrived," as they were about to open for U2 in front of twenty thousand people, at the most prestigious venue in Southern California. It didn't matter that they'd released exactly one single on alt radio, called "Monsoon." Thanks to the power of Graham Young, that single had hit the charts the week before at number thirty-two with a bullet.

Dee had been present for the negotiations since she was working for her father during the summer as his special assistant, as well as taking summer school classes so that she could officially graduate from high school after her second-semester crackup. She'd only been at it a couple of weeks, but so far she loved the job. She relished the chance to spend so much quality time with her father. Most of all, she felt like the job offer from him was a vote of parental confidence, especially given her recent long stint in a psychiatric facility up in Ojai.

Ojai was where you ended up when you went on a road trip to Vegas with your friends and heard so many voices in your head you couldn't tell what was real and what was not. Ojai had been weird. So calm, so quiet, so many people solicitous of her every mood and word. But she'd met some nice people there—it wasn't only old crazies who went batty—the doctors and psychiatrists had been helpful, and the pharmacy well stocked with all the latest in legal psychotropic pharmaceuticals. Now she was on the right meds and felt a clarity that she hadn't possessed in years.

And, for the first time in Dee Young's eighteen years on the planet, she was really and truly in love. In. Love. Oh sure, she thought she'd been in love before; in fact, she had a nasty habit of falling head over heels for whatever latest guy was on her radar. For some bizarre reason, in the past, almost all the guys she'd adored had turned out to be gay—or had gone gay immediately after dating her.

Jack Walker, Dee's new boyfriend, had just finished his freshman year at the same college as Ben Birnbaum, Princeton, and he was definitely not gay.

She'd made a good choice. With rust-colored hair, quirky Elvis Costello–style black glasses, and a thin, lanky frame, Jack was attractive in a very different way than the Beverly Hills rich boys she'd known all her life.

He was smart and extremely ambitious; Dee thought maybe this had something to do with the fact that he'd grown up in a working-class neighborhood in Newark, New Jersey. He was also multiply talented in a wide variety of positions—professionally *and* other ways.

"I've got my fingers and toes crossed," Dee announced, holding up crossed fingers, although crossing her toes inside her leopard-print Christian Louboutin sling-backs proved a little more difficult.

Jack's lanky body was stretched out on the brown microfiber couch in the corner of the reasonably spacious dressing room, next to an elaborate buffet spread.

"I think we're alone now," Dee teased, as she heard the actor Matthew McConaughey—a personal friend of the lead singer, Darwin—introduce Evolution to the crowd. She shimmied on top of Jack until her cheek pressed against his.

"You know, we can hear the band in here," Jack murmured, his hands cupping her butt. "So really, we could stay and multitask. . . ."

He gave her the kind of sizzling kiss that made her melt.

Their only limitation was the length of Evolution's set—a mere thirty minutes. When Jack heard the band announce that their last number would be coming up (they were closing with "Monsoon"), he suggested that this might be a good time to get up and for him to go get some beers. "Can't stand pale ale. I bet U2 has some Guinness in their dressing room. Want to come with?"

Dee smiled, her eyes glimmering. "I need to use the bathroom. Be down in a minute."

"I'll have them poured."

Ten minutes later, she stepped out of Evolution's dressing room just in time to see the band return triumphant from their performance, with a bevy of gorgeous girls in tow. After some quick hellos and a few "good show" hugs—even though Dee could only account for the audio portion, and even then she'd been pretty distracted—she slipped into the corridor.

"Dee? Dee Young? Is that you?"

Someone was calling to her. She turned. A tall, muscular guy with curly blond hair was waving to her. No. It couldn't be. Aaron Steele? What was Aaron doing here? She hadn't seen him since Ojai.

Aaron jogged down the corridor, picked Dee up—it wasn't hard, since she'd never topped a hundred pounds in her life—and swung her around. "Dee Young. I honestly never thought I'd see you again."

"You look great."

He really did look great, especially compared to the first day he'd arrived at the institute. Though everything at Ojai was supposed to be confidential, word of new arrivals traveled fast. Aaron was the son of a screenwriter famous for his humongous belly—ditto beard and ego. Also famous for blasting the gambling industry, the screenwriter was fond of hurling equally harsh criticism at his wife and children, which had contributed greatly to Aaron's arrival at Ojai.

When he had been brought in to the institute, transferred from the psych ward at Cedars-Sinai, Aaron had been in really bad shape. Which made sense, because he'd been on a weeklong bender involving most every drug behind the counter at your local pharmacy and then some that hadn't yet been approved by the Food and Drug Administration, and weren't likely to be approved, either. After his father had discovered him listening to the Ramones' "I Wanna Be Sedated" over and over on his iPod, unresponsive to other stimuli, and he'd been rushed to Cedars-Sinai in an ambulance, Ojai became the logical next stop.

At the Ojai Institute just north of Santa Barbara, Aaron stayed in the facility's equivalent of intensive care. Dee had only met him a day before her release, when they'd taken a walk around the grounds together. It was her last day of treatment; it was his first day out. He was lucid, thoughtful, and charming. He took her hand when they walked—a kind and friendly gesture that almost made Dee want to delay her release so she could get to know him better. She'd always liked his father's films, at least those before the tell-all book.

"You're out?" Dee was thrilled to see Aaron in a normal setting like a rock concert, instead of at a psychiatric rehab facility. "Congratulations."

Aaron shook his head. "Still up there. It's a safe place for me. But I'm starting to get some day passes.

I'm really getting into music, so my shrink thought it would be beneficial for me to be here tonight. I play bass. Did you know that?"

"No, I didn't. But no one's afraid you'll take off?" Dee asked. One thing she remembered from their day together at Ojai—he'd asked her not to hold back. She could ask him anything. He would answer honestly. He hoped she'd feel comfortable enough to do the same with him. It was part of the famous Ojai treatment protocol.

"They know I don't want to. I'm telling you, Dee, that place is turning my life around. I haven't thought about my own future in two years. And now I'm already planning what I'm going to do when I get out: to work on my music."

"I understand." Dee nodded passionately. "If it wasn't for Ojai, I'd still probably be totally messed up. Instead, I'm just moderately messed up."

Aaron threw his head back and laughed like she had just delivered the line of the century. It made her feel amazing.

"That's for sure," he agreed. "The first step to getting moderately messed up is realizing you're totally messed up. I knew there was a reason I liked you."

Impetuously, she hugged him. "I'm just so glad to see that you're going to be okay. What are you thinking about doing when you're out?"

"I've always been interested in the music business. Maybe I'll go into a music management program someplace. Or open my own recording studio. Doesn't your dad do something like that?"

"Definitely. You'll have to meet him sometime. I'd love to introduce you."

"I'd like that. A lot. I've never forgotten that walk we took," he murmured, as they broke apart.

"I liked it too."

"It was special, Dee." Aaron gazed deeply into her eyes. "Can I tell you something honestly? Ojai honestly?"

"Of course." Dee loved Ojai honesty. She'd wished many times that the rest of the world could have the same kind of forthrightness that her doctors constantly preached at the institute. Things would be so much less complicated and easier to deal with.

"I felt myself start to have feelings for you that day, when we were walking. And now that I'm with you, I'm starting to have those feelings again. I know it's crazy— we've only met once, and we've only been talking for a little while. But it wouldn't have been right not to say anything," Aaron continued. "It wouldn't be Ojai honest."

"No, it wouldn't."

"Now that you're out, and I'm on my way to be out . . ." His voice trailed off. "I think of you as an anchor, Dee. Just this wonderful ray of light."

Wow. She had to grin. This was intense.

There was only one problem. She made her voice as gentle as she could.

"I'd love to be your friend, Aaron. I really would. But . . . the fact is, I'm seeing someone. Seriously."

"Well, of course. Isn't it always that way?" He smiled thinly.

"It's been about a month now. More or less."

"Dare I ask who the guy is?"

"Dee! What's the holdup?" A voice boomed down the hallway.

Dee pointed. "That's him," she said softly, then turned and beckoned with one arm. "Hi! I'm here. Come meet a friend of mine!"

A moment later, Jack had joined them. Tall as Jack was, Aaron had him beat by a good two inches.

"Jack Walker, this is my friend Aaron. Aaron Steele." Dee made the introductions. It was kind of uncomfortable. She liked both these guys so much.

"And you know each other from?" Jack asked, before offering his hand for a firm shake.

"Ojai," Aaron explained amicably. "I was there when Dee was there. I'm still there, in fact."

Jack eyed him closely. "Until when?"

"I'm in for life, man. Until my doctors and I agree that it's time for me to leave. That's the nature of the Ojai therapeutic experience. It's a joint decision by the patient and the therapist. You sign an agreement going in. Dee knows all about that."

"Come on," Jack challenged. "It's a psych institute, not San Quentin. You can't leave even if you want to?"

"I could," Aaron allowed. "But the deal is, if you check yourself out before the doctors agree you should, you can never come back."

Dee nodded her confirmation. She'd signed the same

agreement when she'd been checked in by her parents right after she and her friends had gone to Las Vegas.

Jack shrugged. "I'm not real big on the head doctor thing. I know myself better than anyone else could know me. So, Dee and I were just about to suck down some Guinness. Nectar of the gods. You want to join us?"

Aaron looked as if Jack had just offered him a loaded .45 and suggested that he point it at his own crotch and yank the trigger. "Uh, no. I don't think that would be good for me now. Thanks, though. It was thoughtful of you to ask."

Aaron offered Jack his hand again. "Good to meet you. That's a great girl you're seeing. Dee, can I call you sometime? As *friends*? You mind, Jack?"

Jack nodded. "It's her life. I don't tell her who her friends should be."

There was something in his voice that made it clear he did mind, but either Aaron didn't take the cue or he chose to ignore it. "Cool." He took a small piece of paper out of his pocket and scribbled something on it. "Here's my e-mail. Send me your digits, Dee. Enjoy the concert, you guys." He turned and went back the way he'd come, his footfalls echoing in the quiet corridor.

"Strange guy," Jack opined, as Aaron moved off.

"*Nice* guy. He's really pulling his life together."

"Take it from me. He's strange. Hang out with who you want, but . . ." Jack didn't finish the sentence. He put an arm around her shoulders. "Let's take these brews and watch U2."

The Anti-Hollywood Crowd

"**S**o, where are you right now?"

Cammie shifted her new limited-edition silver Razr cell to her other ear so the pedicurist wouldn't overhear. "I'm in the spa at the Century City Plaza Hotel, getting my toes done. In an hour, I'm supposed to be upstairs in the Reagan room at a catered luncheon with the organizers of the New Visions fashion show, where we're going to be picking the designers who'll be showing their stuff at the museum a week from Wednesday night. Now, this is *my* idea of community service."

Adam Flood laughed through the phone. "Hey, it's all in the details. Is this the Beverly Hills version of a *Chained Heat* kinda thing?" he teased, naming a classic Hollywood B-movie about girls in prison. It was heavy on cleavage and lascivious matrons, and, of course, decidedly low on prison uniforms and undergarments.

"Yeah, I mack with some chick who has '666' tattooed on her forehead. Kinky stuff, huh?"

"More like bizarre," Adam commented. "Anyway,

you and Anna got the best community service deal in history."

It's amazing what a couple of highly paid lawyers and a bright DA can come up with together."

He laughed again. "I'm sorry. It's hard to think of you actually being arrested for the heinous crime of trespassing on someone else's sandpile."

"I know! My father is already plotting his revenge against Gibson. Getting on Clark Sheppard's shit list is never a good idea."

It had been two days since Cammie had been arrested with Anna—there was something ironic about *that*, for sure, since Anna Percy would be voted Least Likely Ever to Be Arrested at a monastery. Today they would begin their so-called community service with a catered luncheon here at this hotel, one of the finest in the city. Cammie had decided to take advantage of the location.

Cammie wiggled the toes, then turned her attention back to Adam. She missed him. A lot. He'd gone to northern Michigan with his parents for two weeks. They had been renting a cabin on Lake Superior every year since he'd been a kid. Adam had described it blissfully because he loved it there and, unlike most *normal* high school kids, he actually got along well with his parents.

When he'd first told her about his Michigan retreat into rustic splendor, she'd nodded and tried to keep a perky "wow, what fun!" kind of look on her face, when in actuality she found the idea of two weeks spent communing with nature utterly horrifying.

"So, what have you been doing for fun?" Cammie purred. "Out there in the middle of nowhere."

"Regular cabin stuff: fishing, hiking, and oh, starting on the Pomona freshman reading list—Chekhov, Carl Sagan, the Koran."

Cammie had zero idea who any of those people were. Plus, hearing Adam mention Pomona—the small, fancy-pants college fifty miles away in Claremont that was as tough to get into as many of the Ivy League schools—gave her a minor shiver of insecurity. Adam was an excellent student and would be starting there in the fall. But Cammie wasn't going to college at all. For one thing, she loathed school. For another thing, she was already filthy rich. And for another thing . . . well, those two pretty much covered it.

"Come home soon and I'll show you what you've been missing." Her deliberate giggle made it clear exactly what "what" was.

"A week from Saturday," Adam assured her. "You and Anna have fun on probation. I gotta go—my dad and I are going trolling for lake trout."

Gag me with an earthworm.

"Sounds fun. Call me later if you have cell service."

Cammie hung up and sighed. She really wished he would just pack up his tackle box and come home. In fact, it was bothering the shit out of her that he'd even choose two weeks in the wilderness with his mother and father over spending that kind of time with a far superior friend with exceptional extra benefits. Namely, herself. What kind of guy *did* that?

"You must be Camilla." A middle-aged woman with a chic blond bob, clad in a baby blue knit St. John's suit, clasped both hands around Cammie's own. She had a round face, perfect ivory skin, small dark eyes enhanced with the most understated of cosmetics, and just enough Restylane in her lips to make them look naturally youthful. The gleaming Tiffany-cut rock on her ring finger was the size of a Ping-Pong ball.

"I'm Virginia Vanderleer, head of this year's New Visions fashion show. We're so pleased you and your friend Anna decided to volunteer. She's already arrived. Come join us."

Virginia escorted Cammie to one of the four round tables in the Reagan Room, one of the smaller of the many banquet rooms in the famous Century City Plaza. The white room itself had a high ceiling, heavy red velvet drapes, a parquet floor, and a massive American flag in the corner. There was a large, flat-screen TV at the front. There were two empty seats at the table next to Anna. Virginia gestured for Cammie to sit as she slid into her own seat. Instantly a waiter appeared and placed a jumbo prawn cocktail in front of her.

Cammie said a quick hello to Anna, then Virginia quickly introduced her to the other thirty- and fortysomething women at their table, all of whom were dressed in some variation of pastel designer suit, all of which looked like they had been custom designed for Laura Bush.

Cammie gave a mental shudder. These women dressed like this *on purpose*.

"Excuse me, please," Virginia whispered graciously. "I need to play hostess."

"Cammie." Anna leaned over to her. "Do you get what's going on here?" she whispered. "They think we're just two nice society girls who volunteered to help with the fashion show. They think we're Junior League!" Cammie saw that Anna was wearing a vintage off-white silk blouse and wide-legged white flannel trousers with ballet flats. Diamond studs danced in her ears; Cammie could see them, because Anna had pulled her hair back in a Gwynnie ponytail.

Had someone called her in advance with the dress code?

"Of course that's what they think," Cammie hissed. "Look how you're dressed. They probably want to adopt you. Personally, I wouldn't be caught dead with these fossils if it wasn't court-mandated."

Anna smiled. "This is just the kind of event my mother would do. The only difference is, on the East Coast, old money never, ever wears pastels. Not even in the summertime. It's all white linen."

A few incredibly dull minutes later, Virginia came up behind them and put a hand on each of their shoulders.

"You know, we're always so pleased when you young girls get involved. A decade from now, you'll be running these shows instead of one of us."

Cammie went wide-eyed. "Gosh, Mrs. Vanderleer. How would we ever handle all that responsibility?"

Anna nearly choked on a candied pecan.

"Exactly why it's so important to learn the ropes now," Mrs. Vanderleer replied in her melodious voice.

"Virginia, darling!"

An older woman who looked to be in her sixties—coiffed silver hair, pink knit suit—glided over to their table with a gorgeous young woman in tow. Virginia quickly introduced the older woman as Victoria Chesterfield, head of last year's New Visions fashion show.

"And I want you to meet a simply lovely young woman. This is Miss Champagne Alicia Jones."

Victoria gestured to the beautiful girl. She was maybe five-six, and very slender. Cammie guessed she was fifteen or sixteen, with natural platinum blond hair, glossy and stick-straight; a heart-shaped face with chiseled cheekbones; and enormous emerald green eyes. Her hair was pulled off her face in a low ponytail. She wore lip gloss and perhaps a hint of mascara, but other than that, no makeup. As for her clothes, she wore simple black trousers—a reasonably good Chloé knockoff design—and a black short-sleeve jewel-neck sweater meant to pass as cashmere.

Another trespassing arrestee, but one with less money?

"Ms. Jones is actually a new member of the New

Visions program," Victoria explained. "Once she heard about it, she very much wanted to be involved in this fashion show. We're delighted to have her."

"Nice to meet you," Champagne muttered dutifully. Cammie could see that the girl was a bit intimidated. It was as if she couldn't even contemplate a handshake.

"You look like you could model, yourself," Anna told her.

Now *that*, Cammie noted, made the girl's eyes light up.

"Thanks, but I'm only five-six," she replied with a sigh.

Champagne was escorted back to her table, and then an apricot torte dessert was served. Cammie was not about to waste calories on mass-produced hotel sweets, so she pushed it away. As the others were eating, Virginia explained that they'd be watching a video of twenty up-and-coming designers who were being considered for the event. They wouldn't be seeing the sixties-inspired clothes that would be in their fashion show, but they would get an idea of the talent and style of each designer.

"As many of you know, one of the reasons our project gets so much attention every year . . ." Virginia explained. She had a handheld microphone, and was wandering between the four tables as she talked. ". . . is because we find the most exciting new designers who are just on the cusp of fame. You'll find forms right next to the flowers." She pointed to the tasteful arrangements of white orchids in the center of the tables. "You check off the six designers whose clothes you'd like to see included in the show. We're very democratic about it."

"Why do I think all these designers are going to suck?" Cammie whispered to Anna as the lights were dimmed and the video began.

"Keep an open mind," Anna whispered back.

Well, Anna the Good *would* suggest that. Just once, why couldn't Anna be petty or bitchy like the rest of the world? Was she missing that gene or what?

One by one, different designers appeared on the screen along with their creations.

"Hate it," Cammie told Anna in response to Siobhan McGee's floaty chiffon monstrosities.

Anna nodded her agreement.

Next was Martin Rittenhouse, who screamed metro-sexual. Of medium height, well built, and with thick, black, swept-back hair, Rittenhouse was impeccably dressed in black trousers with a lethal-looking crease, a black cashmere sweater, and a black man-bag slung over his shoulder. He was obviously the kind of guy who took great pains with his appearance. He took great pains with his clothes, too. They were spectacular. He showed a cream-colored fitted lace blouse with a long black silk skirt slit all the way up one leg; a strapless, cherry-red cocktail dress cut on the bias that was to die for; white cigarette pants with a black chiffon bra top under a wispy aqua-and-black paisley shirt; and a lavender suit that would have been too precious, except that there was nothing on under a jacket that was held together with one huge, jeweled safety pin at the waist.

Cammie put a check mark and a perfect star next to his name. Anna checked him off, too. It was immediately clear to Cammie that Martin Rittenhouse really was a rising star. In fact, she made a mental note to buy some of his stuff tomorrow so that she'd be wearing it before the rest of Beverly Hills.

When the video ended, Cammie and Anna compared notes. The only designer they'd both picked was Martin Rittenhouse. Champagne went from table to table and collected the tally sheets. When she took Cammie's and Anna's, she added how nice it had been to meet them, and said that she looked forward to working with them on the show. It seemed to Cammie like the girl had mentally practiced what to say and how to say it before approaching them.

"Let's get out of here before they try to fix us up with their sons. Can you imagine?" Cammie leaned over and whispered.

Anna got up too and looked around. "We just need to thank Virginia—there she is."

Cammie followed Anna's lead. They thanked the older woman for "a lovely afternoon."

"I hope you girls will take Champagne under your wing," Virginia began. "She seems lovely, but . . ." A frisson of concern marred her placid brow. "She's had quite a few problems in the past. Well, I might as well just come right out and say it: Martin Rittenhouse was kind enough to invite a group of our New Visions girls to tour his design studio, and Champagne was one of them. Right before the girls left, Martin noticed that one of his most expensive couture gowns was missing. We checked all the girls' backpacks but didn't find anything."

"So then none of them took it," Anna concluded.

"Well, the thing is, Champagne was missing for quite a while. When we found her, she was downstairs chatting with one of the security guards. We think she may have worked something out with him, given him the gown so that she wouldn't be caught with it, and plans to give him part of the sale price after she sells it."

"You can't really accuse her, though," Cammie pointed out. "You don't know that she did anything wrong." For some reason, she suddenly felt protective of the girl.

"True, true," Virginia agreed quickly. "It's just that our New Visions girls have done some unsavory things in the past. Champagne comes from a very disadvantaged background." Virginia whispered "very disadvantaged background" as if it was something about which Champagne should be ashamed. Like she had any control over the world into which she was born.

"We so want to steer Champagne to a more productive life," Virginia added peppily. "That's why we have New Visions!"

After a round of fake hugs and a final lament over just how wonderful all the promising new designers were, Cammie and Anna walked back outside into the bright afternoon sun.

Cammie heaved a sigh of relief as she handed her parking ticket to the valet. "Honestly, I thought I would suffocate in there."

Anna shook her head slowly, looking uncomfortable. "I think that it's horrible of Virginia to accuse Champagne without any sort of proof."

"That's the second time today I've agreed with you, Anna. What's happening to me?"

"You've decided to dedicate yourself to a life of clean living and good deeds," Anna teased, as she saw the valet pull Cammie's cherry red Lamborghini up to the curb of the roundabout in front of the hotel. "I couldn't be prouder."

The valet got out and held open the door. Cammie tipped him lavishly and made sure he got an excellent view of her black lace thong when she got into the car. There was really only so much clean living she could take in one day.

Kiss and Tell

Anna sat at her antique oak rolltop desk, typing an e-mail to her best friend, Cynthia Baltres, back in New York. It was the morning after the luncheon at the Century City Plaza. This afternoon's community service would consist of her and Cammie meeting a couple of the organizers at the caterer's and tasting a variety of hors d'oeuvres and cocktails that might be served at the fashion show after party. It was bizarre. She realized how lucky she was. Most people getting busted like she had would end up in juvie, or doing the kind of community service that Cammie dreaded—graffiti duty on the freeway overpasses. For her and Cammie? Nothing of the kind. They'd gotten the most benign punishment possible.

Someplace else, the DA might have made an example of the overprivileged, but here, they got the plush gig.

Anna nodded as she finished her e-mail to Cyn, because Cyn would love this kind of affair.

Cyn and Scott, Cyn reported in the same e-mail, were completely and officially over. It struck Anna as amazing, now, the massive crush she'd once had on Scott Spencer. Looking back, she was pretty sure that she'd simply been in need of an object of affection after whom she could lust from afar, because she'd been too big of a wuss to lust from anear. Knowing that Scott wasn't into her made him safe.

Well, Anna had made a choice to stop being so damn safe all the time. Not in the sex-without-condoms sense, or the getting-too-high-to-know-what-the-hell-she-was-doing sense (both of which were, in her opinion, far more stupid than daring), but in the romantic sense. She had decided to throw out the rulebook and have new experiences. She was glad about it, even if she did, at times, feel like she was flying without a net. It was why she'd been willing to tell Ben on graduation night that she didn't want to be with him, that she wanted to be with Caine that night instead.

"Miss Anna?"

She heard the voice but didn't recognize the house-keeper standing in her doorway. Of course, her father was a typical Los Angeleno. He went through domestic help the way domestic help went through Windex.

"I am Julie. New house helper for your father," she explained, in an accent that sounded like it came from somewhere in the vicinity of what had once been the Soviet Union. "There is boy here to see you. He says his name is Ben. He gave me this for you." She handed Anna a folded note.

Ben? She couldn't help it. Her heart pounded in her

chest. But she'd been raised on the *This Is How We Do Things* Big Book (East Coast WASP edition). She knew how to keep her emotions out of her voice. Page one hundred and seventy-two: *Nothing should throw you enough for someone else to notice. If global thermonuclear war erupts, ask what is appropriate to wear to a radiation party.*

She waited until the new housekeeper was out the door to unfold the note. Ben had handwritten it in his familiar scrawl.

Anna,
Good morning, jailbird! Cammie and Sam
told me about your adventure in the criminal
justice system, and that you had your first day of
comm. service yesterday. All serious felons deserve
coffee and rugelach from Nate'n Al to start their
day. I've got some with me downstairs. Just call me
and I'll bring it in. Or we can go somewhere to eat
and talk. If not, then . . . not. I'll leave it on the
doorstep and you can enjoy at your leisure. Take
off the handcuffs if you're planning to eat. Or
leave 'em on and invite me in.
                                        —Ben

Anna refolded the note. Ben was downstairs. *Her* Ben. Except that she needed to not think of him that way now. Too much had happened, and she couldn't pretend otherwise.

She'd actually met him before she'd even arrived at LAX, because they were on the same flight from New York on New Year's Day. He'd been a freshman at Princeton then, and would be a sophomore this coming fall. He wore his brown hair a little shaggy, had eyes the color of the Pacific on a sunny day, and had the toned build of a swimmer. He was also smart and sweet and sexy, and he'd been the boy to whom she'd lost her virginity. She had some great memories of her time with Ben. That was one of them.

Was that the reason that she'd thought he was "the one" for so long, and why she sometimes still thought he'd be the one forever? She sighed. There had been too much deceit, both major and minor. He'd stranded her on his father's yacht not far from Joe's Clams in Marina del Rey on the same night that they'd met. There'd been the Anna Nicole Smith look-alike (much younger, brunette version) who'd surprised her at the front door of his parents' house, and whom he'd actually taken to her junior prom. Not that anything bad had happened with that girl—what was her name, Maddie?—but Ben hadn't exactly been up front with her about it. And then, finally, there was a girl from Princeton who was basically stalking him, but whom Ben didn't mention anything about until it was too late.

It was all too much and too angst-y for her. So when Caine Manning came along via her father's investment firm—a little older and, it seemed to Anna now, a lot more mature—she had been intrigued. Caine was different

from any boy she'd ever known. He drove a pickup
truck. Ben drove a Beemer. Ben lived in Beverly Hills.
Caine lived in Venice. Ben's arms were tan from the
tennis court and the pool at the Riviera Country Club.
Caine's arms were tattooed with reproductions of
Botticelli paintings.

Anna rested her forehead in her hands,

She still held the note. Ben was downstairs. Right
now.

And that's how she came to be sitting across from
him in the gazebo in her father's huge backyard fifteen
minutes later.

"Anna."

Her insides did a somersault when he spoke her
name. His voice gave her goose bumps. His looks, too.
He wore old jeans and a polo shirt the same blue as his
eyes. She was wearing what she'd had on when she got
his note: ancient white cotton pants and a white men's
T-shirt, green flip-flops, a ponytail, and no makeup.

"Nice out here," he commented, passing her a card-
board cup of coffee. He placed the rugelach between
them on top of a white paper bag. "Doesn't even feel like
Beverly Hills."

"I love it, too." Anna ran a finger over the natural
blond wood of the gazebo, wood that had been lovingly
hand sanded to the texture of velvet. "I hardly ever
come out here; maybe I spent too many years living in
New York to even remember to think about a backyard." She sipped the coffee.

Ben bit into a cherry rugelach and stretched out on the long wooden bench seat that circled the gazebo. "So, let's start with the basics. How are you?"

"I'm good." Anna winced. Ugh. What a banal thing to say. How could she possibly feel awkward with him after everything they'd experienced together? She tasted the hot coffee just for something to do and hoped he hadn't noticed the goose bumps on her arms.

"So, community service for *trespassing*?" He sounded incredulous.

She shrugged and pulled her knees up to her chest. "Some vendetta between Cammie's father and this guy, I guess. Cammie and I got stuck in the middle. In some bizarre way I think it's going to be fun. We're helping with a charity fashion show at the Los Angeles County Museum of Art. It's a week from Wednesday night. I love that museum. Anyway, that's our community service."

"Ah yes, the Anna Percy who is up for new experiences. We shared some of those." He sipped his own coffee and smiled.

Damn. Maybe he *had* noticed her goose bumps.

Before the fact, she'd wondered what it would be like to have sex, and then, more specifically, what it would be like with Ben. As it turned out, it was wonderful, amazing, and fantastic. It took her out of her head, something that rarely happened. When Ben made love to her, she was all feeling.

"You ought to come by the club sometime," Ben suggested casually. "Maybe on a Monday."

"You know I'm not really the clubbing type."

He smiled. "That's why I said Monday. I had this idea and we're trying it out, because Trieste is pretty empty on Mondays, anyway. So we're doing some different things in the different rooms. There are poetry readings on the back patio, jazz in the dance room, and short reader's theater plays in the main bar, all of which are actually set in bars. It's pretty cool. Mondays draw a very different kind of crowd. No second-generation club kids, no wanna-bes from the Valley. I think you'd like it."

"This was your idea?" Anna was impressed.

Ben nodded, broke off more of a rugelach, and chewed it before he answered. "I've been going on basically no sleep, but it's incredibly exciting. We did the first Trieste Monday last week, and we've got another one this coming Monday. The owner knows Chick Corea—amazing jazz pianist—and he'll be playing as a surprise at midnight. Then we've got some really cool one-act plays."

Wow. She *never* would have expected this from Ben. He'd never talked about being a club promoter. "Maybe I'll check it out."

He smiled winningly. "I'd like that." Then, ever so casually, he asked, "You still seeing that guy with the tattoos?"

"Caine. Yes. We're . . . dating." It was weird. She felt sheepish saying it.

"Dating." Ben laughed. "Wow, does anybody really *date* anymore?"

Anna stiffened. "Evidently I do."

"Evidently you do. The two of you could come by, then. Drinks are on me."

"Okay, thank you." She sipped her coffee, wondering why he was being quite so accepting of her *dating*, when the person she was *dating* was not him.

"This is amazing!" Anna exclaimed, as the Ferris wheel swung skyward into the cool night.

"Welcome to the best wheel west of the California coastline. Which also happens to be the only Ferris wheel west of the California coastline."

Caine had picked her up at nine as promised. But instead of the pickup truck, he was on a black 1960s BSA motorcycle that he said he'd restored himself, complete with an extra white helmet for Anna. "Put it on," he ordered with a grin.

She did, with some trepidation, never having been on a motorcycle before. Yet within three minutes she was completely comfortable, as Caine followed Sunset Boulevard to Barrington, then cut over to San Vicente and took it east to the ocean, dodging between cars with total confidence. It was a warm night, and she clung to his body, picturing how they must look to passersby. *Like lovers*, she thought. *We must look like lovers.*

He said he had one more surprise in store, and pulled the bike up near the Santa Monica pier, which jutted into the sea off of the Pacific Coast Highway. At the west end was an enormous Ferris wheel.

"A hundred and thirty feet high, and powered by the sun," he told her.

"Even at night?" she joshed. She'd taken enough high school science to know that solar energy could be stored in batteries, just like any other kind of energy.

"Let's go and find out." He looked at the crowded parking area. "Two thousand Los Angelenos can't be wrong."

Fifteen minutes later, they'd walked through the polyglot mass of humanity that was the Santa Monica pier on a warm summer night, paid their admission tickets for the wheel, climbed into one of the yellow cabs, and gone spinning up into the night. It was fantastic. The night was crystalline, and a bright full moon hung in the west like a beacon of adventure. Around and around they went—two, three, four trips on the wheel, Caine happily assuring the operator that he was good for the fare. Then he slipped the guy an extra twenty dollars.

"That's nice of you," Anna noted.

"I have an ulterior motive."

Caine offered no more information than that, but Anna's curiosity was satisfied five minutes later, when the wheel slowed as they reached the top and then stopped dead.

"You paid him for this."

"Guilty as charged. Check out the view." Caine put his hands on her shoulders and turned her around so that they could look east, toward the city. It shone like a constellation in the night, streams of car headlights moving in all directions and up above, Anna could see the lights of the planes as they stacked up to land at LAX.

"It's . . . it's like a dream." Anna found herself thinking of Champagne and wondering whether she'd ever had a guy take her to this wheel, then tip the operator so that the cab would stay perched high in the sky.

"What are you thinking about?" Caine asked softly.

"This girl I met yesterday. Funny name. Champagne. She's in the at-risk girls' program. I guess she begged to help out with the fashion show, and they let her."

"What about her?"

"Just . . . I don't even know her, but the woman who runs the fashion show basically accused her of theft, based on no evidence. She was so patronizing, and this girl seemed so sweet. . . ."

"Fill me in. I'm not tracking."

Anna explained what Virginia had said about Champagne stealing Martin Rittenhouse's gown, even though she didn't have any proof at all. He whistled gruffly. "That sucks. Sometimes people with money act like not having it is the result of a character defect. Such patronizing bullshit."

Anna agreed, and found Caine's reaction so close to her own that she impetuously leaned over and kissed him, the first time she'd ever done such a thing in her life.

The kiss lasted until the wheel started moving again. And then for a while longer after that. It turned out to be both fun and educational. Anna learned in thirty seconds that Ben wasn't the only great kisser in L.A.

Pre-Post-Hot

Cammie found herself that night in an uncharacter-
istic position. She literally had nothing to do.
Dee was off with Jack doing whatever Dee and Jack
did. Ditto Sam and Eduardo, who were crashing at
Eduardo's condo on the Wilshire corridor.

She couldn't even call Adam. He and his parents had
gone on a three-day canoe trip and left their cell phones
behind. Unimaginable, but true. Nor were any of her
other usual suspects available. Krishna and Skye weren't
due back from London until Sunday, while Ashleigh and
Damian were slumming at Hedonism III in Jamaica.

So Cammie decided to go out by herself. Maybe
she'd just check out Trieste, where Ben still worked.
Even after all the press coverage it had received the
month before—coverage that normally turned a hot
club into burnt toast—Trieste remained next to impossible to get into, with Jacinda Barrett reportedly having
to wait forty-five minutes to be admitted and Jessica
never making it to within spitting distance of the VIP
section.

Of course, the best reason to crash Trieste was Ben Birnbaum. Despite being with Adam, the truth was that Cammie still hadn't gotten over getting dumped by Ben at the end of her junior year. Adam brought out the good in her. Ben brought out the bad. Good was often good. Bad was sometimes so much better.

She put on a new outfit she'd found at Fred Segal—a D&G ivory miniskirt and a Robert Graham magenta brocade jacket that ended four inches above the top of the skirt.

She did her makeup, spritzed her strawberry blond curls, then checked out her reflection in her full-length mirror.

I would do me. No higher compliment could be given.

For the last week, she'd been driving her father's new cherry red Lamborghini. Even for Los Angeles, capital of the universe of the internal combustion engine, the Lamborghini was something special. At every stoplight there were admiring stares from passersby. She took it to Trieste, tossed the keys to the valet, and a moment later was waved into the club by the very hot, very bald doorman. He was new, she noted. Very tasty. She favored him with a wink as she shimmied past. No block-long line or velvet rope for her.

As she made her way to the juice bar at the back, her typical club experience began. That is, she was hit on early and often. No to the businessman from France.

No to the lipstick lesbian from Hancock Park. No to the race-car driver from Holland. There was only one guy at Trieste she wanted to hang with. And there he was, behind the juice bar, making the famous fortified fruit smoothies for which this patio was becoming famous.

"Well, well." She sidled up to him, thinking it was impossible for Ben Birnbaum to look anything but hot, even in a basic white Trieste staff T-shirt and black Diesel jeans. "If it isn't my favorite bartender."

"And if it isn't my favorite ex-girlfriend," Ben replied. He flashed a huge, handsome grin. "What can I get you?"

Cammie flashed her most winning smile at him and resisted her natural inclination, which was to say, *You. Me. And the Presidential Suite at the Hotel Bel-Air.*

"What's the specialty concoction tonight from the Ben Birnbaum magic blender?"

"Coconut crème-papaya smoothie with a vitamin B boost. Will make you forget that Jamba Juice was ever invented."

"I'll take a half," she decided, "and the other half Jamaican rum."

Ben laughed. "Make it a quarter, and you got it. Go have a seat, I'll bring it to you."

Cammie spotted an empty pair of red-and-white striped lawn chairs under a eucalyptus tree and commandeered them both, putting her feet up on the one that would be Ben's. While he blended her smoothie, she fended off an approach from a Japanese artist dressed in severe black, and also a cute guy who claimed to be one of the writers of the new hit show *Heroes.*

Suddenly, a half-glass of coconut smoothie materialized in front of her—Ben had snaked it around from behind. "I made it a third rum. Call it a compromise," he murmured in her ear, sending shivers down her spine. "Enjoy."

Cammie raised her glass, which held the same off-white, creamy concoction as Ben's did.

"Here's to ex-boyfriends and -girlfriends," she proposed. "Because you never know."

Ben clinked her glass and then sat in the chair she'd saved for him. "I'll drink to that."

"So, speaking of . . . How are you dealing with Ben-and-no-Anna?" Cammie tasted the drink. It was easily one-third rum. And not bar pour, either. Good stuff.

"The word's out, huh?"

"It's all over MySpace. Also aintitcool.com. And then there was the full-page thingie in the *Hollywood Reporter,*" she joked.

Ben stretched and rubbed the back of his neck, which made his biceps bulge nicely. "I forgot about the Beverly Hills gossip line. The underground railroad had nothing on you guys."

For a moment, Cammie bristled. Just what did he mean by "you guys"? She wasn't that big of a gossip. She was too busy being the star to spend that much time on other people. But she decided to let it go. She wasn't here to bitch. She was here to make nice. Very, very nice.

"Everyone saw you at graduation," Cammie replied strategically, stretching out her legs for maximum visual impact. "Everyone saw Anna get into that guy's—"

"Caine. His name is Caine."

"How biblical. Yeah, I met him at Sam's party out on the *Look Sharpe*. Tattoo Guy. Pretty odd for Anna, but whatever. She blew you off for him?" Cammie was careful to sound as incredulous as possible.

Ben shrugged. "Maybe you ought to ask her."

Cammie took another sip of her coconut smoothie. She felt some coat the skin above her plump upper lip and licked it off slowly, knowing that he was watching. "It's not like she and I are the best of friends, Ben."

He shrugged again. "You're doing community service with her. Which, incidentally, is hilarious. Don't you talk?"

"Two ex-girlfriends comparing notes. I can't think of anything more banal. Except maybe some Penny Marshall movie I'd never see."

"I wouldn't put Anna in the 'ex' column. I'd put her in the 'we're taking a breather' column."

Cammie playfully nudged the toe of her boot into his calf. "Get over it, Ben. I doubt very much that she's tooling around with Tattoo Guy and telling him that she's taking a 'breather' from you." She watched that zinger cause a flicker of doubt to cross Ben's face.

"She's pissed at me," he admitted.

"She pisses off easily. Where's the love?"

He swung his legs off the chair. "She'll either get over it or not. I'm not dwelling on it, if that's what you mean."

"How long are you planning to wait?" Cammie looked at him closely.

"Till I get sick of waiting, I guess."

"That's almost frighteningly mature," Cammie mused. "Is that what happens after a year at Princeton? Because if it is, I'm *never* going to college."

He laughed; Cammie could always make him laugh. That was what kept them together when they were a couple, back when he was a senior and she was a junior. Well, that and physical chemistry so hot it made her feel dizzy.

"Well, I just wanted to say that if you need a shoulder to cry on, I'm here," Cammie continued intimately. "Adam's in Michigan, so I've got the time. And even if you tie me up, tie me down, and kiss me all over, I'm not fooling around with you."

Ben cracked up. "Liar."

"You know, the bizarre thing is . . . I really do love Adam. But what can I tell you, Ben? I'll always have a weakness for you. So don't tempt me, and I'll try not to tempt you. Deal?"

He nodded, regarding her with something that seemed to approach respect. "Deal."

"If I break my promise, the smoothie gods will strike me down with a bolt of liquid lightning."

"Then I'd say you're the one who's almost frighteningly

mature," Ben observed. "Hanging out with Adam did that for you, huh?"

"He's a great guy. He's deep and kind and . . ." She shrugged. "Probably way too good for me."

"Ah, Cammie. There is no one else quite like you." Ben leaned forward in his lawn chair and enveloped her in a quick hug.

She let it go at that. She wasn't about to let on that her mind wasn't nearly as faithful as her body.

Barbie-Doll Curves

S am took her usual table at the Polo Lounge in the Beverly Hills Hotel and waited for the latest petite and dimwitted waitress to wait on her.

Sam had been coming to the Beverly Hills Hotel since she was a little kid, first with her father, and then—by the time she was in middle school—with her friends. Even as middle-schoolers, Sam and her buds didn't have to wait for Mommy or Daddy to drive them. Most were even spared the ignominious humiliation of trailing some nanny or au pair. They simply called the family chauffeur and got dropped off. Then, when they were ready to come home, they'd press speed dial and the driver would be at the hotel there within thirty minutes.

It was a nice tradition for the junior division of Hollywood showbiz royalty.

"Hey, there. Care to see the menu?" asked a waitress with long, wavy chestnut hair, the curves of a Barbie doll, and a sweet Southern accent. She was naturally gorgeous. Sam *hated* that in a waitress.

"I haven't looked at a menu in here since I was six."

Sam wore oversize round black Chanel sunglasses along with her Eve of Destruction jeans and her latest acquisitions from Scoop boutique: a green silk tank top under a Versace black jacket just long enough to cover the widest part of her hips and ass.

Sam whipped off the sunglasses, knowing exactly what would happen. The waitress-actress wanna-be would realize who Sam was and then suck up to her in an effort to gain access to Sam's father and then, hopefully, a role in one of Jackson's films.

"Well, dang, why buck a trend?" the waitress asked with a sparkling smile. "Now, tell me what I can get you. Unless you want to wait." She motioned to the empty chair across the table.

Was it really possible that she didn't know who Sam was?

"The house salad with dressing on the side, the onion soup, no cheese, and an iced cappuccino, no whipped cream," Sam ordered. She had planned on a cheeseburger and fries but had come down with a bad case of size-two-waitress envy. "And you're right, I'm meeting someone. Put the whole thing on my dad's tab."

The waitress's eyebrows headed north as she finished jotting down the order. "Sorry?"

"Tab. Bill. Balance sheet. Account. Signing privileges. My father. Do it."

"Oh, they haven't told me about that yet. I'm new. First day here, in fact. Whose account would that be?"

"Jackson Sharpe."

"Jackson Sharpe," the girl repeated. "Okay, I'll ask my manager. Anything else?"

Sam shook her head. Very odd.

The waitress was just leaving as Sam spotted Parker near the bar, heading for her table. He wore his usual jeans, a white T-shirt, and a red windbreaker, which only prompted more people to make the obvious comparison to James Dean. Sam saw her tarry long enough to flash him a dazzling smile as he slid into the empty seat at her table.

"Damn, that waitress is a knockout."

"The operative term being *waitress*, Parker. Meaning she's not your type."

Okay. That was sort of uncalled for, but it never hurt to remind Parker who had the power at this table. He was always on the lookout for girlfriends with money, which was fine. The thing was, Sam knew that Parker would never describe *her* as a knockout. No one would. Oh, she was no bowser, though she sometimes felt like one, compared to her friends. Pear-shaped. Size ten—and that was only when she was dieting. Thighs that screamed, "Cellulite as gross as cottage cheese!" across a room, even when artfully draped in thousand-dollar pants.

"I saw Cammie at Faux," Parker said, naming a club on Sunset where everything was made to look deliberately kitsch. "Late last night. She told me about getting arrested with Anna. What a hoot."

"Who was she there with?"

"No one. Or everyone, depending on how you look at it. She danced with every guy in the place and half the girls, too."

"Hello?" The Barbie-doll-curves waitress was back at their table, pad at the ready, her eyes fixed on Parker. "Would you like to see a menu, or have you not had to look at it since you were six, too?"

Sam looked at her closely. She had an actual small laugh line near her left eye. Forget Botox. Damn. Her tits were probably real as well.

"I know just what I want," he responded slowly, making serious eye contact.

"Do you?" She smiled like a beauty pageant contestant who knew she'd just nailed the talent portion of the competition. "And what would that be?"

"What's your name?" Parker asked.

"Citron. Yours?"

"Parker." He held out a hand. "It's a pleasure, Citron."

The waitress took it and they started chatting like she didn't have another table to look after, he was eating alone, and Sam was a department store mannequin. Citron turned out to be a recent arrival from Louisiana. She'd bummed around for a few years but would start at Loyola-Marymount in the fall and was waitressing to pay the rent.

"Someone who looks like you has to be a performer," Parker decided, his tone flirty. "Actress? Model?"

Citron smiled. There was another laugh line. "Neither. Singer. Kind of in the Alicia Keyes vein—"

"Excuse me," Sam interrupted. "Did I turn on my invisibility cloak?"

"Oh, so sorry. Is your boyfriend hitting on me?" Citron looked neither guilty nor ashamed.

Sam smiled thinly. "He's not my—look, could you just take his order, bring food, and give us the privacy that we so richly deserve?"

Parker ordered a toasted bagel, fries, and coffee, and then turned his attention to Sam as Citron hustled off to the kitchen. "Sorry about that. Did you ask me to lunch because you miss seeing me at school every day?"

"No, Parker. I invited you because I wanted to watch you hit on the waitress."

"That wasn't hitting—"

Sam waved her hand to cut him off. "I know, I know. If you were really hitting on her, she'd be on a break with you now in one of the empty bungalows. Forget it. Actually, I wanted to thank you again for what you did with Eduardo. I owe you. Big-time."

He made a dismissive gesture. "Forget it. You two are back together?"

"Better than together. He took me to Peru for graduation. To meet his family. I am a woman in love. And I owe it to you."

"Excellent." Parker laced his fingers together. "Couldn't happen to a nicer girl."

Sam frowned. Nice? Her? She should take it as a compliment, she supposed. But the truth was, she'd asked him to lunch to offer him more than just a

thank-you. And the reason was definitely not one a
"nice" girl would come up with. But there was time
enough to get to that.

"Thanks. So what's up with work for you?" she
inquired.

Parker talked about his so-called career for a while.
It was more of the usual. He was auditioning for a
whole bunch of roles, none of which he would get. He
was thinking about getting a crap job to help his mom
pay the rent, but the thought of working as a waiter at
some place where his friends might eat was incredibly
depressing and would confuse everyone since Sam was
his only friend who knew his real financial situation.
Which made it the perfect time for Sam to pounce.

"So listen. You know my dad is remaking *Ben-Hur*,
right?"

Parker gave her a quizzical look and edged his chair
closer to the table. "Of course I know. We had our
prom on the chariot race set. Lay off the wacky weed."

"Here you go, Parker." Citron carefully set his bagel
and fries in front of him and then poured coffee into
his cup.

"Thanks, Citron. What brought you to Los Angeles,
anyway?"

"Katrina," she answered, with not a little sadness in
her voice. "I'm from New Orleans. I stayed with my
grandparents in Memphis for a while. Then with friends
in Baton Rouge. And now . . . here I am."

When it appeared that they were about two conversational steps from the traditional swapping of cell phone numbers, Sam shooed the waitress away once again. To bring her her lunch. Which she had ordered before Parker even showed up.

"Get the digits after," Sam suggested when she took off. "Is that too much to ask?"

Parker watched Citron at another table. "Damn, there is just something about her—"

"Yeah, great. *Focus!* I want to talk to you about something infinitely more important. Namely, a role in my father's movie."

Parker actually froze with his bagel halfway to his lips. "Did you say—?"

"Yeah. Next week. Tom Hanks is coming in to do a small part as a favor to my dad. They go way back. You'd be up for the role of Tom Hanks's son. And you'd have a brief scene with my father."

Down to the white china plate went the bagel, and Parker's eyes widened to the size of its rim. "Tom Hanks's son. And a scene with your father."

Sam nodded and sipped her water. Now that she had his attention, she could take her time. Served him right.

"Tell me more," Parker demanded.

"Oh, so *now* I get your attention," Sam groused. "You'd play a Roman teen. You'd have three scenes: one little one, one where you get into a fight with your father, and one where you help prepare my father for the chariot race. It's not insignificant."

"Damn, I would kill for a screen test."

"You don't actually have to test. I can get you an audition where you'd go up against two other guys. I've already talked to the casting director, and I'd say those are pretty decent odds. Of course, if you don't want to bet on yourself—"

"Are you shitting me? I always bet on myself. When? Where? And can I get sides?"

Citron waltzed over with Sam's order and set it down in front of her. Sam frowned. "Did I not say *dressing on the side*?"

"Did you?" Citron asked, looking neither apologetic nor concerned.

"Forget it. Just take the salad away."

"Fair enough." Citron took the salad with her.

"Sides?" Parker asked again.

"Got 'em right here." Sam opened her oversized Be & D camel suede ruffled shoulder bag and took out several stapled sets of script pages she'd been given by her father's assistant, Kiki Coors. "This is what you need to work on for the audition. I'll call you with the time and place. Sound good?"

Parker looked suspiciously like he had tears in his eyes when she handed him the sides. "Sam, this is really . . . I really . . ."

Sam waved away his thanks and waited for him to take a sip of coffee. This was going to be fun.

"You're the one who has to nail the gig. And in return, I only ask one thing." She smiled sweetly. "That you also nail my stepmother."

Parker nearly snorted coffee out to the hotel tennis courts and had to wipe his nose before talking. Sam desperately hoped that Citron had been watching.

"You want me to— Did you just say what I think you said?"

"She's cheating on my father. I'm pretty sure of it."

"So it's just a suspicion."

"Well, I didn't watch the act," Sam admitted. "But I did see her with her yoga instructor, whose eyes—and probably his hands—know every curve of her ass."

"So you think she's doing him," Parker surmised.

"Do you think I'd be asking you to do this if I wasn't sure? Poppy bitches all the time about how my father is never home. She's taking, like, six classes from Yoga Guy every week. Private classes. At my house. He's definitely showing her more than his full lotus." She leaned closer. "Look, you don't actually have to *nail* her—although the look on your face when I said it was priceless. I don't even want you to trap her."

"What do you want, exactly?"

Good question. "I just want you to . . . open the door, let's say. Be nice to her, very attentive—which, God knows, is one of your great talents—and take your cue from her. I swear, if you come back to me and say she wasn't interested, I'll let it go."

"And if it goes further than that?" Parker raised his eyebrows and rubbed his chin at the same time.

"That has to be her call," Sam decided. "I'm not try-ing to set her up. I'm trying to see how she handles temptation. My guess is, she'll be head over heels for you. And shortly after that, heels over head—metaphorically speaking. Like I said, you don't have to do her."

"Good. Because 'doing' Jackson Sharpe's wife would pretty much guarantee the end of my not-yet-started career."

Sam nodded. "I would never ask you to do that."

Parker riffled the edge of the sides she'd given him. "Far be it from me to question any of this, but . . . what's your goal?"

"For my dad to divorce the Pop-Tart and get her the hell out of my house and out of my life. I wouldn't even mind if we kept the baby around. She's just a baby. We can probably undo the months of damage that Poppy has no doubt done. Do you think babies are too young for psychotherapy?" She grinned. "Perhaps it's not too late to save her."

"At the risk of my losing the gig—how will me flirting with Poppy get back to your dad?"

"I don't have all the details worked out yet. But I'm a director. I can sure as hell direct this." She sipped her cappuccino, thinking out loud. "Let's see. . . . I'll hire a private investigator to take some pictures of the two of you in some public place. Smooching, let's say. But you'll be from the back, the side, any angle where your face can't be seen."

"Absolutely positively I won't be identified?"

Sam nodded. "I give you my word. So, you in?"

Parker nodded emphatically. "You've been good to me so far, Sam."

"And you've been great to me. I'll cover your ass, no matter what," she promised. She meant it, too.

"If I say no . . . no audition?"

Sam had fully intended to say, "No audition." This was, after all, her bargaining chip. But she heard herself say something else entirely.

"Oh, hell. I'll still get you the audition. I owe you, like I said. Besides, Parker, I have a feeling that underneath all that bullshit you throw around, you're actually a very talented guy who's getting overlooked. And one other thing, too."

"What's that?"

Sam smiled. "I helped you. Then you helped me. Now I'm asking you to help me again while I help you. It's the American way. Go for it. Then go over there and give that Southern-fried brain-dead waitress your number. You know you want to."

Model Behavior

"We're here to see Melange."

Anna stood with Sam, Cammie, and Champagne in the all-white PacCoast reception area. All white was no exaggeration. The walls were white, the furniture was white, the phones were white, and the ceiling was white.

The receptionist, whose little desk plaque identified her as Zona, was holding the phone to her ear. "*Excuse me?*" she said rudely, to Sam, and then went back to talking into the sleek white phone. "I know, I *know* she looked like such a total fat-ass." When Zona said the phrase "fat-ass" she looked Sam up and down.

"We've been sent by the New Visions foundation to do a preliminary selection of models for their show at the art museum," Sam explained, tapping her fingers against Zona's desk.

This was true. Mrs. Vanderleer had thought it might be fun for them to winnow down the field of potential models, even if she would be making the final choices. But if Cammie and Anna wanted to recommend, say, four men and four women that would be more than okay.

Anna had been the one to suggest that Champagne come along. After a bit of hesitation, Mrs. Vanderleer had said that would be fine. But they had to keep an eye on her. *At all times*, she'd emphasized. And they had to sign her in and out at New Visions headquarters in West Hollywood. As far as Anna could see, Champagne was just a pretty girl who'd gotten some bad breaks.

Zona looked more carefully at Sam. "Wait. Aren't you . . . ?"

Sam smiled smugly. "This might be a good moment to start sucking up."

Zona opened her eyes wide and slowly lowered the phone back onto the receiver, without even saying goodbye. "I *love* your father's movies!" she gushed.

"Right on cue!" Champagne cried, as if the whole thing delighted her.

"I'm so sorry," Zona insisted. A red blush of embarrassment spread up to her eyebrows.

"Just get Melange," Sam instructed.

The receptionist looked up at the four girls arrayed in a line in front of her desk. "Okay! I'll be right back."

She scuttled through the glass doors into the back offices; miraculously, in her absence, the phones bounced to another location. Normally, Anna hated it when Sam and Cammie threw their celebrity weight around, but this time she had to admit it had been incredibly satisfying.

"It must be so cool to be you," Champagne told Sam.

"It has its upside," Sam admitted.

Zona returned and led them into a large white conference room with a white Formica table, white chairs, and several crystalline white boards. "Have a seat. Melange will be here in a moment."

Before they were even in their chairs, Melange strode into the room. Anna recognized her immediately. When she had been younger, her photograph had graced the covers of countless magazines and bus shelters. She'd been Kate Moss, Cindy Crawford, and Gisele Bündchen rolled into one. Now, at age fortysomething, she was running one of the hottest new modeling agencies in the world.

She also looked much the same as Anna remembered. Five-ten, with a choppy, chin-length bob the color of a burnt sienna crayon, her face wide-eyed and unlined, with the highest cheekbones that Anna had ever seen, and a generous mouth.

"Sam!" Melange put her arms out. The former model towered over Sam but embraced her anyway. "Wow, you look fantastic! I haven't seen you since your father's wedding."

"You look great too," Sam told her, and then quickly introduced everyone, taking extra time with Champagne, who looked like she'd died and gone to heaven.

"I am so honored to meet you," Champagne gushed. "I really admire your work."

"The honor's mine," Melange replied graciously. "Aren't you a beauty! Too bad you're not just a tiny bit taller." She took a seat at the head of the white rectangular table. "It's just fantastic that you're all working on this show. What a great thing to do with your free time."

Champagne nudged Anna and grinned wildly. Evidently Melange was under the impression that they were just a group of do-gooder girls doing a do-gooder deed. "We all really need to do more giving back, don't you think? Did Sam tell you how we met? When I was much younger, Jackson gave me a part in *Hangman's Mountain*. You remember that one, right?"

Anna did. It was a throwback western designed to both mock and pay homage to the melodramas of a bygone era, and she vaguely recalled that Melange had the role of a dance hall girl who was thrown under a steam engine by the grotesquely mustachioed villain within the first half hour of the movie. But Melange had proved incredibly photogenic, and the role had launched her career. Now it was twenty-five years later, and she was apparently returning the favor.

"Anyway," Melange went on, sliding into one of the white leather seats, "we all have to do what we can, when we can, as much as we can."

"Well, we're just really glad that you can help us with this," Sam cooed back, then edged away from the table so she could cross her legs. "So, do you have girls for us to see? And guys?"

Melange nodded. "I called in twelve of each. You're going to narrow it down to eight, right? I'll just have them come in one at a time and you can look at their

books. You didn't need me for this, did you? I've got a
fire to put out on a shoot in Milan."

Moments later, one by one, the models came into
the conference room, starting with the women. They
were all rail thin—no big shocker there—and dressed
down in T-shirts, skinny jeans, leggings, or workout
gear. None of them wore makeup. Each handed her
portfolio over to Cammie, who was closest to the door,
and then waited patiently for the others to flip through
their photos.

Anna found it amazing to see the difference
between how the girls looked in person and how they
photographed. Sometimes she wouldn't even have
been able to tell that they were the same person. From
time to time, Cammie made surprisingly helpful suggestions to the models. To a beautiful girl with long
dark hair, she suggested that the girl brush her hair
back off her face for her next comp card, because
she'd obviously lost a bit of weight since then, and
now her cheekbones stood out even more. The girl
gushed her thanks.

After they'd seen a dozen girls, in came the guys.
They were less clearly variations on a theme, though all
were elevens on a scale of ten in the looks department,
even if some seemed south of the midpoint on the IQ
department. Cammie asked a guy with the biggest chin
cleft that Anna had ever seen the name of the vice president of the United States. When the model answered,
"That old guy," Cammie suggested that maybe he'd want

to read the newspaper or watch *Headline News* once in a while, in case a client cared about such things. The guy thanked Cammie as though no one had ever made the suggestion before.

Finally, they spread out comp cards on the table and picked their eight favorite models—four girls, four guys. Melange rushed back in to air kiss each of them before they left, then walked them to the elevator. After the agency head had departed, Champagne looked back longingly.

"You know what I wish?"

"What?" Anna asked.

"That I really *was* four inches taller. Because maybe I could do what those girls do. You know what my mom did before she went on disability? She was a cashier." Anna saw tears in the corner of Champagne's eyes, which she quickly brushed away. "And that's what she wants me to do too."

Anna sipped her café Americano while Champagne applied some hot pink Rexall lip gloss. There was a Coffee Bean downstairs in the same building as PacCoast, and they'd decided to make a pit stop before heading over to the New Visions offices to meet with Mrs. Vanderleer and Mrs. Chesterfield. Sam had to depart, though. She had a session planned with her psychotherapist.

As Cammie was waiting in line for some elaborate fat-free soy concoction she'd ordered, Anna looked closely at Champagne. "If you were taller, would you really want to be a model?"

With her high cheekbones, wide-spaced eyes, and naturally silvery-blond hair, Champagne really was a spectacular-looking girl. Better looking than some of the girls they'd just picked to be in the show. Yet she was five-six, in a world where models were five-ten.

She shrugged. "I think it would be amazing. Who wouldn't want to?" Champagne raked her fingers through the ends of her hair. "It's not like I haven't tried. I went into this agency on Van Nuys Boulevard that I found in the Yellow Pages—I had to take two buses there from Reseda. It turned out that they were looking for models, all right—porno models. Anyway, I wouldn't have time. I go to school and work two part-time jobs. My mom's on disability, so I work at a doughnut shop on Saticoy from four in the morning till seven in the morning. Then I go to school. Then I work at a 7-Eleven from five until eleven. On weekends, I baby-sit or work overtime."

"How'd you get into the New Visions program?" Anna wondered aloud. Champagne had just laid out a daily schedule that was unimaginable to her. It made her feel very, very lucky. And guilty too.

"There's a teacher at my school—a really cool English teacher, Ms. Martinez. She recommended me. I did really well on some aptitude test for nursing. She thought the program would help."

"Does it?"

Champagne smiled sweetly. "I'm not in jail, am I? Most of my friends have been in and out of juvie. I'd prefer to just stay out."

Cammie came back from the counter with her soy drink. It hadn't taken long for her to get served. At this hour of the afternoon, the café was nearly empty.

"You guys are both rich." There was no malice in Champagne's voice. Only envy. "I know that girl Sam is, 'cause her father is a big movie star. But like, how much do you spend a year on clothes, Cammie?"

Cammie coolly sipped her drink. "Who keeps track?"

"Take a guess, then. Ten thousand dollars? More?"

"Um, probably more. Is there a point to this, Champagne? Except to make yourself feel bad?"

"It doesn't make me feel bad. It makes me feel good. Like, why couldn't I be rich someday?" The girl's eyes shone.

"I agree," Anna told her. "It's great to be ambitious and have goals. If you stay in school and do really well, you can get a scholarship to college—"

"I have what-do-you-call-it . . . aspirations." Champagne looped some hair behind one ear. "You're driving me home, today, to Reseda, right? You'll see where I live—an apartment building that's . . . Well, let's just say I don't want to live there for the rest of my life."

Anna nodded thoughtfully.

"My mom, though," Champagne continued, "she's happy there. It's all we can afford, even with me working so much. *J'ai envie d'être vous deux. Tout les deux. Tout les temps.*"

Anna's jaw dropped slightly. The French was perfect.

"*Ou as-tu apprise ton français?*" she asked.

Champagne grinned. "*Au école. Je suis une bonne étudiante . . . mais sans beaucoup d'argent.*"

"Tell me what she said," Cammie demanded, wiping some of the soy drink from her lips with a napkin.

"I'm a good student," Anna translated bashfully. "And I'd like to be like you. All the time."

A White, Dry Envelope

"**D**ad? You penciled me in?" Cammie reminded her father. She stood with Sam by the side of the tennis courts at the Hancock Park Tennis Club. Her father had a regular Saturday morning doubles game, and he'd just finished his usual Saturday morning three sets—him and Norm Aladjem of Paradigm against Ari Emanuel and Ari Greenburg of Endeavor. The industry partners changed from week to week, but his 9 A.M. to 10:30 A.M. Saturday doubles game was sacrosanct. Definitely, Cammie knew, more sacrosanct than any meeting with her. "Breakfast? Remember?"

"Absolutely!" her father bellowed. He wore a brown Fila tennis shirt and white shorts. "I didn't forget. Glad to see you, kid. Just a sec. Let me say goodbye to my buds."

Clark bounded across the court again—he was one of those completely in-shape Hollywood jock-agent types, with short blond hair, green eyes, and a gleaming smile—and Cammie ruminated on how strange it was that they lived under the same roof but still had to make an appointment for breakfast.

A moment later, Clark was back, his jet-black leather racquet bag slung over his shoulder—he carried four Babolat Pure Drive racquets, like some older version of Andy Roddick. "Walk with me to the clubhouse. I've got a table reserved. How are you, Sam?"

"Ready for coffee."

"Me too."

"I reserved the private room for us," Clark announced. "The Billie Jean King room. Follow me."

There was one white-clothed table set up in the center of the room, its three wicker seats presumably for Clark, Cammie, and Sam. A second buffet table was against the far wall. It was already laden with bagels and lox, scrambled egg whites, scones, sliced prime rib, and a basket of assorted breads.

Cammie sat. She had no appetite but poured herself an oversize cup of coffee. She could make no sense out of the long mystery that was her mother's death, but the time had come to try. It didn't help matters that her father was a notorious liar who would say anything to anyone if it would help to get him what he wanted. Whether she'd get any useful information from him remained to be seen.

"You want to take the lead here, or should I?" Sam asked. She poured herself a tumbler of apple juice and sat down. "You nervous?"

"I was before. Now . . . I just want to get this over with. I got it covered. After all, I heard what your mother said."

"Mother in name only," Sam corrected. "I'm nervous."

"Don't be. I just want to see what my father says when I accuse him of lying—"

"Lying about what?"

Sam and Cammie turned; there was Clark in the doorway. He didn't look angry, though. Just curious.

"Mom. And you. And me," Cammie replied. She idly stirred her coffee.

"Ah. Let me get some juice. We'll talk."

Cammie drummed her fingers on the table as her father poured himself an enormous glass of fresh-squeezed orange juice, set it on the white tablecloth, put down his tennis bag on the parquet floor, and then closed the outside door to the King room before folding himself into a chair and taking a long swallow from his tall glass.

"Guilty as charged, Cammie," he admitted. "I lied about what happened on the boat."

"I knew it," Cammie muttered, and then rested her chin in her hands.

Sam nudged her and mouthed, *Chill out.*

"Let's just say I did something all good agents do."

"Told a half-truth?" Sam guessed boldly. "We got the rest of the truth from Dina. You remember Dina, don't you? Always great when you have to hire a private detective to find your own mother. That kind of maternal connection really brings a tear to the eye, doesn't it?"

Clark drained half his glass. "I've told Cammie this a

million times: never go to a meeting with less information than the other people in the room."

"Sam's mother talked to you?" Cammie was honestly surprised.

Clark nodded emphatically. "Two days after she
went back to North Carolina. I'm up to speed." He
slapped a stomach that would make most body builders
jealous, the product of two hundred sit-ups every
morning. "Hey, I need to fuel up. Aren't you two going
to eat?"

Both Cammie and Sam shook their heads no. Then
they had to wait again, while Clark filled his plate from
the buffet selections. Sam's mother had indeed come
for graduation, after not having seen Sam for many
years. They had met her at her crappy hotel in Sherman
Oaks. After what Cammie had learned from the police
report about her mother's death-by-drowning on a
yacht off the coast of Santa Barbara ten years ago, she
had to find out the truth. The police report had said
that Dina—Sam's real mother—had been out on the
boat that same night.

When they'd met Dina, she'd confirmed that she had
indeed been a passenger that night. Then she'd shared
more information than Cammie and Sam had bargained
for. According to Dina, Cammie's mother had been clinically depressed. The reason that Jeanne had jumped had
a lot more to do with blood chemistry than with any sexual musical chairs that evening—or any other evening—
despite the wife- or husband-swapping that was so popular

back then among Hollywood parents. In fact, Clark had confessed to Cammie that he'd done little more than play gin rummy with Dina that same night.

Clark brought his food back to the table. "Nothing like playing tennis to work up an appetite." He shook his napkin out, placed it on his lap, and dug into his egg whites.

"Dina said that Mom was depressed," Cammie began pointedly. "True or bullshit?"

"True."

Which, of course, did not necessarily mean it was true at all.

"Prove it."

"Figured that's what you'd say." Clark took a huge bite of his everything bagel, washed it down with some coffee, and then unzipped his black leather tennis bag. Out came a manila folder, which he passed to Cammie. "Take a look at this."

Cammie did, even as Sam edged her chair closer so she could check out what was in the file. It held a sheaf of papers much thicker than the original police report. As Cammie leafed through them, she could see they were from Cedars-Sinai Hospital as well as from various well-known Beverly Hills doctors and psychiatrists, all detailing treatment of one Jeanne Sheppard for severe depression. There were prescriptions galore, plus at least one mid-five-figure receipt from the Ojai Institute, the same psychiatric facility that had helped Dee get her life back on track.

"Holy shit, she was at Ojai," Cammie murmured softly, the enormity of her mother's mental health problems so apparent here on paper in black and white. How ironic it was—in some sick way—that her mother had once been at the same mental hospital where Dee had gone. Maybe that was why Cammie had felt so creepy being there. A sixth-sense kind of thing. "I didn't know about any of this."

"We did our best to keep you isolated from it," Clark explained. "Like, if your mom had to go in-patient, we'd send you to visit friends up at Mammoth, or to a summer camp or something. Maybe that wasn't fair, but we didn't want it to be a burden. You were just a kid. We were trying to keep you that way." He gave a sad little laugh. "I can't say we entirely succeeded."

Cammie kept reading, though her hands felt as numb as her heart. Here was the proof she'd been looking for. For the briefest instant, she thought that maybe her father had faked all this—she wouldn't put that past him. But it couldn't be. There was too much evidence. It would have been too easy to check. This *was* the truth. There'd been no foul play on the Strikers' yacht. Jeanne Sheppard had jumped overboard.

"You should have told me." Her voice was hoarse, and the back of her throat ached.

"When you're a mother . . . If you're a mother . . . The idea of you being a mother . . . Well, maybe you'll understand then. You just want to protect your kid." Clark sighed.

Suddenly, Cammie slammed a hand down on the table so hard that orange juice splashed and coffee sloshed. "I could have the same fucking thing that mom did. Did you ever think of that? What if it's genetic?"

Her father's cell rang. He checked the number and then swore softly. "It's my partner. We're in this intense negotiation over online video streaming rights for *Hermosa Beach.*"

Cammie felt so sad that no words could have made it past her constricted throat anyway. Her father was going to take a business phone call. Now? She watched in mute horror as he snapped open his Razr.

"Margaret? I'm with my daughter. . . . No, *you* wait. I'll call you back. . . . When I can . . . Learn a little patience. It's a goddamn virtue." He closed the phone again.

Cammie wasn't sure if she had just imagined that her father had blown his partner off for her, or if it had really happened.

"Okay, so where were we?"

"You were hanging up on Margaret." Cammie smiled. It gave her some serious satisfaction just to say it aloud. "And your daughter was proud of you."

"I do have to talk to her. But I have one more thing for you." He ducked down again for his tennis bag.

"About Mom?"

Clark shook his head and handed her another envelope. This one was letter-size, white, and very dry. There was handwriting on the outside of the envelope that Cammie hadn't seen in years but remembered like her own name. Red pen, the color her mother liked so much because she was a teacher. Perfect cursive. *Camilla*. Not Cammie. Camilla.

"Not about Mom. From Mom," Clark explained gently.

Her heart careened around inside her chest; her mouth went to another level of dry. Her ears rang from the blood that rushed to them, so loudly that she could barely hear what her father was saying.

"Mom . . . ?"

"She wrote this right after you were born. I wrote one, too. The plan was, we'd give them to you on your wedding day." He smiled sadly. "But somehow, I don't think Jeanne would mind if you got hers now. In fact, I think she'd rather like it.

"Damn. I miss her. I was a better person with her." He stretched his neck and then stood. "Come on, Sammy-antha, let's take a walk and give Cammie some time alone with her mother."

Cammie started to tell Sam to stay, that she could read over her shoulder, but then stopped. Her father was right. She'd let Sam read it later. This time, she wanted to be by herself and relish her mother's words. Whatever they turned out to be.

"You good?" Sam asked.

"No. But you should go."

"Cammie, you'll come out when you're done?" her

father asked. He gestured toward the door. Clearly, he'd be waiting for her.

She nodded blankly. Her father had just called Sam by her childhood nickname that no one used anymore. She hadn't even known that he remembered.

And then she was alone in the room with her mother's missive. Carefully, she opened it.

My dearest daughter,

I am awed and amazed that you have made me a mother. My own mother once told me that I wouldn't understand her until I became a mother myself. Already I feel like I understand that, at least a little bit. I loved you from the moment I saw you, Camilla. To love this much is beautiful, and wonderful, and painful, and the scariest thing in the world, all at the same time.

It thrills me to think that I will be raising you with your father. He is the smartest man I've ever met in my life. I hope that you have come to realize that, having traversed teen years that could not have been easy. They never are.

If you are reading this, it must be your wedding day. I pray you picked a man worthy of the wonderful young woman I know you will grow up to be. What I want to tell you is this, my darling daughter: Love him fiercely, but not with all your heart. Save a piece of it for yourself. Don't let marriage be an excuse to stop living and growing. Every day that you are alive is another day full of possibility. Cherish it. Make the most of it. Use it wisely and well. And one day when you are very, very, very old and you leave this world for whatever is out there, leave it a better place than you found it.

You are my hope and my joy and my future.

All my love forever,
Mom

Could I Have Your Autograph?

Parker Pinelli was a man with a plan.

People had commented on his good looks for as long as he could remember. First it was, "Better watch out, he's gonna be a heartbreaker one day." When one day came around, he was six feet tall, a hundred sixty-five pounds, and just in ninth grade; a young-Brad-Pitt-James-Dean-but-taller look-alike. That was when girls and women of every age, size, and shape began to throw themselves at him. The first time someone old enough to be his mother had hit on him was when he was fourteen, at a commercial audition for some breakfast cereal. The fiftyish casting director said he looked tense, asked him into her private office, and began to give him a massage. He'd freaked out and bolted.

Needless to say, he didn't get the gig. But on the long bus ride back to his crappy apartment on the fringes of Beverly Hills, he started to feel remorseful about leaving. It was a national commercial. If he had booked it, he'd have gotten a check every time it aired, as well as compensated for the job itself.

He'd been hungry when he got home. As usual, there was nothing in the refrigerator except some nasty-looking leftovers his mother had brought from the Apple Pan diner, where she was currently waitressing, and a frozen chocolate cake she'd ordered from QVC. The furniture looked more worn and threadbare than usual, and that was saying a lot. He couldn't avoid it. His mother, younger brother Monte, and he desperately needed the money the commercial would have brought in. That casting director had wanted something. He'd wanted something. They could have exchanged. It was the American way. Instead, he realized he'd blown it by running in the wrong direction.

By the time his next audition rolled around, this one for a well-known amusement park down near Anaheim, Parker had gotten over his jitters. And since then, because women and men of all ages hit on him, he'd pretty much been able to pick and choose whose affections—and favors—to court.

Such was the power of really great looks. He saw it with Sam's friend Cammie Sheppard, who had it with guys. He had it too, with both girls and guys. That was just the way it was. To ignore that power would be to ignore the fact that the earth was round, or that two plus two equals four.

When he got to high school, those same looks helped fool Sam and her friends into thinking he was one of them. When Sam discovered Parker's secret during the trip to Las Vegas, he figured he was fucked. It was too delicious a secret—that he was actually poor—to expect anyone to keep. But she'd promised to keep her mouth shut, and they'd looked at each other differently ever since.

Parker's plan was to become a movie star. An Orlando-Brad-Leonardo-level movie star. But there was always a hitch. While he could generally finagle auditions, he rarely made it past whatever assistant was making the first round of cuts. Parker was just another great-looking piece of Hollywood meat. They never really *saw* him. The phone never rang, and, quick as he'd gotten his hopes up, he was on to the next casting call.

Until now.

Thanks to the deal he'd cut with Sam, he'd screen tested yesterday at Transnational Studios for the role of Marcus in *Ben-Hur*. He'd done homework and discovered that the role didn't exist in the original but had been added during one of the uncredited rewrites.

By three o'clock—just twenty-four hours ago—the call he'd been praying for had actually come. The role was his. The pay would be ten thousand dollars and he should report to the Palmdale set today.

That was when the tears had flowed. He tried not to think about the part of the bargain that would come later, in which he had to start a seduction of Sam's gold-digging stepmother.

But the worst-case scenario—in which Jackson found out Parker had hit on his wife and got Parker blacklisted from Hollywood for life—wasn't far from his mind, which had to be part of the reason he was sweating as he stood under a blue tent canopy on the *Ben-Hur* set, dressed in a white Roman toga, about to shoot his first scene. In it, Marcus would help Judah Ben-Hur dress for the climactic chariot race.

He'd been messengered the entire script the night before, and he'd read it through twice. It was the year A.D. 1. Judah Ben-Hur, after years of being imprisoned by the Roman procurator Messala, now had the chance to defeat him in a chariot race. Parker had read his own scenes so many times that he had not just the lines but the stage directions memorized. He could see the pages in his mind's eye.

EXT. CHARIOT GROUNDS—RACE PREP AREA—DAY

MARCUS, NOSAN's son, enters and bows to BEN-HUR, who is checking the condition of his horses.

                    MARCUS
If I might be of service . . .

                    BEN-HUR
What is it, Marcus?

                    MARCUS
I would be honored if you would allow me to help you prepare for the race, sir.

[BEN-HUR turns and looks askance at
MARCUS.]

                    BEN-HUR
Why would you, a Roman and the son of a
Roman, choose to help the Jew?

                    MARCUS
Because, good sir, I have my own brain and
my own heart. I have seen your goodness,
even after all that they have done to you.
I make my own choice, to be here, now, with
you.

[BEN-HUR sees something true in the youth's
eyes. He takes MARCUS by the shoulders,
then embraces him.]

                    BEN-HUR
I would be honored, Marcus.

   That was the entire scene. But a two-shot with
Jackson Sharpe—and an emotional one at that—was
exactly the jump-start Parker's career needed. Who
knew where it could lead? This was the kind of scene
that could end up an Oscar clip. He could be watching
it on TV next February. Hey, he might even be at the
Kodak Theatre for the awards, with the rest of the *Ben-Hur* cast, cheering Jackson as he was called to the stage.

This was his big break. He'd waited eighteen years for it. He would *not* blow it.

Since Jackson was directing as well as starring, he sat behind one of the cameras with his director of photography, assessing the lighting, wearing a tunic similar to Parker's, though more ornate.

A curvy assistant with a riot of curly black hair spouting from a ponytail on the top of her head came over and asked Parker if he needed anything—sparkling water, protein shake? He shook his head. And then, finally, he saw that Jackson was ready. He stepped out from behind the camera. His makeup was touched up, lint removed from his tunic, and his hair rearranged into Caesar-style bangs. Parker had the same haircut—he'd been shorn in the hair trailer at five-thirty that morning, after a fantastic breakfast at the craft services trailer and tent.

Because, good sir, I have my own brain and my own heart . . .

"Places, everyone! *Ben-Hur*, scene forty-three, take one," called the second assistant director. He held a slate in front of the camera so that the scene could be easily identified.

"Quiet, please! Quiet on the set!" shouted a blond dreadlocked PA. That cry was picked up all around the set, until no one at all was talking. It was so quiet, in fact, that Parker could hear the sound of the horses breathing and whinnying.

And . . . action!"

He mounted a small crest to where Jackson brushed one of the horses that would be pulling his chariot. Then he fed the other one a carrot.

Marcus. I am Marcus. Not Parker.

"If I might be of service?" he asked Jackson.

Jackson turned. *Wham.* Parker felt the unexpected full force of the man's movie-star charisma.

"What is it, Marcus?" Jackson asked.

"I would be honored if you would allow me to help you prepare for the race, sir."

Parker felt Jackson's eyes look him up and down, as if he might be carrying a dagger under his tunic. Jackson/Ben-Hur had to be thinking that Marcus might be an assassin. It was a novel interpretation, but thrilling.

"Why would you, a Roman and the son of a Roman, choose to help the Jew?" Jackson asked.

"Because, good sir, I have my own brain and my own heart. I have seen your goodness, even after all that they have done to you. I make my own choice, to be here, now, with you." Parker bowed slightly. If Ben-Hur was afraid that he might be a killer, it seemed the right thing to do.

Jackson came close to him and looked him in the eyes. Then he embraced him with a show of love and respect. "I would be honored, Marcus."

"And . . . cut!" The assistant director ended the scene. "Okay, back to one. We'll do it again. Same thing."

As he went back to "one," meaning the place at the bottom of the swale where he'd started out the scene, Parker thought the scene had gone quite well.

They ran the scene four times, until Jackson was happy with his work.

"That's a wrap!" called the AD. "Set for scene fifty-six! Thank you, Marcus!"

"Nice job," some people called to him as he strode off the set. Parker had no idea whether or not they meant it. Suddenly, he felt just like another small-part actor. They probably didn't even know his real—

"Can I have your autograph?" a voice squealed.

He turned. There was Sam, grinning wildly in Diesel jeans and an aqua silk Stella McCartney shirt. "You kicked ass in that scene with my dad. I was watching on the monitors." She motioned to the producers' tent over to the left, where the film's financiers could watch the shoot and listen though headphones.

Parker was thrilled. "You watched the whole thing? And you really think it went okay?"

"I'm telling you, you were great. The camera loves you."

Parker felt so relieved that he threw his arms around Sam and gave her a huge hug. "How can I ever thank you for this?" he whispered.

"You know exactly how," she whispered back.

He smiled. Tit for . . . well, for tit. Although touching Poppy's was more than he hoped he'd need to do. At any rate, he was ready to fulfill his part of the bargain.

She took his arm as they walked across the set toward the so-called base camp, where everyone associated with the film parked their cars. "Day after tomorrow, you're shooting again, right?"

"That's the schedule. Two more scenes. Starts early in the morning, like 4 A.M. They're supposed to finish by six—"

"Perfect. Because my dad's throwing a party at our place. Turns out a few people who are doing cameos—Tom Hanks, Jean Reno, Maria Bello—won't be around for the official wrap party next month. So he figures it's the least he can do. There'll be a zillion people. It'll be a great opportunity."

"You mean—"

"Hells, yeah. Come over and get to work. Let's see what the Stepmother from Hell is really made of."

Toga, Toga

"Miss Sam? Would like some help with your toga?" The new maid, Marcella, stood at the door of Sam's twelve-hundred-square-foot suite.

"Come on in and call me Sam." She reached around but couldn't seem to grasp both sides of the belt at her waist. "Could you just fasten the belt in the back for me, Marcella?"

"Surely, Miss—I mean, Sam," she said softly. Marcella tightened the fabric belt that had come with the toga, which gave the black silk material some shape. It fell in graceful folds to her ankles, with a slit up one leg, which was just about as much of her thigh as Sam planned to expose, thank you very much.

It had been Poppy's idea to make the party in honor of the cameo stars in *Ben-Hur* a toga party and hold it at her father's estate. Because of course the newly svelte, Bodhi-yogafied post-baby-weight Poppy would look fabulous in a sheer toga.

"Great." Sam smiled at the maid. "Thanks for the help."

"Anything else?"

"Just welcome to my father's house. And good luck."

"Thank you." Marcella slipped out of her room.

That afternoon a small army from Party Central, Fleur Abra's newest party-planning venture, had turned their backyard—if you could call four acres, complete with pool, tennis court, putting green, and koi pond a "backyard"—into a virtual Roman coliseum.

Of course, everyone was supposed to come in a toga.

When she'd invited him, Sam had had a hard time explaining the concept of a toga party to Eduardo, but being the good sport that he was, he'd said he'd rent something from a costume shop. God knew Los Angeles had plenty of those. And tonight would be the night Parker would start making his move on Poppy. Sam couldn't wait for Poppy to expose herself as the cheater that Sam knew her to be.

Sam eased herself to the center of her three-way, full-length mirror and checked out the rear view.

"Sam? You look amazing!"

Dee practically flew through the open doorway. She wore a darling pink toga the size of a postage stamp, sandals that laced up to her knees, and a garland of fig leaves around the crown of her head.

"So listen," Dee said, perching her tiny butt on the edge of Sam's green marble vanity. "Jack couldn't come. There's some kind of crisis at Fox on some new reality show, and he'll be there until midnight at least. Does the name Marshall Gruber mean anything to you?"

"Is it a rare African disease?" Sam moved to her

silver tray of perfumes and decided on a limited-edition Prada that hadn't yet been released to stores. "Is Marshall Gruber curable?" she asked, as she sprayed her pulse points.

Dee giggled. "It's a person. The guy from Ojai who was my chaperone at prom?" she prompted. "Tall, skinny—"

"Oh yeah. Napoleon Dynamite. The one you ditched so you could run off with Jack."

Suddenly it all came back. Marshall had been the comic relief of an evening that hadn't ended comically. "He hooked up with someone on the beach right? Skye, maybe? I was pretty polluted—"

"I think it was Skye, but whatever. Jack and I were already . . . busy."

"Which is kind of out there, considering you had just met the guy."

"Yeah, but who *doesn't* get wild on prom night?" Dee asked rhetorically. "Besides, for me and Jack it was this instant thing. You know. A thunderbolt of love."

"Or else you'd been locked away in the funny farm for so long that anything male looked good."

"Oh no," Dee insisted. "Jack and I are the real thing. Anyway, Marshall will be driving Aaron Steele down from the Ojai Institute. Did you ever meet him? Aaron, I mean, not Marshall."

Sam shook her head. "I don't think so. His father used to be a good writer and then he lost it. I think it happened when he wrote that tell-all book dissing everyone in Hollywood—like they were going to work with him after that."

"Do you know if Skye will be here?"

Sam grinned. "Skye plus Marshall equals you alone with Aaron?" she figured. "What about how you and Jack are soul mates?"

Dee sighed. "I don't know. I think my soul might be expanding its horizons. So? Skye?"

You're in luck. She is."

"Miss Sam?" Marcella appeared once again in the doorway.

"Yes?"

"*Señor Eduardo está aqui.* He is waiting downstairs for you. *En la biblioteca.* In the library. Also, your father wishes that I tell you the guests are arriving and the party is beginning."

"*Muchas gracias*, Marcella. And *por favor*, Marcella. Please, lose the 'Miss' thing with me. Really. It makes me nervous."

"Okay, Miss—I'm sorry. Okay, Sam."

Marcella fled. Sam and Dee spent the next five minutes touching up each other's makeup, and then they went downstairs together. Sure enough, they found Eduardo waiting in Jackson's teak-paneled library. He looked elegant in his rented classic white toga.

Eduardo kissed Sam's hand. "You are ravishing."

"Oh!" Dee cried. "That is so romantic. Jack never tells me I'm ravishing."

"That's because he is an American," Eduardo explained.

"He would sound ridiculous. The party is under way. Shall we?" He offered both Dee and Sam his elbows. *"Mujeres y caballeras? Con migo, por favor."*

Sam and Dee took his arms; they wound their way through the house and down the steps from the deck to the backyard. The party had indeed begun. There were hundreds of people in various togafied states of dress and undress in the backyard.

"Dee! There you are!"

A guy Sam had never seen before jogged over to Dee and hugged her. He wore a white bedsheet knotted at one shoulder. Had to be Ojai Guy. Only someone without access to a costume shop would make a toga out of a sheet. He was tall and well built, with the perfectly naturally blond highlighted hair of a surfer.

"Is it really you or am I dreaming?" the guy asked, staring at Dee.

"It's me," Dee replied. "And I'm so glad you're here. Sam and Eduardo, I want you to meet my friend Aaron Steele. Aaron, this is Sam Sharpe. She's kind of our hostess, or at least her dad is. And this is her boyfriend, Eduardo Muñoz. He said Sam looked ravishing."

Aaron laughed and shook Eduardo's hand. "I thought I was the only one who could say stuff like that."

Dee shook her head. "Nope. You're American. You'd sound like an idiot."

"I'm not American. If you asked my dad, he'd tell you I was from Mars," Aaron joked. "Sam, it's great to meet you. I think your father paid for my father's Bentley."

Sam laughed. She knew exactly what Aaron was talking about. Jackson had asked the immensely talented and immensely egotistical James Steele to do uncredited rewrites on two of his pictures—he'd gotten high six figures for about a week's worth of work.

"Aaron! Aaron! The deal is that you have to be in my line of sight at all times." Marshall came loping over to them. Now that she saw him and heard his distinctive high-pitched voice, Sam remembered Marshall only too well. His Adam's apple was so large he looked as if he'd swallowed a Ping-Pong ball, and he was the only guest in sight not wearing a toga. Instead, he sported plain black trousers and a hideously tacky short-sleeved white shirt with a single chest pocket. There was no misidentifying him, either—around his neck hung a name badge identifying him as MARSHALL GRUBER, STAFF INTERN, OJAI INSTITUTE.

Yet Aaron took his arrival in stride, even with impressive kindness. "Right, Marshall, sorry. But honestly? If I'm with Dee, you've got no worries. I know Dee. She's a rock."

Huh?? Was he talking about the same Dee that Sam knew? Maybe Dee really was changing.

"How about we dance?" Eduardo asked Sam. They excused themselves; he took her hand, and led her down the brick path to the dance floor. Earth, Wind, and Fire were doing a cover of "Since I Fell for You."

Eduardo sang softly in Sam's ear as he took her in his arms.

She pulled back and looked into his eyes. "You can sing, too?"

"I am a man of many talents," he teased, and pulled her close again. Over Eduardo's shoulder, Sam saw Anna dancing with Caine. Anna looked amazing in a long white gown, very simple, knotted under the bust. Caine looked like he'd rented his toga from the same costume shop where Eduardo had gotten his.

"Interesting party," Eduardo went on. "Do you think anyone will really climb into the wine goblet?" Eduardo motioned to an enormous wine goblet filled with grapes that was set up off to the side.

"No doubt. Some starlet will be first. She'll fling off her clothes to show off the boobs she paid for. Any publicity is good publicity in La La Land."

"You have such disdain for the water in which you swim," Eduardo mused. "And yet you want to become a film director."

"I won't be like *them*," Sam declared. Then she laughed and added, "Everyone says that."

"I think it's possible," Eduardo encouraged.

Sam smiled up at him. "I do too. I think. I hope." That is, if she weren't addicted to the attention and the swag that came with being Jackson Sharpe's semi-famous daughter. Who knew?

"Are you chilly?" Eduardo asked solicitously.

"I'm fine. I'm with you, aren't I?"

They danced some more, until Sam saw Parker cut

through the dancing couples. She grinned, because he was wearing the same tunic he'd worn for his movie scene with her father. He'd probably cut some sort of a deal, or charmed one of the costume assistants. That was just so Parker. He looked incredibly hot in it. That was also so Parker. He tapped Eduardo on the shoulder.

"Hey Eduardo, mind if I cut in? That's what it's called, isn't it? I have zero designs on your lady, man," he added hastily. "I just want to talk to her."

"Relax, Parker. You're the man who helped make peace between us. Now, if you kiss her like you did on prom night, I'll have to call in the Peruvian Air Force for some close combat support."

Sam was amazed that Eduardo could joke about Parker kissing her. She'd almost lost him forever over it. Man. Eduardo was confident. She loved that about him.

"So, how goes seducing Stepmommy Dearest?" Sam asked, when Eduardo had departed.

"Sad, really. I ran into your stepmother by the hot tub. Heavy eye contact and some very unsubtle conversation about just how relaxing a hot tub can be."

"You're kidding." Sam wasn't surprised to hear that Parker had made progress, but she hadn't expected it this soon. Jeez. The party wasn't a half-hour old yet.

"Look, I hope you appreciate that this is hard for me," Parker said. "To let your dad's wife hit on me—"

"You're doing him a favor," Sam insisted. "And me. How far did it get?"

Parker sighed and then showed Sam the back of his hand. On it was written an unfamiliar cell phone number.

"Hers?" Sam asked.

Parker nodded.

"I don't even recognize that phone number. Did you give her your number, too?"

"She asked for it."

"Wait for her to call you," Sam suggested. "And don't worry. I will not let you down. No matter what, no one will know it was you."

The song came to an end. People stopped dancing to applaud. Suddenly, a crowd started chanting as a girl who played a handmaiden in the movie, chosen for her eye-popping and entirely unnatural curves, did a swan dive into the goblet. Two buff guys were already climbing a ladder to join her.

"And . . . off comes the toga," Sam said, watching the girl swing it over her head.

The crowd whooped its approval.

"Where's Cammie?" Parker asked, scanning the crowd of strategically sheeted people.

"I'm not sure. I invited her. She'll show. I'm going to catch up with Eduardo. Thanks, Parker. I mean it."

"Cool. I'll keep you posted. I'm going for some mead." He gave her a little wave and headed for one of the bars. Meanwhile, Sam drifted toward the buffet, looking around for Eduardo. Instead, she saw her father and Poppy with their arms around each other, talking and laughing with the British producer of *American Idol*.

Go ahead and fake it, Sam thought bitterly, staring at her stepmother. *I am so onto you.*

"Great party!" Dee exclaimed, strolling up next to Sam. She was hand in hand with Aaron, who was looking at Dee with something approaching adoration.

"It's awesome," Aaron agreed. "But I'll tell you, once you get straight, you really notice how this whole industry is fueled by booze and drugs. It's real messed up."

"Facing reality is so much more meaningful," Dee agreed.

Only Dee could say a sentence like 'Facing reality is so much more meaningful' with a straight face.

"What did you do, Dee? Memorize all those motivational posters on the walls at Ojai?" Sam winked at her friend.

Aaron laughed. "Hey. You can't possibly know how Dee and I feel. You've never been there."

Marshall ran over to them before Sam could respond. "I'm gonna dance with Sam's friend Skye. But only if this is a trust moment."

Aaron nodded. "Totally. Dee's on it. Right, Dee?"

"Right."

"Sam! Hey!"

There was someone calling to her—she peered through the torchlit darkness at an approaching toga. "Sam Sharpe?"

"That's me," she acknowledged. It was a guy in his midtwenties, decent looking enough, with close-cropped brown hair, brown eyes, nice cheekbones, and horn-rimmed glasses that didn't exactly go with his toga but worked anyway. He put out his hand for Sam to shake.

"I really wanted to meet you. I'm Norman Shnorman."

Norman Shnorman. Where had she heard that name before . . . ?

"We've never met," he went on. "But you've read me." Norman smiled winningly.

"Excuse me?" Sam didn't understand.

"I'm pretty sure you're writing the coverage on my screenplay. *Burnt Toast.* Norman Shnorman isn't my real name of course. It's Jonah Jacobson."

Norman Shnor—*oh my God.* That piece of shit set in *Brokeback* country about the bikini model and the sheriff's son? This guy wrote that piece of shit? *What a talentless loser. They should take away his keyboard for life.*

But wait. He had the same last name as the third in command at Transnational, Andrea Jacobson, who had funding power on all Transnational pictures. Jackson was in fear of Andrea putting one of her storied size-twelve feet down at any moment.

"Your mom is Andrea?" Sam asked brightly, just to be sure.

"Yeah. She encourages me to use my real last name when I'm submitting. But I turned it in as Norman Shnorman. Not that anyone would ever have the name Norman Shnorman. But I hate when people see my real name and then bullshit me because my mom works at Transnational." His eyes bore into Sam's. "So, tell me honestly. What did you think of my screenplay?"

Reserved for Bono

There were times when Jack wished that he had done what his father, a fireman in New Jersey, had wanted him to do: join the Newark Fire Department, become a fireman, maybe work his way up in the department to a stationhouse chief, or maybe even a battalion chief. Then do his twenty years, retire with a nice pension by the time he was forty, and then kick back and enjoy his life.

Days like the one he'd just had made him wish that he were a firefighter.

His internship was in the reality television department at Fox. It was a plum gig and there'd been a ton of competition for the position. Little had he known what it would mean in reality to be a Fox intern. Ninety percent of the time, he found himself interviewing contestants for a new reality pilot called *Triple Threat,* where the idea was to find the most triply-talented person in America. He spent hours watching videos they sent in, or watching them in person during the hours of the Los Angeles auditions. His job, along

129

with six other interns, was to write down the name of anyone who was either in the realm of the possible or so awful as to be amusing.

Triple Threat made for triple-plus-ungood dreary days. And long ones. He'd left the studio tonight at one in the morning. There'd been no hope of getting to the toga party at Sam Sharpe's house. Though Dee had invited him, the party was to end reasonably early, because the next day was a shooting day on Jackson's movie.

It wasn't a total disaster. He'd called his friend Ben and suggested a drink. Ben had immediately suggested the Golden Turtle, a former dive bar turned way cool club on West Eighth Street downtown. Would one-thirty be okay? No problem with Ben. He'd be there.

"What'll you have?" the blond bartender asked. Jack felt lucky to find a bar stool. There were plenty of beautiful people in the darkened interior, which was a maze of semicircular conversation nooks, partially exposed brick walls, and tiger-striped couches.

"Bourbon. On the rocks." He held up two fingers. "Two of 'em."

She smiled lazily. Jack thought she was cute, but he wasn't into very short hair or lip piercings, both of which this bartender had in abundance. And besides, he had Dee.

"Two?" the bartender asked. "One for you and one for—?" She pointed at herself.

"Meeting a friend," Jack explained.

She shrugged. "Maker's Mark'll work?"

Jack nodded and then felt a hand on his shoulder as the bartender put the two drinks in front of him.

"Hey, buddy. Feels like old times, drinking with you at one-thirty in the morning."

"Yeah, yeah. Only diff is, we don't have an eight-thirty hourlong calc exam the next morning," Jack quipped.

Ben hopped onto a bar stool and motioned to the second bourbon. "For me?" Then they clinked glasses. "How youse doin'?"

Jack laughed. That was such a New Jersey thing to say. It was one of the reasons he could actually stand Ben—he wasn't a pretentious richie asshole. Of course, there was only one legitimate response to "How youse doin'?"

"How *youse* doin'?"

They turned simultaneously. Behind them were a couple of truly beautiful girls. One was very much Jack's type, in the Dee Young mold, albeit with red hair and bigger breasts. She wore a barely there slip dress paired with spike-heel dominatrix-style boots. The other reminded Jack of Anna Percy. She was tall, blond, and lithe, almost regal looking, in a sleeveless black sweater and stovepipe jeans.

"Drinking alone?" The redhead raised her eyebrows. "That's not good."

Well, this was par for the course. So often back in New Jersey, he and Ben would pick up girls together. Tonight, it didn't seem like there would need to be a Herculean effort. But what about Dee?

"You know what?" Ben smiled at the girls. "How about we buy you drinks another time?"

"How about if we make the 'another time' in ten minutes, at our place?" cooed the Anna type.

"We're very best friends," added the Dee type. "And we like to do everything together."

The insinuation was hard to miss.

"Another time," Ben repeated. "We've got some things to work out."

"Each other?" the Anna type asked pointedly.

She was clearly disappointed, and probably not used to being turned down. In fact, this might have been the first time.

It was the strangest thing. Jack couldn't have cared less when the girls slunk away. When he thought "girl" he thought "Dee." Damn. How had this happened?

"So you're not interested?" Jack asked Ben as the girls slunk away. He knew he was covering his own anxieties about Dee, but what the hell.

Ben sipped his bourbon. "Anna."

"What's up with that?"

Ben shrugged. "She's seeing another dude. Some guy named Caine. It won't last."

"You're confident."

"I don't know, man, I can't explain it. There's just something about Anna. . . . Okay, you never hear me say this shit, and you know it. I feel like . . . she's the one."

That's how I feel about Dee.

"Ben, let me just go on the record and say that you're too damn young for 'the one,'" Jack said, speaking to himself at least as much as he was speaking to Ben.

"Maybe," Ben mused. "But maybe when the real thing comes along, you're a fool to let it get away." He took another sip of Maker's Mark. "Anyway, this guy Caine. He's a suit with tattoos, doesn't know who the hell he is. I'm not losing her to that poser."

Jack motioned for the bartender to bring another round. "I kind of have this thing myself. With Dee."

"What? You fell for the girl?" Ben hooted. "Mr. Two-dates-is-a-relationship-and-three-is-I'm-outta-here?"

"I did not expect to feel this way." Jack grabbed the fresh drink and took a long swallow. "And I don't know what the hell to do about it. We ran into this guy she knows—he was all about her, I could tell—and I was ready to take the guy's head off."

"What are you talking about? What guy? I know all about Dee and her guys."

Jack outlined for Ben what had happened with Dee in the basement corridor at the Staples Center, when she'd run into Aaron Steele.

"Aww, relax. Maybe it's just a rehab thing," Ben suggested. "Like soldiers who go through a war together or something."

"It's more," Jack insisted. "He was looking at her like she was a cold drink and he was a hot day."

Ben laughed. "Hey, I know that feeling."

"Me too," Jack agreed. "That's why I don't want him having it about Dee."

"He touch her?" Ben asked.

Jack shook his head.

"She touch him?"

"Not that I remember."

"What happened right afterward?" Jack felt Ben's eyes bore in on him.

"Umm . . . we went to U2's dressing room. We drank a couple of cold Guinnesses. Then we spread out a blanket on Bono's couch and did it."

"It doesn't sound like there's a big problem here," Ben concluded. "And even if there was, there ain't shit you can do about it, my friend."

Jack felt his fingers tighten around the tumbler of bourbon. The idea of that asshole touching Dee . . . Aw, jeez. He had it bad. Really, really bad.

Ben drank down the last of his bourbon. "Look, in the end, she either wants you or she doesn't. Same thing with me and Anna."

"I don't know," Jack mused. "Maybe you need to fight for love. How long you willing to wait?"

"Five months, three weeks, four days, seven hours, and eleven minutes—don't know." Ben stretched. "But if she is the one, then in the long run, that wait won't mean a damn thing."

"Gotcha." Well, great if that worked for him. But no

way would Jack stand by while some other guy—and certainly not a head case from Ojai—moved in on his woman. Jack had fought for everything good he had in his life. If it came down to it, he would damn sure fight for Dee, too.

Wax On, Wax Off

"Try this on." Cammie offered Champagne a black satin Bebe dress, cut very narrow through the hips, with a neckline that plunged nearly to her navel. "It's you."

"This is the most beautiful thing I've ever seen," Champagne gasped.

"Then stop gawking and get your ass in the changing room," Cammie ordered. "It doesn't cost anything to try something on."

Then, on a wooden hook behind her, she spotted a pair of black leather gloves long enough to reach past the elbow and halfway up the bicep. You had to be a certain kind of girl to pull off the dress-gloves combination, but Cammie had a hunch that Champagne was exactly that kind of girl. She tossed Champagne the gloves. "Let's see it with these. Or I'll send Anna after you with an ice princess stick."

"Go ahead, Champagne," Anna urged. "I want to see you in the dress, too."

It was late the next afternoon; they were ransacking the Anastasia boutique at the Beverly Center, before heading toward the Bloomingdale's wing. When Anna and Cammie were driving Champagne home to the valley after yet another meeting with Mrs. Vanderleer and Mrs. Chesterfield—this one about selecting the music that would accompany the runway models—Champagne had politely begged for a window-shopping expedition to the Beverly Center. She claimed she'd never been there. Considering what the girl had told them about her background, Cammie believed it.

"My prediction: She's going to sizzle in that," Cammie told Anna.

"She's a beautiful girl. And she's smart. We should steer her toward using her brains to get somewhere."

"Please, Anna, spare me the modeling-is-so-superficial speech."

Anna shrugged. "Well, it is. Besides, Champagne's been through a lot. Think what a great social worker she'd make."

"If she isn't a thief," Cammie joked.

"I don't think she took that dress, Cammie."

"Of course she didn't. But it's so easy to make assumptions." Cammie tossed the hair off her face. "She was at PacCoast with us. She wants to be a model like that. It's a new dream. Why shouldn't a person go after a dream if that's what she wants to do?"

"Because a person isn't tall enough," Anna reminded. "Why follow a dream that's impossible for you? Isn't that a huge waste of time? Isn't she setting herself up for a big disappointment?"

"Fuck that kind of negative thinking," Cammie decreed. "Following rules is boring. Champagne could be the exception—a successful model who's on the short side."

Anna smiled as she flipped through a rack of ivory lace shirts. "You know, I actually agree with you. If you can't try to be exceptional when you're sixteen, I don't know when you would."

"Exactly."

Huh. Maybe Anna had more sense than she'd figured. Or maybe being away from Ben Birnbaum was actually good for her.

"Didn't you ever have a crazy dream, Anna?"

Anna held up an ivory lace shirt. It had lovely eyelets instead of nasty buttons. "Coming out here in the middle of my senior year was pretty crazy."

"Oh yeah, that's wild. Dream bigger," Cammie ordered. "Life's short."

Cammie knew how true that really was.

Life was too damn short sometimes.

"What do you think?"

Champagne. She'd poured herself into the Bebe dress and the gloves, and somehow had matched them with a pair of electric blue suede stiletto-heeled open-toe pumps that elevated her from five-foot six to almost five-ten. The dress clung to every curve; no evidence of a panty line spoiled the view.

"Champagne . . ."

Anna could barely form a sentence, so Cammie did it for her.

"What Anna meant to say is, 'Go back in the changing room and put the dress on a hanger. The gloves too. Box up the shoes.' Where did you get them? They don't sell shoes here."

"The salesgirl saw me in the dressing room and ran across to Ferragamo so I could try them on with the dress. I think she knows the manager."

"The whole thing looks fantastic on you!" Anna exclaimed.

"Really?" The girl's voice was small, almost dazed.

Suddenly, Cammie knew what she wanted to do. She stepped over to Champagne and put her hands on the girl's shoulders, not saying a word until the younger girl looked her in the eye. "Listen to me. I know what you want. And I think I can help you. But you have to do everything I say. Wax on, wax off. Wax on, wax off."

Champagne grinned. "Like the *Karate Kid*? I love that old movie. You want me to be like Daniel-san? He lived in the valley, too. But I don't understand."

"And I'm the teacher, whatever his name was."

"Mr. Miyagi," Champagne reported. "How are you going to help me?"

"Here's how you start. Bring that stuff to the counter. Then we're going to pick out some simpler outfits for everyday. If you're going to be seen in public, you need to have something decent. Then we're going to Ferragamo and buying the shoes, too."

Champagne shook her head. "That's incredibly nice of you, but I can't let you buy me this stuff."

"Well, 'buying' might be a bit of an exaggeration," Cammie admitted. "I'm investing. In you. Consider this an advance against your future earnings as a model. And 'no' is not an option."

Champagne stood there, stunned. "But . . . everyone says I'm too short. How would I ever pay you back?"

"Champagne?" Cammie asked.

"Yeah?"

"Wax on, wax off. Move your ass. Now."

"Adam! It's me." Cammie laid back on her bed wearing just a satin La Perla thong, her feet arched against the wall behind her headboard, her head propped up on a massive pile of plush rose pillows, and her curls spread out on the luxurious cotton summer bedspread below. Her enormous bedroom was immaculate—not that Cammie ever cleaned it herself—the windows flung open to capture the last rays of sunshine of this gorgeous Los Angeles summer evening.

"Hey, Cammie. How goes it back there in La La Land?"

"Well, let's see," Cammie purred. "I'm on my bed. No one else is home. I'm not wearing anything but a thong." She smiled, knowing what that mental image would do to him. "When are you coming back?"

Silence at the other end of the line.

"Adam?"

"Well, I'm not sure, exactly," came his voice.

"Meaning, I've tempted you to come back early? Great idea. Just steal your parents' canoe, paddle it to the bottom of the lake, hitchhike to Detroit, catch a plane to LAX, and we'll do a rerun of my current state of undress tomorrow," she suggested. "Same time, same place. The front door will be open. Don't knock."

"Hard to resist," Adam admitted. "But the thing is, I might stay a little longer here in Michigan."

Longer? What was he talking about?

"How much longer?"

"Dunno, exactly. You know, it's just that . . . well, this place is, like, sacred to me. I've come every summer with my parents since I was in grade school. Now that I'm starting college in the fall, everything is gonna change. My parents said maybe they'd try to rent the place on the lake for an extra month, seeing as how it might be our last time."

It was more of a battle to stay calm this time. "That would mean you wouldn't be in Los Angeles until *August*?" Fuck. What about how she was supposed to be so irresistible? "That's a long time, Adam."

"I know. I'd miss you a ton."

"Well, you don't *have* to stay an extra month."

Cammie tried not to let irritation color her voice, but really, look at his choices. Blackflies and bullfrogs versus naked and boyfriend-deprived *her*? What guy in his right mind could resist?

She swung her feet around and found herself facing the wall of her room that had been moved in its entirety from their old house in Beverly Hills when that house had been sold. Back when Cammie was in elementary school, her mother had painted a mural on it of the characters from *Charlotte's Web*. Cammie had refused to move to her father's new mansion unless the mural came with them. Workmen from the Getty Center had orchestrated the move as if the mural had been painted on the ceiling of the Sistine Chapel.

"Hey, here's a plan," Adam offered. "Why don't you come here? We've got plenty of room."

Her? Come *there?* To *Michigan?*

"Are you on drugs? I consider maid and/or room service basic human needs."

Adam sighed. "Yeah. I know."

Shit. There were so many things she wanted to tell him face-to-face that would be ruined by the phone. About the amazing breakfast with her father. And the even more amazing letter from her mother, like a song from the Great Beyond.

"Cam?"

"Yeah?"

"There's something I need to tell you."

Oh no, he was *not* breaking up with her by cell phone. If he even tried, she was going to press in star seventy-one pound eleven and his cruddy LGX 5200 cell would blow up and take his brain with it. Hey, it might work.

"I'm not breaking up with you," he added quickly.

"Never entered my mind," Cammie lied. She stood and drifted to the open window. Why wasn't Adam outside right now, smiling up at her?

"Being back in Michigan. It's . . . weird."

"And?" she prompted, because obviously there was more.

"And . . . it's making me kind of . . . nostalgic, I guess. I miss it here."

She was in Los Angeles, and he missed Michigan. It was time to talk some sense into this boy.

"Adam, can you do me a favor?"

"Sure, Cam. Anything."

"Tell me exactly where you are right now."

"I'm on one of the bunk beds in the cabin."

"What'cha wearing?"

"Jeans. T-shirt."

She could picture him perfectly. Tall and on the thin side, with a basketball player's gangly arms and a star tattoo behind one of this ears; spiky, dark brown hair, and a warm smile.

"I can tell you for a fact that the view is a lot better from my bedroom," she declared. "I believe you when you say you're not breaking up with me. But do not bullshit me. Are you having second thoughts about coming back?"

She heard him sigh. That was confirmation enough, no matter what his words would be.

"I wouldn't mind going to U of M," he said softly. "You'd like Ann Arbor. It's a very cool—"

There was a limit. He'd just smacked into it. Not to mention the fact that she didn't have the grades to get into U of M, and she didn't think any amount of money or sexual favors could get her in, either. Adam knew that full well, too.

"Adam."

"Yeah?"

"Foreign countries aside, there are only two digits that will ever go at the front of my zip code—9 and 0. I'm allergic to flyover country."

"Yeah. I thought that's what you'd say."

"And yet you asked anyway."

"Sometimes people change, Cammie. You're judging a place you've never been to and don't really know."

They talked for another minute or two, but Cammie felt like a helium balloon five days after a birthday party. And when she hung up, she felt even worse. Not even the thought of retail therapy could make her do anything else but lie on her bed and stare at Fern, Avery, and Wilbur on the wall. They didn't move, so she didn't either.

Midnight Special

"**I**sn't this a little *Mission Impossible*?" Caine asked, as Anna took out the set of keys that Sam had given her. She was wearing black jeans and a black T-shirt, which seemed appropriate for a stealthy operation.

"I'm doing Sam a huge favor," Anna reminded him. "She said not to come until midnight. She wanted to be sure the office was deserted. It's midnight, almost. Here we are."

She said these things matter-of-factly, but honestly—she was nervous.

"I think we woke up the guard at the front desk," Caine said. "What's the point of having a guard if he sleeps on duty?"

"So that desperate criminals like you and me can sneak in."

Anna chuckled as she turned keys in both locks. The door to the offices of Action Jackson Productions, on the second floor of a nondescript building at the low-slung Culver City movie studio complex that housed Transnational Pictures, swung open.

Once again, Anna asked herself what the hell was she doing. Yet the answer was clear: she was doing something huge for Sam that Sam dared not do herself.

At the end of the toga party, Sam had corralled her and told her all about her encounter with Norman Shnorman, aka Jonah Jacobson, whose mother held the purse strings at Transnational. There were enormous budget problems on *Ben-Hur*, and it simply wouldn't do for Andrea, aka Bigfoot, to see negative coverage on her son's *Burnt Toast* from an Action Jackson Productions script reader. Someone had to change the coverage in a hurry. But Sam didn't dare do it, because it could so easily get back to her father that she'd been at his production offices at midnight. Someone would surely mention it to him, even if just by way of making conversation, and she'd have to concoct some elaborate lie. If Anna went . . . well, no one knew her, so everyone would just assume she was some assistant doing something. And surely that wouldn't be worth mentioning to anyone.

Which is how it was that Anna and Caine had presented their credentials to the guard on the ground floor of the studio offices, gotten themselves cleared, and were letting themselves into the deserted production offices. Just as Anna got the door open, Caine's watch beeped twice. He pushed the sleeve of his black hooded sweatshirt up his tattooed arm and glanced at his wrist.

"Midnight," he declared in a doom-filled voice. "The witching hour."

"Very funny."

Anna snapped on the lights. Though she was officially an Action Jackson employee, she hadn't yet been inside the offices. They were surprisingly spare.

They went into Kiki's utilitarian office—there wasn't even a window—and Anna quickly found the script in the drawer where Sam had said the covered scripts would be.

Caine pushed his hair off his forehead. "Hot in here. Don't they believe in air conditioning?"

"Oh, that's just me," Anna quipped, proud of herself for being lighthearted in the midst of this unusual midnight outing. Anna dug out the script to *Burnt Toast* and was pleased to see Sam's coverage still stapled to the upper righthand corner.

"So, what now?" Caine asked.

"Can you boot up that computer?"

"Yes, ma'am. Love taking orders from a high school graduate." Fortunately, Caine was grinning.

"Let's redo it from the top," she decided.

"Fine with me."

"How are you on the keyboard?"

"I bring new meaning to the word *fast*."

"Great. I'm not an expert at this, but I'll dictate and you type."

"I await your brilliance."

"Hmm . . ." Anna looked at Sam's coverage. It was scathing.

"Okay, let's start like this, as an overall summary:

'Use script to paper the walls of Versailles. It's magnificent.' Or is that overkill?"

"Is there such a thing as overkill here in Tinseltown?" Caine asked.

"Right. 'Norman Shnorman deserves to be amongst the pantheon of top film industry writers for life.'"

"I could weep," Caine deadpanned.

"In this case, weeping is good," Anna mused. "Just type at the same time."

She dictated a few more paragraphs, described the plot as "original, thoughtful, funny, and highly moving all at once," and the characters as "fresh, clever, highly castable, and relatable by young and old alike."

"My mother couldn't write a recommendation that good," Caine noted when he was finished. "Want me to read it back to you?"

"Just print it." Anna felt a little sick to her stomach.

Caine pressed the print button; Anna heard a printer hum behind her in the receptionist's office.

She hurried to the receptionist's desk with the script, tore off Sam's original coverage and ran it through the paper shredder, stapled the new coverage to the script as soon as it was fully printed, and then brought it back to the filing cabinet and stuffed it—as best she could figure out—back where she'd originally found it.

No one would be the wiser, she decided. And Sam was off the hook.

"Anna?"

She turned. Caine was standing a few feet behind her. "Yes?"

"Really no ethical qualms about doing this?"

"Honestly? A ton," she admitted. Frankly, she was surprised—and touched—that Caine even thought to ask her.

By way of response, he wrapped his arms around her. Anna flushed and leaned her forehead against his chest. She could feel her heartbeat speed up under her simple black Calvin Klein T-shirt.

"I just don't feel comfortable lying," she murmured. "And this feels like lying."

"I love that about you, Anna. I really do. But you're going to find out that there are worse things than lying."

She wasn't sure she liked the sound of that, and edged back far enough to see his face.

"Really? Like what?"

"Like . . . some lies can be told for a good cause. Like, saying a bride is beautiful when she's not. Like that. So . . ." He kissed her softly. "We done here, Madame Criminal Mastermind?"

"Maybe," she teased, and kissed him back. There was something really strange about kissing Caine in Jackson Sharpe's production company office. But maybe it could be . . . good strange.

She kissed him again.

The next thing she knew, they were on the couch, one of his hands tangled in her hair, the other holding her T-shirt. He slipped one strap of her camisole off a shoulder and kissed the soft skin of her neck. The other strap fell. Her pulse raced between her collarbones. When he went to tug the camisole over her head, Anna pulled away.

"The guard could come up," she explained, breathless from what they'd started.

"Not to worry. I re-locked the door." Caine pulled her close again.

How did she feel? What did she want? She put a hand on his chest.

"I'm not ready for this," Anna admitted.

"Here?" Caine asked.

"Anywhere."

"To be continued, then," Caine said easily, and hoisted her from the couch. "There's a great new jazz club on Hillside Avenue in Los Feliz. Wanna check it out?"

"Definitely." Huh. He had sure given up on seducing her easily enough. What did that mean? She had no idea.

Five minutes later they were signing themselves out at the guard desk in the lobby. The uniformed guard wasn't sleeping this time. In fact, he gave them both a knowing nod, followed by a lascivious wink at Caine. Anna felt embarrassed. Had he thought they'd made use of the mythical casting couch in Jackson's office?

Caine was right. She had too many scruples. For Hollywood, *and* for fooling around in a Hollywood producer's office.

Room 928

"**R**oom 928?" Jack asked the clerk behind the carved wooden counter, who wore a black suit and a name tag identifying himself as Ji Min. "I specifically requested 928."

"Let me check, sir."

As Jack dealt with the clerk, Dee surveyed the hotel lobby. In all the time she'd been in Los Angeles, she'd never been inside the Hotel Roosevelt on Hollywood Boulevard, though she'd driven past it countless times. The lobby itself had an enormous four-story ceiling, marble fixtures, and sleek black furniture. When she looked up, she saw a marvelous crystal chandelier old enough to be the original. Maybe it *was* the original—on the ride over, Jack had told her that the hotel was eighty-five years old. He'd also told her that it was supposedly haunted.

Was she up for an adventure? Always.

Dee had chosen her clothes with a sex-with-ghosts kind of theme. Her Stella McCartney baby doll dress was constructed from translucent ivory silk. At certain angles, when the light hit her just so, she almost appeared to glow.

"Okay, here you go." Dee saw the clerk hand over an envelope with a key card. "Room 928 it is. Enjoy. If there's anything we can do to make your time more enjoyable here, let us know."

"I will," Jack assured him.

"What's so special about room 928?" Dee asked

Jack smiled and wriggled his eyebrows mysteriously. "You don't know the story?"

On their way up in an elevator as modern as the hotel was classic, Jack told Dee about the legend of room 928. Supposedly, the actor Montgomery Clift had lived in that room back in the 1950s, back when he was filming *From Here to Eternity* with Natalie Wood. Soon after the hotel was renovated, people who stayed in 928 began reporting a peculiar presence. One woman swore she had been reading in bed, felt a tap on her shoulder, turned over to say good night to her husband, and realized that it couldn't have been her husband, because he was snoring with his head under the quilt.

Another time, a psychic awoke at five in the morning to see a shadowy apparition that resembled the silhouette of Clift sitting in a chair near the door. But the chair hadn't been anywhere near the door when he went to sleep. The psychic reported that the ghost stood and glided into the bathroom. There it disappeared.

These stories didn't make Dee nervous. Actually, they thrilled her. There'd been a time in her life when she'd loved the paranormal and the occult. This visit to the Roosevelt was bringing all that back.

Room 928 was the last one on the right at the end of the hall. Jack opened it with his key card. Then, with no warning, Dee felt herself being swept up in his arms and carried over the threshold of the doorway. She giggled.

Five minutes later, they were "adventuring" all over room 928, kissing on the white-draped bed with the round French-style green bolster pillows, the matching white love seat, and even the window ledge that looked out over Hollywood Boulevard and the hills beyond. Finally, Dee lay cradled in Jack's arms.

"I have news for you," she teased. "Really big news."

"What's that?"

"I'm pregnant. It's either yours on Montgomery Clift's."

Instead of laughing, which is what Dee had expected, Jack got very thoughtful. "Interesting," he admitted. "Minus the Montgomery Clift part, I mean."

"Come on, I was joking," Dee told him, as she nuzzled against his neck.

"Yeah, I got that. But think about it. My sister Margie—you know about her, she has brain damage—is never going to have children. That leaves me. My parents have always talked about how cool it would be to have grandchildren. The more the merrier, actually."

Whoa. Dee remembered how early in the school year, she'd tried to fake a pregnancy. She was so ashamed of that now. But at that time she'd been halfway to the Ojai Institute but hadn't even known it. Now, she realized she'd had a biochemical imbalance back then. Between her meds and excellent therapy, she was a completely different person now.

Jack, however, had no such imbalance. Which meant that he was serious. Which was really, really weird.

"That idea doesn't totally freak you out?" Dee asked.

Jack swung his head back and forth like a bobble-head toy. "Once upon a time, yeah. But now . . . I could see being a father sometime. Not just with anyone, though. With you."

"You mean like . . . a decade down the road or something. Right?"

"Maybe," Jack agreed, nuzzling her neck. "Or maybe we'll be on our third or fourth kid by then."

"I validate your feelings," she said seriously, just as she'd been taught at Ojai. "But . . . I'm so not ready for anything like that."

"I didn't mean tomorrow, Dee. I meant . . . some-time."

"Oh." Dee tried to smile, but it didn't feel right on her face. Were they seriously talking about *babies*? She hadn't even officially finished high school yet!

"You ever thought about where you wanted to live?" he asked.

"You mean like now or what?"

"What." Jack pressed his lips to her forehead.

"Umm, my parents' house in Beverly Hills? After they retire and go to their place on Oahu?"

"Yeah. But you've been back east, though. Ben told me you visited him at Princeton. What'd you think of New Jersey?"

Ben had mentioned she'd been to Princeton? She wondered what else he'd told Jack. Surely not that they'd slept together. After all, it was only one time. Ben wouldn't tell Jack. Or would he? She had a feeling now that it would upset Jack. A lot.

"Princeton was nice."

There. That seemed neutral enough.

He smoothed the wispy blond bangs from her face. "I like the shore. Belmar, Asbury Park. It's not all the fake shit you find out here. Back there, people build things and get their fingernails dirty. People with real jobs, fixing cars, building houses, driving buses, working for the phone company. Like that."

Okay, this was entirely too bizarre. Dee stretched her toes into the high-thread-count white Egyptian cotton sheets. She slept on similar ones every night, and, not to sound terrible, she expected that state of affairs to last forever. She wondered what kind of thread-count sheets one might find at the MegaMart in Belmar, New Jersey? Could thread count veer into negative numbers?

"But . . . you go to Princeton! You're at Fox for the summer. You want to make a lot of money! You told me so!" Dee found herself really upset.

"Yeah," he admitted. "But there's so much—the bullshit out here is just so thick. Maybe I can play the game for a while. But after that, I'm thinking about returning to the real world."

"In New Jersey," Dee clarified, just to be sure. "Like after you make money to help your sister?"

"I figure she can live with me. Or you know, when the time comes . . . us."

Holy shit. He *was* serious. Dee did some deep, meditative breathing. This didn't make any sense. She was the one who always seemed to be pulling him closer. He was the cool college guy who wasn't interested in commitment. Back in her bipolar days, she might have thought that she was in a science-fiction movie and aliens had eaten Jack's brain.

"Jack?"

"Yeah?"

"I'd rather screw the ghost of Montgomery Clift than live in Belmar, New Jersey."

Silence. She felt Jack's arms tense.

"Oh man!" He laughed a little louder than was necessary. "You think I was serious?"

"Yeah," she admitted, though she felt uncomfortable doing it. "Kinda."

She still wasn't sure, frankly.

"Didn't know I could act, did ya?" Jack wrapped his arms around her; soon they were kissing again.

From Dee's point of view, kissing Jack was vastly superior to talking at the moment. So she made sure his lips were well occupied.

Soon, she'd put the weird conversation about weddings

and babies and living in New Jersey out of her mind. They ordered room service and sneaked into the hotel pool to skinny-dip after hours. They raided the minibar and finally fell asleep around three in the morning. The ghost of Montgomery Clift did not make an appearance. But all through the evening, no matter where they were, Dee felt like another kind of apparition was following her around, casting a peculiar shadow. It was the niggling suspicion she had that Jack hadn't been bullshitting at all. And that was a worse nightmare for her than any encounter with a spirit from the great beyond.

"So, I need your help."

"Maybe I should get those words on tape," Anna quipped.

Cammie bit her lip and clenched the wheel. Asking Anna for anything was not her idea of a good time. On the other hand, they *were* getting along better. Nominally.

"Actually, I'm serious."

It was the next morning, and they were on their way to the beach in Carpinteria to Virginia Vanderleer's second home (she had four) for a fashion show organizing committee brunch. There wasn't a good reason for the brunch—everything that could be organized had been organized, and the show would take place the following Wednesday evening—but Mrs. Vanderleer had insisted that this brunch would build what she called "committee solidarity."

Cammie wore a black Cheeta B. shutter-pleat camisole with a tiny plaid schoolgirl-looking miniskirt, and black Miu Miu sling-back sandals. Anna had on a White and White mint green beaded cardigan that looked vintage, and black silk Harari slacks. They looked, Cammie thought, as different from each other as they actually were.

"It's Champagne," she explained, as she shifted into the left lane to blow past a teal blue Ford Taurus that was barely going sixty. "I want to help her. And yes, this is Cammie Sheppard talking. So your next question is, 'What's in it for you, Cammie?'"

"Actually I'm still back on you having what sounds like it might actually be a selfless desire," Anna declared, as she fished her sunglasses out of her cherry red Kate Spade hobo bag.

Cammie zipped in and out of traffic; the Lamborghini hugged the road like three-ply cashmere. It was definitely worth the quarter-mil her father had paid for it. "Okay, first of all, you don't know me. And second of all, I refer you to first of all. So let's not pretend we're close friends."

"Whew," Anna teased. "I feel much better now. You being nice could be a sign of the apocalypse."

Cammie bit back a bitchy retort. "Here's the thing. We both know Champagne wants to be a model. And we both know she doesn't have a clue about how to reach that goal. I know she's on the short side. But she's got the look."

"Agreed. And?"

"And she needs a manager. Someone to help her, show her the ropes, someone who believes in her, who can maybe even make it happen."

"And?"

"That's where I come in."

Anna nodded. "Fair enough. So where do *I* come in?"

"Contacts. As in, who you know. I've pretty much got the Los Angeles thing covered. I know all the agencies here. The ones I don't know, Sam knows. But you know the East Coast thing, the New York thing."

Anna gave Cammie a blank look. "You are an Upper East Side of Manhattan snotty rich girl, are you not?"

Anna blanched. "Yes to everything except the snotty part, I hope."

"Fine, fine. But, you probably have more connections in the business back there than you even realize. I'm thinking it might be hard for Champagne to get a break as a runway model, no matter how great she looks. But print—print is a definite possibility."

Anna was silent for quite a while, and Cammie didn't press her. Finally she spoke. "I'll think about it. I'd like to help Champagne, that's for sure." She tapped a finger against her naturally full lips. "Maybe I do know someone—

"But there's something I'd like you to do for me, too. I know you want Champagne to be a model."

"*She* wants—"

"Right, got it," Anna agreed. "And I hope she

succeeds. But I don't think we should drop the girl if the modeling thing doesn't work out. So you have to be willing to help her . . . no matter what. And I don't mean hand her money. I mean help her help herself."

Cammie frowned. "Are you going all New Visions Foundation on me?"

"I hope what I'm doing is the right thing."

"How gruesome," Cammie muttered, but actually, it was fine with her. She wasn't about to drop Champagne now. Up ahead, she saw a turnout to a Phillips 66 gas station. She pulled into it, though her father's driver made sure every morning that every vehicle in the family fleet had a full tank of gas.

"Need gas?" Anna asked.

"Nope." Cammie turned the engine off, took the keys out of the ignition, and tossed them to Anna. "I'm assuming you can drive a stick. Take 'er to Carpinteria from here."

"I really have barely driven a stick—"

"Oh, for God's sake, just do it! Live a little!"

Anna didn't say anything. She simply got out of the car and traded places with Cammie. "You know what?"

"What?"

"You're right about me," Anna admitted sheepishly, turning the ignition key so that the engine roared back to life.

"Of course I am," Cammie agreed. "Carpinteria is about fifty miles away." She grinned at Anna. "In this baby? You should be able to do it in thirty-two minutes."

Does He Do *This* to You?

"**C**amilla, lovely to see you," Raymond cooed softly, kissing Cammie on both cheeks and then holding her at arm's length to survey her outfit.

Raymond was *the* hair guru in Beverly Hills, and the acknowledged king of Rodeo Drive. You simply could not get a booking with Raymond unless you called at least three months ahead, and even then you usually had to know someone or be able to promise a really impressive favor, involving money, fame, sex, or all three.

The hairdressers who worked under Raymond would be doing the hair for the fashion show. Today, Mrs. Vanderleer had brought Anna, Cammie, and Champagne to the salon so that she could see the "look" that Raymond had in mind for the models at the show next week.

Raymond looked Cammie up and down. He already had several of his assistants fawning over Champagne and her gorgeous platinum hair, settling her into a chair toward the rear of his salon. The younger girl had been obviously thrilled with the attention. Anna too had been eased into a chair for a shampoo, cut, and overall beautification—not that she needed it, Cammie thought. As for Mrs. Vanderleer, she'd slipped out for a quick shopping jaunt to the Christian Dior and Chanel boutiques down the street, though Cammie had overheard her warning Raymond not to turn his back on Champagne for too long. She'd be back in a few hours to assess the efforts of Raymond's crew and offer her comments for improvements.

"More beautiful than ever, Cammie. Volunteer work suits you." He motioned Cammie toward his own chair. "Ready to be transformed into a sixties icon, darling? I've got some wonderful ideas for you, if you're feeling courageous."

Cammie slid into the chair. "I'm always courageous."

"Now this is another one of the wide-eyed looks we want for the fashion show," Raymond was telling his stylists, as they gathered around Anna. "Very sixties mod, but we exaggerate the lines for dramatic purposes. Any questions?"

Anna had new long, fringy bangs. As for the rest of her blond hair, it had been teased and sprayed, then twisted and pinned up in back, with pieces falling loose around her face. She'd had three sets of false eyelashes glued to her top lids and two sets on the bottom. Thick eyeliner headed for her temples, pink blush highlighted the apples of her cheeks, and a faint coat of pink lip gloss completed the look.

She was ready to get up and wash it all off when a short male assistant came running into the salon, a black garment bag in his hands.

"Try this with it. It's from Gucci. *Vogue* was going to use it for their 'Everything Old Is New Again' layout, but they went with the fifties instead of the sixties."

"What size are you?" Raymond asked.

"Four," Anna replied.

"It's a four, should be perfect!" the assistant chortled.

"Go, go, go!" Raymond shooed her toward the unisex bathrooms at the rear of the salon.

There, she pulled off her jeans and T-shirt and pulled on a very short black A-line dress. It was trimmed in white, the sides were completely cut out, and it barely cleared her butt. The only mirror in the bathroom was shoulder-high, so she couldn't see what she looked like.

Anna hesitantly walked out of the bathroom in her bare feet. There was a moment of silence, followed by rapturous applause from the hair designers, and even the regular salon customers. Even Mrs. Vanderleer, who'd arrived back from her shopping trip just a few minutes before, was applauding wildly.

"Damn!" Champagne exclaimed. Raymond's minions had transformed her with a radical sixties blunt cut and flat ironing: she looked like a London model from the 1960s.

"Is that a good 'damn'?" Anna ventured.

Raymond nodded vigorously. "It's fabulous."

"You look fantastic. Come and see." Champagne took her by the arm and walked her to the full-length mirror near Raymond's hair stand. "What do you think?"

Just as Anna went back to the bathroom to change, her cell rang. She fished it out of her jeans and checked caller ID.

She leaned against the wall and flipped her phone open.

"Hi."

"Hey." Ben's voice floated easily through the phone. "I'm at La Dolce Vita, just down the block. You're at Raymond's salon?"

Anna frowned. "How do you know where I am?"

"Cammie. She said you'd be there most of the day."

Anna hadn't known that Cammie and Ben had been talking. Not that there was any reason that she should. But still.

"So, you're just about done there, right? Want to grab a bite?"

"I . . . can't. We're supposed to go to the museum after this for some kind of a walk-through." That was the truth—Mrs. Vanderleer was going to drive them over and show them the actual gallery where the fashion show would be happening.

"Well, at least sneak downstairs so I can say hello, okay?"

Anna considered his request. Well, why not?

"Five minutes. Okay?"

She made it down in three.

He was waiting on the sidewalk outside the salon entrance. When he got a look at her—the hair, the makeup, the dress—his jaw literally fell open. "That's . . . you . . . oh my God . . . you're . . ."

"A girl wearing way too much makeup?" she ventured, her vow not to care what he thought vanishing as quickly as she'd made it.

"Hot. Like incendiary-hot hot. Only hotter. Like, spontaneous-combustion hot."

Anna grinned and put her hands on her hips as two older guys walked by on the sidewalk, both in expensive looking suits. They both turned to get another good look at her. Wow. Anna couldn't deny that it gave her a fantastic, powerful feeling.

"Don't do this too often," Ben joshed. "You might have to hire a bodyguard. I might have to volunteer for the gig."

"Hey, they're just trying stuff out on me for the charity fashion show," she explained, pushing back a pale tendril that had blown into her eyes.

"Does the head-turner in the hot dress have plans tonight?"

Anna shook her head.

"So?" Ben asked quietly. "I'm not working. We can do whatever you want."

"Sorry. I just . . . I can't."

Ben stiffened. "Is it that Caine guy?"

Anna nodded.

"Come on, seriously." Ben scowled. "The guy's a poser. Tattoos and a pickup truck, but he's a financial analyst? Please."

"I like him. A lot."

"The same way you 'like' me a lot?"

"I don't know."

Ben moved closer. "How long are we going to play this? A week? A month? Until the summer's over and I go back to Princeton?"

"I'm not trying to 'play you.'" Surely he knew her better than that. "But I can't be with him and with you at the same time. It's not fair to anyone."

"All's fair," Ben murmured.

Just as Anna was mentally filling in the rest of this quote—"All's fair in love and war"—Ben's hand was on the back of her neck, his lips brushing against hers so softly it made her insides ache. She forced herself to push him away, breathless.

Ben smiled. "I'm not playing fair, Anna. I'm playing to win."

The Natural

"You're ready?" Sam asked.

"Yeah," Parker replied into his cell, a cheap LGX 3200 model he'd had forever.

"Where is she now?"

Parker put the phone in his other hand and looked in the direction of the bathrooms off the lobby of the Ritz-Carlton Huntington Hotel. It was the most luxurious hotel in Pasadena, selected precisely because no one from Beverly Hills ever went to Pasadena, unless that person was a lady who lunched or was shooting a movie on location.

He was there with Poppy Sharpe, Sam's stepmother, Jackson's wife. Thank God he didn't actually have to go to a room with her.

"She went to the 'powder room,'" Parker relayed. "Those are her words, by the way."

"Good. When you see her come out of the 'powder room,' I want you to end this call. Don't even say goodbye. You can see her coming?"

He peered across the hotel lobby, with its Axminster

carpets, dark wood wall paneling, and Viennese lighting fixtures. At this hour of the afternoon, the premises were very quiet. The previous night's guests had checked out, and the current night's arrivals were still a couple of hours away.

"Definitely," Parker confirmed. "A straight shot. I'll see her."

"Great. Then do exactly what I told you. Let's go over it again. She'll want you to register. Don't bother. Tell her to wait in the Lobby Lounge. There's a beige couch in there with three burgundy pillows. If you can get her on that couch to wait for you, that's the best. If not, get her someplace close. When you come back to her, kiss her. Then, do whatever you need to do for her to take you home. I suggest feigning intestinal distress."

Parker felt a bead of sweat roll down his brow, despite the lobby's very excellent air conditioning. Sam had everything covered, but he was nervous anyway. "Are you here, watching someplace?"

"No. Definitely not. I've got someone else there for me. And Parker? When you get home, call that waitress from the Polo Lounge. The one named for the fruit. You haven't called her yet, right?"

"No."

"You want to. Call her. Okay?"

"Okay."

"Great. Now do what you have to. Oh—one more thing."

"Yes?"

"If she gets cold feet, don't try to talk her into stay-ing."

"Got it," he agreed.

"This is all up to her, remember. If she backs away, just call and tell me."

"You've got a photographer here, then?"

He could almost hear Sam grin. "Listen for the click. Okay, you better go."

He and Poppy had been exchanging e-mails and phone calls on Poppy's private line ever since the night of the *Ben-Hur* toga party. It had all been at Poppy's initiation, too. She'd even arranged one meeting in an out-of-the-way bar in the valley, where she'd rubbed his thigh under the table. Finally, she'd invited him to meet her at a hotel.

It was sad, really. She was married to one of the most famous men in Hollywood. She was beyond rich and had given birth to Jackson's baby. The man deserved better.

"Sam?"

"Yeah?"

"Here she comes."

Damn. She looked good but had the morals of a bonobo. Okay, so he wasn't much better sometimes. But that was to help his career. What was her excuse? Still, he had to admit that she was hot. She was just twenty-two, and definitely back in shape again post-baby. She'd worked a little urban flava into her look by shimmying into a Baby Phat catsuit with a plunging back, matched with metallic bronze stiletto heels. Her red hair was pulled back into two low pigtails, and her lips were coated in some shimmery gloss that pretty much begged to be kissed.

She strode right toward him with a "come and get it, big boy" look on her face. "Gotta go," Parker whispered quickly, turning away to pocket his cell. Then he swung back in the opposite direction and greeted Poppy with a big grin. "Hey." He planted a kiss on her forehead.

She snaked her arms around his neck and kissed his mouth. "You gonna check in for us?"

"Sure. Come on. Wait in the Lobby Lounge. I'll walk you there."

He let her take his arm and strolled with her across the lobby, his perma-grin turning into a floodlight. Acting, he repeated to himself. You're acting. But knowing that Poppy was both married and this easy made him lose just a little faith in love. He felt her soft hand on his arm.

"You okay?" she asked.

"Oh yeah, sure."

"You know, human beings have needs," she told him with a straight face. "If you block the flow of energy by not expressing yourself physically on a regular basis, it builds up toxins. I'm totally serious."

"Uh-huh," Parker agreed, as if he was actually interested in her lame New Age excuses for why she was cheating.

"Besides, I knew from the first moment I saw you that our auras were the same color. You're just so cerulean." She put a hand on his chest. "I'm sure Jackson still screws around on the film set," she continued. "After all, that's how we met. You're not having second thoughts, are you?"

The actor in him kicked in. "I'm great, babe."

They reached the Lobby Lounge, passing the big sign advertising their famous formal afternoon tea at four o'clock. Beige couch, burgundy pillows . . . Bingo, there was his drop zone, near a massive arrangement of several dozen roses. He steered her toward it and dared to try out a line. "I was just thinking about what the next two hours—naw, four hours—are going to be like. When do you have to be home?"

"I left a message for Jackson that I wouldn't be back from shopping until after nine. Of course, he won't be back from the movie set until ten. Not to worry. I've got three nurses for Ruby Hummingbird." Her arms went around his neck again. She gave him a kiss with way too much tongue. "Mmm. You're hot."

"Yeah, you too," Parker said, his eyes darting this way and that. The lounge was empty, save for an elderly woman in a green floral dress, sitting alone with a cup of tea and the *Los Angeles Times*. Yep. That had to be her. The PI with the camera. Nice disguise. "Wait here and order a cocktail. I'll check us in and be right back. But I need one more kiss first. A good one."

Poppy obliged, this time biting his lower lip in a way

that felt more predatory than sexy. As she did, he heard
the soft click he'd been waiting for. And then another,
and another, and another. His work was done. So he
winced.

"What's wrong?"

Now he grabbed his stomach and grimaced. "Dunno.
Something I ate, I guess. Gotta find a bathroom. Right
now."

"He's a little temperamental," Anna observed, as she
and Cammie stood a hundred feet away from where
Phillip Champion, the renowned fashion photographer,
was working with two assistants and Champagne.
Phillip looked like a giant teddy bear, with long, shaggy
chestnut hair, and a stomach straining under a wrinkled
navy T-shirt. At the moment, he was yelling at his assistant because he didn't like the way she'd buttoned the
gauzy white shirt Champagne wore; he was as fastidi-
ous about the appearance of his models as he was not
about his own.

Already Champagne had modeled a diaphanous
royal purple Versace gown while she lay on some rocks,
and a magenta fur coat that apparently had nothing
under it. After those outfits, the white gauze shirt and
black linen trouser combination almost seemed tame.

"More than a little," Cammie agreed. "But the best
always are. And don't give him any attitude, because he
gives enough already. He had to cancel a magazine shoot
for *Allure,* but he did it as a favor to me, so deal with it."

"This is me, dealing," Anna assured her, holding her hands up in a gesture of acceptance.

It was the same evening. Before they'd even left Raymond's salon, Phillip had returned Cammie's call to say he was free that evening, and that he wouldn't be available again until September. Could they meet him at Palisades Park, in Pacific Palisades, at six-thirty? The light would be perfect. Cammie had quickly filled Champagne in; Anna had decided to come along just out of curiosity.

"Wait, I'm going to do an actual modeling shoot?" Champagne had asked, completely confused.

"I just said that," Cammie repeated. And then she launched into a Champagne-centric pep talk, so good that Anna was impressed in spite of herself.

That was how they had ended up in this beautiful, small park perched on the cliffs overlooking the Pacific Coast Highway, the beach, and the ocean beyond. Anna had been a bit little concerned that Champagne wouldn't have the right clothes, but Cammie told her not to worry. Phillip had it covered.

Anna's cell rang. "Hello?"

"Anna, it's Lizbette's assistant, Lindsay," said a young female voice with a crisp British accent. "Lizbette says to tell you it's a go. Upload the images to her—she'll get back to you in a jiff. You have the e-mail address?"

"I do. I'll send them as soon as I've got them."

"We'll look forward to seeing the photos then."

Lindsay clicked off.

"You'll send what?" Cammie demanded.

"Well, my mother is a good friend of Princess Lizbette Demitrius. Her company is—"

"Hold it right there. Lizbette Demetrius of Demetrius International?" Cammie grabbed her arm. "Holy shit, Anna. They're one of the biggest upscale cosmetics companies in the world."

Anna nodded. "Exactly. Well, I know her rather well—I've known her since I was little, actually. She and my mother have been friends forever. So I called her about Champagne."

Anna thought Cammie almost looked stunned. That was really very satisfying.

"She told me they're launching a new cosmetics line called Principessa, which is being marketed to younger women. I thought Champagne might be right for it. Height's not an issue because it's all print, and—"

"You're a genius!" Cammie threw her arms around Anna and hugged her wildly.

She laughed. "We aren't really going to become new best friends, are we?"

"God no," Cammie assured her. "But I love that you did this. So Lizbette wants us to send her some photos?"

"Exactly. This shoot would be perfect."

"She'll have them tomorrow if I have to spend the night in Phillip's studio myself."

"Hey guys!"

It was Phillip, walking up a dirt path toward them.

He shook his hair out of his eyes. Three different cameras hung around his neck, and there was a light meter clipped to his faded leather belt.

"How'd she do?"

Anna heard the anxiety in Cammie's voice, and realized again how much she had invested in this.

Phillip grinned, then glanced behind him before he answered. Champagne was still at the other end of the park with the assistants. "I'm glad you called me. I hope this isn't the last time I get to work with her. She's one of the most natural models I've ever seen. Great bones. The camera absolutely loves her."

"I knew it, I knew it!" Cammie pumped a fist in the air.

Phillip looked confused. "Hey, I've known you a long time. Since when are you so interested in another beautiful girl?"

"We're . . . volunteering together," Cammie replied with a straight face, which made Anna laugh.

"Okay, whatever, keep your secret," Phillip said. "Anyway, it was a pleasure. The chick is a natural. Big future ahead of her. If she were four inches taller, she'd be making five grand a day. *Every* day, for the next fourteen years. What do you have in mind for her?"

Cammie shrugged and shot Anna a look that seemed to say Anna shouldn't open her mouth, so she didn't. "Not sure yet. Can you print tonight?"

"No need, it's all digital." Phillip popped the media cards out of each of his cameras and handed them to her.

"Here. Enjoy. Use Photoshop or Camedia or whatever you want. Tell your dad to call me soon. I'd love to do lunch."

"Will do. And thanks, Phillip. I owe you one."

"Good to know." He turned to regard Anna. "Great look, by the way. Love the hair." Then he gave them a two-finger salute and headed to his Jeep.

Cammie stretched her arms above her head, then drifted over to a bench, "So, here's the plan. Go tell Champagne to get her ass in gear so we can drive her back to the valley. I don't want to be up all night. And I want five shots on your friend's desk when she gets to work tomorrow."

Anna folded her arms and regarded Cammie coolly. "Excuse me, I wasn't aware that I was your employee."

"Sorry, I was channeling my father," Cammie admitted. "I'm trying to remember why I dislike you intensely. Other than the Ben thing and the ice princess thing."

"Well, one out of two isn't a problem at the moment."

Cammie's eyes narrowed. "I'm assuming you mean Ben. And you can tell me whatever bullshit you want about Tattoo Guy. There was someone on the staircase behind you this afternoon at Raymond's. Me. I saw him kiss you. You kissed him back, so don't deny it. It meant something."

Anna hadn't realized Cammie had been spying on her. But she kept her cool.

"I don't know what it meant," Anna admitted. "Besides, you're in love with Adam."

"True." Cammie leaned back against the bench. "If I wasn't, my life would be so much easier. Anyway, thank you for what you're doing for Champagne. I owe you one." She regarded Anna coolly. "Just keep this in mind. You screw around with a guy like Ben for too long, you're the one who could end up getting screwed."

The Price Is Right

"What do you mean, we don't get paid?" shrieked Tinkerbell, the tallest and most angular of the models. Her silvery hair was cut into something between a Mohawk and a shag. "Is this some kind of a joke?"

It was the next evening, and Sam, Cammie, Anna, and Champagne were all with Mrs. Vanderleer at the Los Angeles County Museum of Art. Mrs. Vanderleer and her committee had decided that the fashion show would take place in a gallery that would be reconfigured to hold a dozen or more large works by the sixties pop artist Roy Lichtenstein.

Of course, Sam didn't have to be there. But she was the one who had arranged for the models for the fashion show, and she was still feeling just a little guilty that Cammie and Anna had been busted without her. So she'd offered to meet them for this rehearsal, in case there were any problems with the models from PacCoast.

The rehearsal had gone beautifully. That is, until now, when the models decided to demand pay for a gig that was supposed to be volunteer.

"What part of the word *charity* in 'charity fashion show' eludes you?" Sam asked Anastasia.

"The part where I agreed to work for free," the skinny brunette sniffed petulantly, curling out what looked to be a lower lip made puffy with some serious Restylane injections. "I haven't worked for free since I was in sixth grade."

"For real." Malcolm, a male model with a ripped body made for underwear ads, agreed. "Charity begins at home, you know what I'm saying?"

"But there must be some misunderstanding. Everyone is volunteering their time," Mrs. Vanderleer explained. She wore another of her pastel ladies-who-lunch outfits. "So are you."

"Oh, I don't think so," a different male model sneered, fluttering what Sam was sure were eyelash extensions. His name was Ambrosia, and Sam hadn't realized he was quite so fey until this very minute, though his unisex look had made him famous on the party circuit.

"I really do not see what the big deal is. What's your day quote?" she asked Anastasia, who had the best tear sheets, meaning she was the most experienced and probably had the highest rate.

"Five thousand a day," Anastasia said coolly.

"And the rest of you?"

"We don't share our quotes," Tinkerbell snipped.

Malcolm nodded. "Call our agency."

Sam would have liked to call his face a bull's-eye and

put her fist through it, but she took a deep breath and held on to her cool. She forced herself to casually smooth her hands over her cropped wool FCUK jacket while taking a deep, calming breath. So what if it cost her a few thousand bucks to hire the models. She'd do it through her father's production company and make it a tax write-off.

"I will pick up the tab for the models," she told Mrs. Vanderleer. "Consider it a donation and my pleasure."

"And I'll help," Cammie added.

"I can help, too," Anna volunteered.

Mrs. Vanderleer rubbed her forehead. "Could I speak with you a moment, Sam?"

"Sure."

"Privately."

They left Anna, Cammie, and Champagne, and walked through the Lichtenstein gallery and into the next one filled with Andy Warhols; a giant soup can painting was being mounted on the far wall. Mrs. Vanderleer shut the door behind her so they wouldn't be overheard.

"As I said earlier, I very much appreciate your help with this project," the older woman began in her usual patrician tones.

"Look, Mrs. Vanderleer, this is my responsibility. I promised you the models from PacCoast, so I'll deliver the models from PacCoast," Sam said, cutting to the chase. "I'll just consider whatever they charge a charitable donation. And I'll make sure that PacCoast gets a call from my dad. Personally. I can't believe Melange is screwing us like this. Don't blame the models. Blame the person in charge."

Mrs. Vanderleer nodded. "I will. And you've already gone above and beyond. However, I can't let you pay for these models, much as I appreciate your generosity."

Sam folded her arms. "Because?"

"Because money is not the issue. The publicity has already gone out about this event to every media outlet in town. It specifically says that everyone is donating his or her time. If the models are paid by you or anyone else—any one of the women on my committee could write the check—it will look as if I misrepresented the event. And that won't do, not for me or for the organization. Donated time means donated time."

"So what's your plan B?"

"I wish I knew. Let's go back in. Maybe I can convince them."

"Good luck," Sam said dubiously.

When they came back into the gallery, Mrs. Vanderleer marched over to the gathering of models and put on her most persuasive voice.

"I'm sorry this didn't work out the way you expected. We appreciate your time. But this is a charity event. For everyone. And especially for the at-risk girls in our program. Through New Visions, we are providing opportunities for young women age twelve to twenty-one to better their lives. We give assistance with school and academics. If there are at-risk behaviors, we try to eliminate them.

We insure that they get adequate health care and emergency psychological help. In situations where these girls
are burdened with adult responsibilities, New Visions
will assist with everything from training to respite care.
Please. That's just the beginning of what we do. Look
into your beautiful hearts. Help me out now, and I'll be
able to help you out later. You have my word."

"No fee? No modeling." Tinkerbell grabbed her
Tylie Malibu python purse, then slipped on a pair of silver Gucci aviator shades and strode out of the room
without a backward glance. Anastasia was right behind
her. A few of the others hesitated, but within a minute
all of the models had followed her.

"Well, that went well," Mrs. Vanderleer declared,
once they were gone. She pressed her lips together so
hard they turned white.

"I have an idea," Cammie began. "What if it's your
girls?"

Mrs. Vanderleer arched a brow. "Meaning?"

"Meaning that your foundation is supposed to help
at-risk girls, right? What if you brought three or four of
those girls—three, because I'm sure Champagne here
will want to participate—and we use them as the models, instead of professionals?"

"What?" Champagne gasped.

"You can do it," Cammie assured her. "I'll show you
everything you need to know."

Sam nodded her agreement. "Great idea. Wouldn't
that be more interesting, anyway?"

"I don't know." Mrs. Vanderleer frowned. "Some of my girls are size sixteen or eighteen. I don't think that would do at all."

Anna turned to Sam. "I wonder . . . could we contact the designers and see if we can get the clothes for the show in a variety of sizes?"

"They don't design clothes in those sizes," Cammie put in.

"Some of them do, actually," Mrs. Vanderleer mused, tapping a perfectly manicured finger against her lips.

Anna nodded. "Well, then, I think it's a great idea. Isn't the goal of your program to be affirming to these girls? So modeling says that they're beautiful just the way they are."

Mrs. Vanderleer frowned again. "And Cammie, you're confident you can teach them what they need to know?"

Cammie nodded.

The older woman seemed to make a decision. "Assuming we can work out the details, I give this a tentative yes. Though I'd feel more comfortable, Cammie and Anna, if you'd be backstage with my girls. And out on the runway too. As positive role models."

Sam saw Anna blanche. Mrs. Vanderleer apparently had no idea that a court order had brought Cammie and Anna there in the first place.

"Definitely," Cammie said. "I'm in. Anna's in too, and Champagne. Right?"

"I guess so," Champagne acknowledged. She looked very nervous.

"If Champagne will do it, so will I," Anna told Mrs. Vanderleer.

"That's great. But we're not done. There's still the little problem of the male models," Sam pointed out. "I don't think we want to troll San Quentin for hot inmates doing ten to twenty-five for armed robbery."

"Don't need to. I know a whole bunch of hot guys," Champagne said casually.

"Who are these 'hot guys'?" Mrs. Vanderleer asked warily.

"Just . . . you know . . . friends."

"I don't know. . . . " Mrs. Vanderleer was starting to sound like she was sorry she'd ever considered anyone other than the professional models in the first place.

"Look, let me give it a try," Champagne wheedled. There was a twinkle in her eye that Sam had never seen before. "I'll bring their photographs, Mrs. Vanderleer. I'll go see them tonight at work. Cammie and Anna can come too."

"Just where do they work, Ms. Jones?" asked Mrs. Vanderleer.

"They're firemen," Champagne said. "That's why they're so hot."

Sam had just started up the Big Bird–yellow Hummer in the museum parking structure when her Treo sounded with a cell call. She didn't recognize the number.

"Sam Sharpe," she answered.

"Sam? It's Melanie Mayes. Your detective. I haven't

heard from you since I did the job in Pasadena. Is everything okay?"

Melanie Mayes. Whom she'd hired a few weeks ago to track down her mother in North Carolina and whom she'd hired again to pose as an old woman reading a newspaper in the cocktail lounge at the hotel in Pasadena, and take photographs of Poppy and Parker. Melanie was one of the most outstanding private detectives in all of Los Angeles, scrupulously honest and frightfully expensive. She had left a "mission accomplished" message that very same night.

Sam hadn't called back to acknowledge it. When Sam first had the photo idea she'd been a hundred percent gung-ho. But now a teeny-tiny ten (okay, twenty) percent of her was having second thoughts. If she leaked those photographs to the *Galaxy* . . . what kind of a person would that make her? Besides a typical Hollywoodista, that is?

It was infuriating. Sam had that cheating Poppy Seed in her open palm, ready to be crushed, and she couldn't bring herself to do the deed.

"Hello, Melanie. I appreciate it. So what do I owe you for this job?"

"A buck fifty." Translation: fifteen hundred dollars. Not bad for an hour's work.

"You want me to e-mail the pictures to the *Galaxy* from a secure server, or do you want to do it yourself?"

"Neither," Sam instructed. "Kill them."

"Yeah?" Melanie sounded surprised. "You want me to destroy the photographs?"

"Exactly." Sam sighed. "I can't do this, Melanie," she confessed. "I'd like to, but I can't."

"Are you sure?" the detective asked. "I'm the one who took the photos. Your name will never come up."

"Kill them," Sam repeated.

"Fair enough. Listen. They're on a digital media card."

The next thing Sam heard was a loud crunch, like a boot heel coming down on a piece of ceramic underfoot.

"That was the card. I just stepped on it. It's now in five pieces. Those pictures are gone. In fact, they never existed." Melanie told her.

"You've still got my credit card number?"

"I do," Melanie acknowledged.

"Put the bill through. And thanks, Melanie. I'm sure you did a great job."

Sam's voice was hollow. She'd either done something kind and noble, or she'd just made the stupidest mistake of her young life. She said goodbye, called Parker, and left him the world's briefest message, saying that the photos were destroyed, but that he still had her eternal gratitude. When she hung up again, she sat in the Hummer, staring into space.

Kind, noble, or stupid. The worst part of it was, there was absolutely no way to know for sure.

We Call It the Fire Drill

"Turn left up ahead." Champagne pointed to the next intersection. Anna was driving her repaired silver Lexus; it was funny to recall how she had met Caine in the first place, when he'd driven to her rescue after a car accident. Plus, the accident had occurred right about where they were at the moment, on Sawtelle near Washington Boulevard. It was a gritty section of town, bisected by the 405 freeway, home to auto body shops, liquor stores, roofing and hardware wholesalers, and the occasional adult entertainment establishment.

They'd come directly from the fashion show rehearsal. Anna had on chocolate brown Ralph Lauren cords and a cream-colored sleeveless cotton Chloé shirt her best friend, Cyn, had gotten her for her sixteenth birthday. Cammie wore something she'd picked up at the Beverly Center—a Juicy Couture tube top that exposed about six inches of her perfectly tanned midriff, and a microminiskirt made from the same cherry red silk. Trendy, Anna knew, but cute and comfortable all the same. Champagne sported skinny-legged blue pants of dubious designer origins with a blue Dodgers T-shirt. Anna guessed that she'd had it forever.

She had to admit she was rather looking forward to visiting a firehouse, since she'd never been in one before. She stopped at a red light. "Do they really slide down those poles?"

Champagne, who was sitting next to her, looked startled. "How did you know?"

"It's in every movie about firemen."

"Oh, right." Champagne smiled. "Yep. They definitely use the pole. They use the pole *all the time.*"

"Are you sure you know where you're going?" Cammie called out, suddenly alert. "Because this is one scuzzy part of town."

"Definitely," Champagne confirmed. "Can I ask you guys something? Did you see the photos yet? The ones that Phillip guy took in Pacific Palisades? That was so much fun. I can't believe that models get to do that for a living."

"Uh-huh," Cammie replied. "We saw them. You rocked."

Her face lit up. "Really?"

"Even Phillip said so," Anna happily assured her.

"Wow." Champagne marveled. "And he works with a lot of top models. So now what do I have to do? Or was that it?"

"We're not going to rush anything," Cammie told her. "A young model needs to be brought along slowly."

Anna knew that wasn't exactly the truth. The night after the photo shoot, she and Cammie had gone back to Cammie's house with the three digital camera media cards that Phillip had given them. It was the first time that she had been in the Sheppard home since she'd come to Los Angeles, and she admired the decorating scheme that had been instituted in a recent renovation by Cammie's stepmother. Every room was done in shades of a single color, but each room had a different overall theme. The living room was modern white on white. The kitchen was French classic, burgundy on burgundy. The family room was industrial gray on gray, with only slight variations across the board.

Cammie didn't offer to show Anna her room. Instead she made espresso in a French press, then carried it and two cups downstairs to the lowest level, which not only featured an indoor lap-swimming pool that connected to the larger outdoor pool, a British billiards table, and an array of classic pinball machines, but also a corner office filled with computer equipment. This wasn't her dad's actual home office—Cammie explained that her father had one of those up on the main floor. But it did have a high-powered P4 Dell box with endless memory, a forty-inch Samsung plasma monitor, and an HP Photosmart professional photo printer.

Cammie had sat down at the computer and worked for five solid hours, reviewing each and every one of the photographs of Champagne that Phillip had taken, often asking Anna for an honest opinion. Anna was surprised.

Even more than that, she was impressed. Cammie had always seemed to her the personification of indolent rich Beverly Hills youth, for whom determination meant deciding which day spa to visit. But here, she watched her making a huge effort for a girl she barely knew.

"Do you think Champagne will appreciate all this?" Anna had asked, motioning to the monitor.

Cammie shrugged, scrolled over to another photo on the monitor, and opened it up. A stunning extreme close-up of Champagne in profile. "No clue. Grateful would be nice, but not necessary. The girl has a dream. I'm her fairy godmother. Maybe. If it works, she'll have a new life. If it doesn't work, she'll have had some fun. I'd call that a win-win, wouldn't you?"

Maybe this was why Adam was so into Cammie. Maybe be he had fallen for this side of the girl—a side that Anna couldn't say she had ever seen before.

Finally, they decided on five photos to send to Lizbette back in New York. Two were extreme close-ups of Champagne's captivating face, one a profile from the neck up, one a full-length picture of her lying back on the rocks in the unzipped evening gown, and the last another filmy full-length portrait, where she looked young, vulnerable, and innocent in the white gauze shirt. Cammie had skipped right past the fur coat and panties thing, saying overt nudity was most likely *not* a look Lizbette would embrace for her cosmetics line for young women.

When they were finally done, Anna had saved all the

photographs in a zip file and e-mailed the file to Lizbette's American headquarters back in New York. That had been two days ago. In the meantime, she hadn't heard anything. Cammie had wanted to call after twenty-four hours, but Anna knew this was exactly the wrong thing to do. Women like Lizbette never wanted to be pushed. It was Cammie's job now to wait graciously, and that was exactly what they were going to do. Anna also decreed that they should not mention the cosmetics or the new campaign to Champagne. There was no reason to get Champagne's hopes up unnecessarily.

The light changed, and Anna made the right turn. They passed more warehouses and low-rent business storefronts. "Whatever you say, Cammie. Okay, just ahead is the firehouse," Champagne instructed. "Turn in there."

There was no sign. Just a small nondescript warehouse and a jammed parking lot.

"This is the firehouse?" It didn't look like any firehouse Anna had ever seen.

"Definitely," Champagne assured them.

Anna was lucky to find a single unoccupied spot at the far end next to a Dumpster. When she got out of the Lexus, she heard pounding music coming from the warehouse. There was also a flashing neon sign that she noticed for the first time: THE FIREHOUSE: EAT, DRINK, AND BE RESCUED!

Cammie was grinning as she pushed the curls off her face. "Okay, what the hell is up with this?"

Champagne went wide-eyed and hitched a thumb toward the sign.

"Firemen," she replied innocently.

"So, let me make sure I'm following," Anna observed, as she dropped her key ring into her ancient dove gray Chanel leather purse. "Your friends are *strippers*?"

"Nah. Not *strippers*," Champagne said with a smile. "I wouldn't call them that."

Cammie winked. "Anna is disappointed. Right, Anna?"

"Not really."

Anna saw Cammie link her arm though Champagne's. "Good. So, let's head on in and see if these guys can put out some fires. And . . . whether any of them are model material."

Champagne grinned. "Fires, I don't know about. Model material? Just wait."

Anna was thrilled that her worst expectations were dashed.

Far from being a seedy strip joint, the Firehouse was much closer to a cross between the famous New York City bar Coyote Ugly and the original Hard Rock Café. Done in a firefighting theme, the walls featured bright murals and posters from firehouses and fire crews the world over, in a score of different languages. One end of the enormous room was dominated by an actual turn-of-the century horse-drawn fire engine that had been gutted so that diners could sit at tables inside. The main bar had bar stools shaped like firemen's hats,

and the menu featured only spicy foods ranging in hot-
ness from "hot" to "radioactive."

As for the help, Champagne had been right. There
was plenty of model material. The waiters and bar-
tenders wore jeans, red suspenders, and firemen's
boots. That was it. All of them were bare-chested, all of
them had chests well chiseled either by months in the
gym or the Almighty, and all of them were—as adver-
tised—exceptionally good-looking. In the parlance of
the Firehouse, definitely hot. Loud rock and roll played
over the sound system, and the firemen-waiters boo-
gied to the music as they delivered food and drink
orders. That wasn't such an easy thing to do, because
the tables were filled with rowdy cocktailers and patrons,
nearly all of them female, nearly all of them dressed like
they'd just come from work.

As the three girls were led to an empty table by the
fireman-host, the rock music stopped, a fire bell clanged,
and red lights whirled. Four firemen-waiters came sliding
down a floor-to-ceiling fire pole, all of them holding shot
glasses full of red alcohol. Not a drop was spilled. They
jogged in a conga line over to the table that had ordered
the shots and presented them to the delighted women
with chivalrous bows.

"Been here before?" the host asked Anna jovially, as
he seated them. He was a little older than the other
firemen, with dark brown hair, a chiseled jawline, and a
set of deep dimples when he smiled. His hat indicated
that he was the "chief."

Anna shook her head.

"Order shots all around, you get that treatment," he advised. "We call it the Fire Drill. Have fun—your waiter will be here in a minute."

It didn't take Anna long to get into the carefree and energetic mood of the club. Everyone was having fun, judging from the laughter, clapping, and raucous cheering whenever the firemen did their Fire Drill, which seemed to happen every five minutes or so. There was an obvious bachelorette party three tables away, complete with a blond and silicone-buxom bride-to-be in a veil. Yes, her mind did ponder what it meant to objectify people—male or female—which this club definitely was doing. Yes, she did wonder what kind of guy would choose to work here. But honestly? She was having—

Champagne stood abruptly and cupped her hands. "Hey, Bryson! Come wait on us!"

A shaggy-haired blond waiter who couldn't have been older than twenty cut through the crowd toward them. He wore the same jeans-and-suspenders getup as all the other staff. When he got to the table, Champagne flung her arms around him for an enormous hug and introduced him to Anna and Cammie.

"You guys know each other, I take it," Cammie observed, smirking.

"We definitely do. What's up, doll?" He kissed Champagne on the cheek and then looked back at the table. "So, how do you guys know my cousin?"

"They're . . . friends of mine," Champagne explained.

"From her summer volunteer thing," Cammie added.

"Very cool."

"Bryson—before we order, I need to ask you something!" Champagne had to shout to be heard as the music cranked up again.

"Sure, anything! But quick—I've got tables."

Champagne stood, took a few steps away, and motioned for him to join her. Anna's first instinct was to go with the girl, but Cammie put a hand on her forearm. "I think she's got it covered."

"Done! We've got our models!"

Anna turned. Champagne stood behind her and Cammie, looking triumphant. "Bryson said yes. And he's bringing four of his buds!"

"I'll call Mrs. Vanderleer first," Cammie assured Anna. "And I'll take some pictures with my cameraphone. She won't be disappointed."

Anna was proud of Champagne for her coup. She'd really come to like the plucky younger girl. Champagne so genuinely wanted to be helpful, once again Anna couldn't imagine how anyone who'd talked to this girl for more than three minutes could possibly think she was a thief. "Nice job!" She had to shout over the music, which the DJ had just taken to an entire other level. How did you do it?"

"Bryson's not just my cousin. He's my friend!"

* * *

They stayed for quite a while, ordering hot wings, tamales, and Cokes. Bryson brought over a couple of other waiters who he thought might be good for the show. One was tall, with close-cropped dark hair, and the other was shorter, with a gorgeous smile and incredibly wide shoulders. Each was a remarkable male specimen. Cammie was Cammie. She flirted outrageously. Anna was quieter but friendly. She was listening to one of Bryson's friends—Granite was the name he went by—tell a joke, when the music stopped, the fire bell clanged, and the red light whirled. By now, everyone in the place had started to clap rhythmically whenever the Fire Drill bell sounded. Anna clapped right along, until the last fireman came down the pole.

Then she stopped. Because she realized that she recognized the Botticelli tattoos on the arm of the final fireman.

The Opposite of the Last Sentence

Anna watched as it took a moment for Caine to register what he was actually seeing—Anna, probably
the last person he ever expected to see at the Firehouse,
at the Firehouse. Watching him.

He did a literal double take.

He delivered the shots, took his bow, and then
bounded over to her table. Anna could say this for him:
His sangfroid was as steady with his shirt off and
women cheering as it was with his shirt on at the top of
a Ferris wheel on the Santa Monica pier.

"Hi. I never—"

"Yes, I'm sure you never did think you'd see me
here," Anna finished his sentence for him.

She didn't need to hear the rest of his sentiment, even
as she introduced him to Champagne and reacquainted
him with Cammie. The evil smile on Cammie's face—it
had to be *so* obvious that Anna had no clue that Caine
moonlighted at this place—made her feel mortified. Caine
said he'd love to get her a drink at the bar and would meet
her there in three minutes. She took her time in rising.

She was grateful for the chance to think a little bit first. So many thoughts were running through her overloaded brain. Her problems with Ben had stemmed from a lack of honesty in their relationship. She'd been so sure that Caine was older, wiser, different. Did any guys tell the truth . . . ever? But what did Caine owe her, really? It wasn't like he was working for a male escort service. He wasn't even a stripper.

She slid onto the stool next him—he offered her a bottle of water. "Sorry for the surprise. Buy you something stronger? I've got about fifteen before I'm due out there on the floor again." Again, he seemed to have recovered quickly from his initial surprise at finding her there.

"I'm good." She looked at him curiously. "So, boring money manager by day, object of female lust at the Firehouse by night?"

"I have a wide variety of interests." Caine laughed, then got the bartender to pour him a glass of orange juice.

"Why didn't you tell me?" Anna asked directly.

He shrugged. "Didn't seem relevant. Yet. It's kind of early for us to be baring our souls to each other. Three weeks? But now that you're here, ask away."

"Why . . . why do you do this?"

"I've got massive debts from undergraduate and grad school. This is how I'm paying them off. It's honorable work." He took a sip of his drink.

"Umm . . . my father has to be paying you well. He

says you're a genius. Maybe you should ask him for a raise." Anna tried to stop her tone from sounding preachy, as she knew it did. "Did you think you *couldn't* tell me?"

"I thought it might bother you, yeah," Caine admitted reluctantly, and drank some more of his juice. "Look, don't take this the wrong way, Anna, but you're very young and—"

"Inexperienced. You were going to say 'inexperienced.'"

"Am I wrong?"

"I'm not . . . entirely inexperienced." She felt heat rush to her face. "I was . . . with Ben."

Caine grinned. "Ah. You mean *with* in the biblical sense. So if you had been *with* me in Jackson Sharpe's office the other night, it would be the second time."

"If you mean my second guy, yes. You would be the second guy."

"That's what I figured." He nodded sagely. "Which is fine. But that's why I decided to let you take the lead on all that, so that you'd feel comfortable." He downed the last of his juice and motioned to the bartender for another. "Would you like something stronger? You've barely touched that water."

She shook her head. Across the room, Anna saw Cammie dancing with a buff Latino fireman to Santana's "Smooth." Caine put his hand on her arm to get her attention, then quickly withdrew it. "Honestly, I'm an adventurous guy—always have been. I hitchhiked across Europe when I was sixteen. When I was eighteen, I drove my motorcycle cross-country with a girl I met along the way. Working for your dad, living this suit-and-tie kind of life . . . it's new for me. So if you were looking for a straight-arrow financial planner—"

"I wasn't looking for anything," she protested. She didn't want him to think she was presumptuous. "And I plan to have a lot of adventures myself."

"Oh, you do, do you?"

She gave him a look that her mother would be proud of. "Don't you dare patronize me. I thought you were better than that."

Caine nodded slowly. "You're right. I apologize. I really would have gotten around to telling you about this. I think."

"Let me ask you something. If I had wanted to . . . go further in Jackson's office that night . . . would we have?" Anna folded her arms.

"Hell yes," Caine replied. "When you kissed me on the Ferris wheel, after what I said about you making the first move, I thought that was, you know, *the first move.*"

"That's what I thought, too. And if and when we ever . . . it would be because I felt something for you so real and so deep that my body would be following my heart." She slid off her bar stool. "I may be young. But I'm not stupid."

"I never thought—"

"I don't know what you thought," Anna confessed. "But what's clear to me is that you didn't care what *I* thought. We don't have to get serious for you to take me seriously."

"Fair enough."

She raised eyebrows that had been perfectly shaped on an outing with Sam to Valerie's salon on Rodeo Drive. "And one more thing, Caine."

"Yes?"

"I have to say, that's quite an outfit you have on."

By the time Anna dropped off Cammie and Champagne and pulled her Lexus into the circular drive in front of the double doors of her father's white stucco mansion on Elevado Drive, it was nearly midnight. The only way she had endured the last hour was to tell Cammie in no uncertain terms that the subject of Caine-in-the-Firehouse was strictly off limits.

Tomorrow, maybe. But not tonight.

Cammie got the message. She studiously avoided mentioning Caine the entire ride home. That didn't mean she wasn't thinking about him, though. More than once, Anna caught her with a completely shit-eating grin plastered on her face.

As she put the car in park and killed the headlights, she glanced over at Django's guesthouse—a two-bedroom wooden bungalow built by the Craftsman Company back in the 1950s, shortly after the main mansion had been constructed. Django Simms was her father's driver, a guy about Caine's age who hailed from Louisiana and was a wondrous keyboard player. With his short dark hair bleached white blond, and his lanky figure, he seemed an incongruous match for his boss. But Jonathan trusted Django implicitly, and Anna had come to like him a lot.

He was standing in front of his own door, talking to a young woman. This was no shocker. Django was a girl magnet. When Anna stepped out of the Lexus, he softly called her name and waved her over. Why not meet Django's latest? His love life had to be less complicated than her own.

"Hey, Miss Anna, you're getting home late," he noted in his Southern drawl. Per usual, he looked fabulous, in old jeans and a fifties-style bowling shirt. His light blue eyes shone in the moonlight. "Fun night?"

"Odd. Very, very odd." She held out a hand to Django's latest conquest, who was stunning in a very natural way—long chestnut curls held up by two pearl chopsticks stabbed through them, and very curvy under what looked like standard-issue black pants and a neatly tucked in white button-down blouse. "Hi, I'm Anna Percy. Ignore the 'Miss' thing—it's Django's idea of a joke."

"You're Anna? I've heard so much about you!" She was beauty-queen pretty and had a Southern drawl that matched Django's. "I've been wantin' to meet you since I got to town. I'm Citron, Django's sister."

For some reason, Anna was shocked. Django never

talked about his family. She had no idea that he had a sister. All she really knew about him was that he played the piano masterfully. Now he was allegedly trying to get a record deal here. His work for Jonathan was his day job.

"Nice to meet you, Citron." She regarded Django and offered a little smile. "A sister? Aren't you the mystery man?"

"Now, see, I was going to introduce you to my little sister tomorrow. She just got here from Louisiana. She's working as a waitress over at the Polo Lounge."

"Good tips," Citron put in. "Even though I think I'm supposed to know a lot of people that I don't know. Not yet, anyway."

"She's living with a couple of friends of mine in mid-Wilshire, but I'm fixing to ask your dad if she can move in here with me for a while. There're two bedrooms, and she's on a budget," Django explained.

"I'm saving up to make a demo," Citron chimed in. "I'm a singer."

"Rock and roll?" Anna asked.

Citron shook her head. "Jazz, mostly. Not that there's much call for it in the music stores. Even less on the radio. I aim to change all that. Maybe."

Anna smiled. "So, I can see it's just a musical family. Well, nice to meet you, Citron. I love your name."

Citron breathed in the clean night air. "This is a beautiful house that your father has. In a real different way from down home. We had a big place there, too, but ever been in Louisiana in the summer? You can wring your clothes out after a walk on a clear night, it's that humid. And summer means April to October. You end up taking a lot of showers. Of course, after Katrina, most of my friends left. It's kind of a lonely place now."

They continued talking for a while, then Anna bade them good night and walked back to the main house. It was white with red shutters, and at night it was completely illuminated by bright white floodlights. Impossible to see from the road, it was guarded by shrubbery so tall and thick it served the same purpose as a barbwire fence.

She was surprised to find her father still awake. He was stretched out on the claw-foot beige couch in the living room reading a Tom Clancy novel and listening to a Gary Burton CD on the new Bose surround-sound system. Anna padded across the marble floor, past the white Steinway grand piano that never got played except when Django stopped over, and sat down by him. Her father rarely had time to read for fun. She was also surprised—and not in a good way—to see and smell marijuana smoke wafting from the huge blunt in the ashtray on the new Moroccan carved wood coffee table. Judging from the powerful reefer odor in the room, and the pair of roaches that flanked the joint, this hadn't been her dad's first one of the evening.

"Hey, Anna," he greeted her, his voice dreamy. He wore an old pair of black Levi's and an even older Yankees sweatshirt left over from their days in New

York. With his spiky hair and two days' growth of beard, it would be easy for a stranger to mistake him for a writer, or maybe a music industry executive. Instead, Jonathan Percy was an accomplished investment advisor sought after by the richest of the rich.

"You're stoned." It was an observation, not an accusation.

"Couldn't sleep. You're up late. Out with Caine?"

Anna almost admitted that she'd been out watching his protégé Caine Manning slide down a fireman's pole in jeans and suspenders but decided to keep her mouth shut.

"Hey Dad?"

"I've told you before. I want you to call me Jonathan. You've been here—how long have you been here?"

"Since New Year's."

"Uh-huh." He picked up the big fat doobie, sucked down a big fat hit, and offered it to Anna. She took a big fat pass. "Jonathan," he repeated, blowing out more smoke than the caterpillar in *Alice in Wonderland*. "Call me Jonathan. Please."

"I'll try, *Dad*."

He grinned. So did she. "That's my Anna," he pronounced. "Raised right."

"Did you know that Django has a sister?"

He nodded. "I think so. Or maybe it was a brother."

"It's a sister," she assured him. "She moved here from Louisiana. I just met her out by the guesthouse.

She's a singer, and she seems really nice. I told her she could stay there for a while with her brother—I knew you wouldn't mind."

"That's cool. Seem nice?"

Seem nice? Hadn't she just said that? Anna made a mental note to avoid whatever it was that her father was smoking.

"Very. Well . . . I guess I'll go up now. See you in the morning."

"Wait, Anna. When's that fashion show thing you're working on?"

She was surprised he was even tracking what she was doing with her days. "Wednesday night. County art museum. The modern art section."

"I'm going to come, I think. If I can rearrange my schedule. Anyway, have a good night." He took another monster hit of the joint, and returned his glassy gaze to his book.

That was it for the All-American father-daughter moment, and Anna climbed the stairs to her room. She pushed off her shoes, threw her purse on the bed, and slid into the brown Duxbury chair at her rolltop desk. She tugged her shirt over her head with one hand while bringing up her e-mail with the other. Life could be so insane. There was an e-mail from Sam—once this fashion show was over, she and Anna needed to really get cracking on their script reading. In fact, maybe they could put in a serious session on Tuesday. Plus, if Sam hadn't adequately thanked Anna for changing that coverage on *Burnt Toast*—well, Sam owed her. Big-time. Of course, if either of them had a brain, they would have realized that no one named their kid Norman Shnorman in the first place. Maybe they needed to improve the circulation of blood to their brains with a spa day.

While she was reading Sam's, her inbox lit up with a new-message indicator. When she saw the "from" line, it made her heart race. The subject line couldn't have been clearer: *The photographs you sent me.*

Dearest Anna,
Received and reviewed photos of Champagne. She
is truly lovely and exactly the kind of fresh face we
need to launch Principessa. I plan to be in
Los Angeles for your fashion show, and perhaps I
can meet her in person beforehand. I just saw your
dear mother in Milan last week. She's the patron of
a new young artist. His work is dashing and so is
he, but I'm sure she told you all about it. Look
forward to seeing you, and to meeting the glorious
Champagne. Thank you for thinking of me first.
Please say hello to your father for me. With your
permission, I'll have my assistant telephone you to
make arrangements for the night of the show.
Cheers,
Lizbette

A Little Short on Role Models

"**O**kay, okay. Listen up!"

Cammie assembled her so-called models—four other girls suggested by Mrs. Vanderleer from the New Visions at-risk program. Including Champagne, Anna, and Cammie herself, there would be seven women modeling at the fashion show, plus five guys from the Firehouse.

It was Monday afternoon, which meant the event itself was only two days away. They were in a dance studio in Santa Monica that Mrs. Vanderleer had rented for this rehearsal. The walls were mirrored, and the floor had been taped with the outline of the T-shape of a catwalk, indicating the correct width and length on which they'd be working. The girls wouldn't face an actual catwalk until they were on it, but Cammie had to make do with what she had. What she had to do was train rank amateurs of all sizes, shapes, and social strata in how to avoid falling on their asses during the fashion show.

What she needed was four months. What she had was four hours.

Cammie felt pretty confident, however, about her own ability to walk these girls through the art of the catwalk. She'd done a fair amount of runway work herself back in junior high school, when she was among the tallest of the girls she knew. Alas, after she topped out at five-foot five, a serious runway career was almost impossible. Stunning as she was in person, she wasn't all that interested in print work.

In prep for the session, Cammie had asked for a TV monitor and combination DVD/VCR, so she could show the girls some video of professional models doing their professional modeling thing. She had also finagled some video equipment so that the girls could be filmed and then get a chance to review themselves. She wasn't surprised when Mrs. Vanderleer came through with everything she'd asked for.

Her models were identified by name badges. Exquisite and Mai both hailed from the Bellflower section of Los Angeles. Each was striking. Exquisite was taller, with close-cropped dark hair and startling green eyes. Mai was shorter, but with a perfect figure much like Dee's.

The other two girls were from East Los Angeles. Daisy was quite tall—close to five-ten. While she was far too voluptuous to be a runway model, easily a size twelve or maybe even a fourteen, and had a serious gap-toothed look, she wore the jet-black Escada knockoff dress she'd chosen for the rehearsal exceptionally well. Her friend Consuela was more boyish and athletic, with beautiful lips and thick, glossy hair.

"Listen up." Cammie strode to the taped catwalk area. "First, everyone got measured and fitted this morning, right? And they took your shoe sizes? If anyone didn't get measured, see me when we're done. "Your shoes should be ready tomorrow. I've asked for them all to have scratched soles."

Exquisite waved a hand.

"Yes?"

"Why scratched-up soles? Won't that make the shoes look worse on the catwalk?"

Cammie smiled. "Smart question, Exquisite. The scratching is for your protection—to give you traction. New shoes are slippery. Which leads me right into the not-falling-on-your-ass thing. I've done it. Every model has done it. It isn't pretty."

Champagne had a question. "Do we get to keep the shoes?"

Cammie smiled to herself. She'd spoken with Mrs. Vanderleer about exactly this, and had extracted a promise from the organizer that the girls could indeed keep their shoes.

"Definitely. The shoes are yours."

The grins from the girls were as brilliant as the sun. Cammie actually felt her heart squeeze. She couldn't even remember a time when the acquisition of a single pair of shoes mattered to her.

"Okay, let's talk posture." She put one palm flat against her stomach, the other on her lower back. "Stomachs tucked in, shoulders back. An invisible

string from your toes to the ceiling. Take a look at
Anna. Wave, Anna."

Anna, who stood at the rear of the throng, raised
one shy hand.

"Anna stands like this like this all the time without
even thinking about it," Cammie pointed out. "It's natural to her. Watch her and learn. But first, do what I'm
doing now."

All around the room, hands obediently went to tum-
mies and lower backs. This was good. The girls were
taking this seriously.

"You guys, you should stand like this all day and
night between now and Wednesday night," Champagne
advised. "You'll want to look great for the guys."

"When will we meet them?" Daisy asked excitedly.
"They're firemen, right?"

"Wednesday night, at the show," Cammie reported.
"Please. Stay focused on what we're doing here. This is
important."

Cammie, Anna, and Champagne were publicly stick-
ing with the myth that the guys were actual firemen
who did a little calendar work on the side. If Mrs.
Vanderleer found out the truth, she'd possibly cancel
the whole show, lest models from the Firehouse somehow negatively impact the reputation of her foundation. Champagne had relayed the firemen story to her
cousin Bryson, and he had schooled his buff-bodied
friends.

As the girls worked on their posture, Cammie

circulated through them, pushing a hip here, moving a shoulder there. She was pleased to see that Champagne got it naturally. "Now, for the all-important walk. One foot goes directly in front of the other, eyes straight ahead to an invisible horizon line. Like this. You've seen it on TV. Pretend you're Gisele."

She moved to the DVD player and started a disc of top models on the runway, then put one hand on her hip and did the walk herself, executing a perfect 360-degree turn at the point of the T.

"Can we all try that walk?"

All around the room, the girls tried it. Most of them failed miserably. Consuela nearly twisted an ankle in her heels.

"It's not easy," Cammie warned. "Consuela, get right up and do it again. Remember, the heel of the front foot has to come to the toe of the other foot on every step. Shoulders back, stomachs in, butts tucked—everyone practice and I'll come around and help you. Anna, come help me, please."

Anna cut through the crowd and then whispered to her hastily. "Me? I've never done this before in my life!"

"Yeah, but you've got that ballet posture thing going on, and you've already picked it up, so help," Cammie implored.

"Fine, but I'm modeling under false pretenses." Still, she went to help the other girls, some of whom were still teetering like half-cut trees in a winter gale.

"If you swing the back leg out before you bring it

around to the front, it will help. And look straight out," Cammie advised Champagne. "Never down at your own feet."

"Right, straight out," she echoed, walking with such focus and such intensity that some of the other girls followed in her wake, copying her movements.

An hour later, Cammie began videotaping each girl in turn on the mock catwalk. And fifteen minutes after that, they sat down to watch the tapes.

The girls were self-conscious and very self-critical when they saw themselves on tape. But interestingly enough, they were also extremely supportive of one another, offering suggestions and acting as more than cheering sections.

Then Champagne's tape came on.

She never changed her expression, but stayed cool, calm, and collected. She kept her head completely still and let her body move beneath her. At the far end of the runway, she did a little shift with her hips that turned her to the left, and then another that took her back to where she'd begun.

Cammie flicked off the monitor. The studio was silent, until Exquisite broke the quiet. "Was that your first time doing that, Champagne?"

"Please. I've done it *thousands* of times," Champagne replied loftily. Then a sad smile crept onto her lips. "In my mind. In the last week. Thanks to Cammie."

The girls laughed and hooted.

"Go, Cammie!" Daisy exclaimed. "You're our leader!"

Cammie didn't know much about any of them, except for Champagne. But if they were in an at-risk program, they had to be facing challenges far bigger than whether to wear Chloé or Alaïa. They were from neighborhoods that Cammie never ventured into, even with a driver, and had family incomes that probably didn't equal in a year what her father earned in three days. Yet here they were, giving it their all, excited because they'd get to be in an actual fashion show and take home a single new pair of designer shoes.

In another time and place, she would have been contemptuous. Now, though, Cammie just felt good. They were having fun. She even suspected that she might have something to do with it. "Guys, there's nothing I can tell you except this: What Champagne just did, you can all do. Bye-bye, Giselle, Kate, Tyra, and Heidi. Here are Champagne, Consuela, Mai, Daisy, and Exquisite!"

I'm going back to the same club twice in two weeks, Cammie realized as she opened the front door to Trieste. *I must be slipping.*

This time, though, there was no velvet rope, no doorman, and no line of would-be club kids stretching down toward Hollywood Boulevard. Just a small black-lettered sign on the door that read, TRIESTE MONDAY, 9 TO 11, $10 COVER, CASH ONLY. And then, in red marker scrawled underneath, in case anyone didn't know what they were getting themselves into, were these words: NO DANCING, NO ROCKING, TALK HARD.

She'd spoken with Ben late in the afternoon, just to see how he was. Okay, she admitted to herself, she'd really phoned him because she couldn't bring herself to call Adam again—she didn't want to appear the least bit needy or desperate. To her surprise, Ben had invited her to the club that night to check out this new thing he'd been organizing called Trieste Monday. "Dress casual," he'd warned. "It's different."

Cammie scoffed at "dress casual." Like she *ever* dressed the way people told her to dress. She wore Earl jeans rolled to the knees with skintight patent leather Gaultier boots and a snug little white BCBG top, all the better for a summer night. She pinned her Raymond-styled strawberry blond curls half up and half down, the better to show off her new Jacob the Jeweler chandelier earrings made of an intricate pattern of tiny, diamond-studded palm trees.

Though there was no doorman, there was someone stationed just inside the front door. A burly guy with a beard, thick glasses, and a ready smile was taking cash in a shoe box. Ben had said she'd be on the guest list, and the guy checked her name off when Cammie gave it to him. "Cammie Sheppard? Ben said you can find him in the play room."

"The playroom?" Cammie repeated.

"The play room. Where they're doing plays. It's the first room you'll come to—you can't miss it."

"Ah. You mean the army hospital room."

The burly guy laughed. "Not tonight."

He was right. As she made her way into the club, Cammie saw that the glitzy lights had been turned off and all the props removed from what had been one of the hottest, most elite dance floors in the city. Instead of a mock army mobile hospital, rows of simple steel folding chairs had been erected, and a crowd of sixty or seventy people was intently watching three actors performing a scene.

"Thank you to our great Trieste Monday audience!" A familiar voice boomed over the club PA system ten minutes later, when the scene ended. *Whoa.* Cammie grinned. Ben. "And thanks to our fine volunteer cast performing the ten-minute play *No Pain, No Gain* by Stephen Greene. Next performance will be back here in twenty minutes, featuring new actors and a new script. Please visit our jazz and art rooms! Thanks for being here on Trieste Monday."

The enthusiastic crowd clapped again. Most everyone stood, either to stretch their legs or to check out one of the other attractions. A moment later, Cammie felt a tap on her shoulder.

"You came."

She turned. There was Ben, in black trousers and a black T-shirt imprinted with the club logo. He was giving her that delicious, irresistible Ben smile. "Yeah, I caught most of it. I liked it."

He looked pleased. "The writer does a lot of TV. He's brilliant. But he really wants to write for the stage."

"Funny how no one seems to want what they've got. Does he have any idea how many playwrights would kill to write for TV? Just ask my father."

"No doubt. You want a drink?"

She pursed her lips. "I thought there was no partying here tonight."

"Follow me. I've got special privileges."

He took her hand and led her through a door behind the makeshift stage and then down a narrow, ill-lit corridor to a small office at the far end. To her surprise, the office was remarkably elegant, with a buttery brown leather sofa, a small bar, a sound system, and a desk tidier than Cammie had thought humanly possible. The only giveaway that they were in a nightclub back office was the bank of ten security monitors. If the customers didn't know they were being watched, they should.

"Whose is this?" She settled into the delicious folds of the sofa.

"My boss's. But on Monday night, it's mine. Pick your poison."

"Champagne?"

Ben smiled. "Definitely."

There was a fridge under the bar. Down went Ben. Out came a bottle of 1995 Clos du Mesnil, plus a pair of chilled champagne flutes.

"Your boss keeps *that* in his fridge?"

"Nope. You said you'd stop by, so I stocked up. Is this still your favorite champagne?"

If only Anna could see her now.

"Yeah."

Pop went the cork. Out came the bubbly. There was nothing like Clos du Mesnil and no year like 1995.

She raised her glass to his. "To Ben Birnbaum, for his exquisite preparation and wonderful taste in friends."

They clinked, and Cammie took a long sip. Liquid bliss slid down her throat. Too bad Adam didn't indulge. Some people had no idea how good it was to be bad.

"So, how is this Monday night thing working out?"

"So far, so good." He sat down next to her. Not too close, Cammie noted, but close enough. "I'm psyched about it. I have all these ideas for sort of a modern version of a salon, you know? With poets and rappers and playwrights. But not that experimental shit that no one can stand, like you'd find in Santa Monica or at UCLA. Very Hollywood. Which means quality."

"So open your own place," she suggested, crossing her left leg over her right, toward him.

"Princeton first, my own place second, third, and fourth. But yeah, I'd be lying if I didn't say I'm thinking about it. So, how's the fashion show prep going?"

Cammie tensed slightly. She and Ben had been an item for many months back when he was a senior in high school and she was a junior. She knew every tiny nuance of Ben's voice, and she'd felt the shift in his tone, minute as it might have been.

This was his way of asking about Anna. She was sure of it.

"We did Modeling 101 today. Oddly enough, it was fun."

"How'd Anna do? How's Anna doing?"

As if the lack of eye contact wasn't a dead giveaway.

There was so much she could tell him. Like how Anna had found out that Tattoo Guy was a money manager by day and a bare-chested fireman-style faux-stripper waiter by night. But that would only fuel his hopes of a Ben-and-Anna reunion.

"How do you think, Ben?" she asked lazily.

"She was great."

"She was great," Cammie agreed, thinking about the Ben/Anna liplock she'd seen outside of Raymond's salon. "What is up with the two of you anyway?"

"What could possibly be up? She's with this Caine guy."

"That much I know."

He nodded and sipped some of his champagne. "I'd like to be able to just walk, you know? But . . . damn, I just can't."

"Gee, you found it easy enough to walk away from me."

"I was younger, dumber—who the hell knows. It was high school. If it bothers you to have me talk about her—"

"No, it's fine," Cammie lied.

"Because you're so into Adam. Yeah, I get that."

"Right." That she and Adam were currently less than tight and that he seemed to be opting for blackflies and lake trout guts over her was another thing she didn't plan to share.

Ben stood up and paced the small office. "I never expected to fall so hard for her. But . . . it happened. And I've made so many dumb-ass mistakes." He shook his head. "If I could go back and undo them, I would."

"God, you sound like me." Cammie leaned her head back against the forgiving leather. "Do you think it's possible for two people to be in love and stay in love? Or does that only happen in bad movies that no one likes but people who own hundreds of teddy bears?"

"You're asking the wrong guy. My parents? I don't think they've really been in love for a long time. Plus, my dad's always either gambling and chasing tail, or at a twelve-step meeting undoubtedly chasing tail. I'm a little short on role models."

"I'm not," Cammie replied thoughtfully.

Ben returned to the couch. "I *know* you don't mean your stepmother, Patrice."

She laughed. "Not hardly." Then she hesitated, wanting to tell him about the letter her mother had left for her, but at the same time not wanting to open up that much. It wasn't like Ben loved her the way he loved Anna. And she really did still love Adam. At least she thought she did.

"I remember so many things about my mom. Her perfume—Rive Gauche. When I catch a whiff of it—it doesn't matter where—I get this visceral memory of her." She twirled the stem of her champagne flute thoughtfully between her fingers. "And her smile—how her eyes would take in my face as if seeing me was the most important and beautiful thing in the whole world. I remember how she used to draw pictures for me, and sing me to sleep, and really listen to me, in a way that maybe no one else ever has. And I mean, I know that isn't romantic love. But it was real. I had it. And I remember it."

"It sounds great, that's what it sounds like."

"I know. Maybe we need to call that something else besides love. Because it's crazy to think you can fall in love with someone and have that and toe-curling good sex, too."

Ben grinned widely. "There is no one else on the planet like you, Cammie."

"I'll take that as a compliment."

"You should." He hand brushed against her cheek and he looked deeply into her eyes. "It sucks that you lost her, Cam. It really sucks."

"But it would suck worse if I'd never had her at all."

Slowly, she watched Ben's face come toward hers; she remembered exactly what it felt like to kiss him, the texture of his lips, the way he would sigh from the back of his throat, his hand tangled in her hair. And she wanted it, she really, really, really—

Just before his lips brushed against hers, she pulled back. So did he.

"Bad idea." His voice was husky with desire.

"Yeah."

He picked up his champagne again. "Don't take this the wrong way. But you are not the shallow, self-involved chick you used to be."

"What, you're allowed to grow up and I'm not? Besides, you were with me mostly for the hours between 10 P.M. and 6 A.M. So what does that say about you?"

Ben nodded. "I deserved that. But the thing is . . ."

"What?" She drained her glass, not wanting to admit how shaky she felt from their near kiss.

"If things were different and we got together again . . ." His eyes met hers; Cammie felt as if they were piercing her heart. "It would be *so* much more."

The Smell of Rive Gauche

"So anyway, I really love Jack, but I think I'm starting to love Aaron, too. Does that make any sense?" Dee asked.

She was curled up on the oak daybed, wrapped in an aquamarine cashmere throw, while Cammie dug around in the five-hundred-square-foot closet. They were in one of the guest rooms at Clark's estate. It was done in cool blues and greens, wallpapered in the palest of blues the same shade as the carpet. Though she had a huge walk-in closet in her own bedroom, Cammie's wardrobe was so extensive that she'd kept the overflow in here. She and Dee were here because she'd been unable to find what to wear to the fashion show in her own walk-in. The decision was especially important, because now there was going to be that face-to-face with Lizbette Demetrius beforehand. Anna had forwarded the email from Lizbette—Cammie had been so psyched—but they'd decided not to say anything to Champagne. Why make the younger girl nervous?

"Does that make any sense?" Dee repeated.

"Yeah. It makes sense."

Cammie had no idea what she was talking about. Not because Dee was incoherent again, but because she had too many other things on her mind.

There was Lizbette's arrival tomorrow for the fashion show.

There was Adam. This morning, she'd broken down and tried to call him, but she hadn't been able to get through.

There was her almost-moment with Ben the night before at Trieste.

"Do you think it's possible to love two boys at the same time?" Dee went on. She smoothed the fabric of the belted silk Rebecca Taylor day dress she was wearing. It was sheer enough that Cammie could see Dee's tiny silver nipple rings.

Cammie didn't answer. Instead she held up a hanger with an emerald green Albert Nipon suit with a shrunken jacket and short, pleated skirt. No. Too matchy-matchy. Maybe the Nicole Miller lavender sheath? Too short. Barely thong-protecting.

"Like, suddenly Jack is getting all clingy," Dee continued. "Usually I'm the one who does that. And Aaron—well, he needs me in a way that Jack doesn't. I'm usually the needy one. My whole life is changing."

"Hurrah for great meds," Cammie observed absentmindedly, as she considered an Akris Punto houndstooth skirt. Nope. Too day-at-the-races.

"Totally. I just wish could talk to my mom about

stuff like this." Dee took a sip of the iced mocha she'd brought with her from the Coffee Bean.

That comment actually got Cammie's attention. "I feel that way all the time."

Dee looked surprised. "You do?"

"What's so shocking about that?" She shut the closet door and stood with her hands on her hips, feeling dissatisfied.

"Well, you never talk about her," Dee pointed out.

"What's to talk about? It's not like it would change anything."

"Yeah," Dee responded gently. "My mother is a ditz. But at least I have her."

Cammie went over to her window, which overlooked a decent swath of her backyard. Near the guesthouse was a cluster of clementine trees. Her mother had loved that fruit. She recalled a day when she and her mom had sat together at the modest butcher-block kitchen table of their old house in Santa Monica. She'd been how old? Eight, maybe? There'd been a huge black ceramic bowl on that table that had been filled with clementines. They'd eaten and eaten the sweet fruit, until they both had stomachaches. She even remembered what her mom had been wearing—a raw silk shirt with oversize buttons in a pink that was so pale it was almost white, and a floral skirt with inverted pleats. Where had that memory come from?

When they'd moved to this whale of a mansion— when Cammie had insisted on taking the partially finished *Charlotte's Web* mural with them—they'd also brought her mother's clothes. Those clothes were boxed in storage up in the attic. Or at least they were supposed to be, unless her father or the stepmother from hell, Patrice, had tossed them away.

For all this time, Cammie had never gone up there to look at them. The idea of doing it was too sad. But now, for some reason Cammie couldn't quite put her finger on, it seemed right.

She was halfway to the door before she called to Dee. "Come on!"

The attic space was lit by harsh bare lightbulbs, and the air smelled musty, like old newspapers. There was furniture that Cammie remembered from her childhood—an ornately carved armoire, an oval-shaped full-length antique mirror, and the gilded brown rocking horse she'd named Alex, after *The Secret World of Alex Mack*, her favorite TV show when she was a girl. There were the boxes. Scores of them. Identical and white, obviously packed by professionals, stacked against the far wall.

Dee wandered over to a large support beam and squinted at a sheet of paper taped to it. "Wow, whoever moved you guys in here was really organized. There's a master list here. All the boxes are numbered."

Cammie hustled to join her. She ran a finger down the list of a hundred and fifty-six packing boxes. It didn't take long to find what she was looking for—

three consecutively numbered boxes labeled JEANNE'S CLOTHES.

"You want your mother's clothes?" Dee asked, as Cammie's finger stopped on those numbers.

"It's a sentimental blip." Cammie didn't want to admit the clutch in her stomach. "What my father would call 'a nonrecurring phenomenon.' Just go with it."

"You didn't see your mom's ghost, did you? Because that would be way cool. Especially if it was at the Roosevelt in Hollywood."

"Dee?"

"Yes?"

"Help me find the damn boxes."

As it turned out, finding the right boxes was a snap. Whoever had put together the master list had also been wise enough to secure a box cutter to the pillar, so Cammie could even break the packing tape seals with ease.

Her heart pounding, she opened the first one. It was full of sweaters, mostly polyester or cashmere blend—they hadn't had enough money back then for her mother to wear really good cashmere. Cammie found a red one with a boat neckline she remembered and held it to her nose. It still smelled just ever so slightly like Rive Gauche perfume. She closed her eyes and inhaled deeply. Amazing.

The second box held a variety of things—shoes, costume jewelry, the silver filigreed brush and comb set her mother had kept on her vanity. Cammie replaced it all with care; maybe she would use them herself one day.

The third box held more clothes. Some she didn't remember, but some she did. She examined each piece with care. And then, halfway through, she found exactly what she'd been looking for. The pale pink shirt with the oversize buttons. The full skirt with the inverted pleats.

She took them out carefully, as if the fragile memories they held could shatter if a single wrinkle was undone or a single thread came loose.

"My mom wrote me a letter," she said as she fingered the clothing like it was precious gold. There was no sadness. She just felt giddy. And excited. As if her mother had come home after a long trip, and she was so excited to see her.

"But she's—"

Dee didn't need to say the word for Cammie to know what she meant. "She wrote it when I was a baby, and I wasn't supposed to get it until my wedding day. My father gave it to me. A couple of weeks ago."

"What did it say?"

"Basically that I should be more than the selfish bitch I've been all my life," she confessed with a bitter laugh. "You think she knew how I was going to turn out ahead of time?"

"Probably she was just telling you what was important to her. Don't you think?"

"Maybe she was just worried that I'd be way too much like my father." Cammie raised her gaze to her friend. "My mother was clinically depressed, and I never even knew it. Just so you don't feel alone in your iffy mental health."

Dee shrugged and pushed the shaggy bangs out of her eyes. "You can't imagine how many people tell me now that they take something for depression or anxiety or whatever. I'm like the new mental health confessional. So, did your mom get help?"

"Not enough. Not nearly enough. I only wish I'd been old enough to help her."

Cammie pulled off her Michael Stars shirt and pulled down the royal blue Juicy Couture shorts she kept meaning to throw out, except that they were just so comfortable she couldn't bear to part with them. She slipped into her mother's pale pink shirt and buttoned it, then stepped into the skirt and zipped it up.

"How's it look?"

Dee smiled and pointed to the other side of the attic where the old furniture had been stored. "I could say great, but you'll want to see for yourself. There's a mirror over there, I think."

The antique mirror was covered in a fine sheen of dust. Cammie used her other shirt to wipe it clean, then took in her reflection. The ensemble fit perfectly. In fact, as she looked at herself wearing her mother's clothes, she saw how much she looked like the mother she remembered.

"I miss her," she said simply.

"When I was my sickest, I couldn't see what was real and what wasn't, couldn't make enough sense out of things to get help. Maybe that's how she felt, Cammie. Maybe she just couldn't help it. But she loved you so much from the time you were really little, when she wrote you that letter. And no one can ever take that love away from you."

She would never have expected to get wise counsel from Dee. Cammie had always called the shots in their friendship. But here she was, giving Cammie exactly what she needed.

"Oh God, I'm such a *Lifetime* movie. Tough teen finally grieves over the loss of her mother. Who'd play me?"

"Keira Knightley?" Dee ventured.

"Too old."

"Hilary Duff?"

"Too—go on to the next."

"Dakota Fanning?" Dee tried again.

"Too annoying."

They both laughed.

Who would have believed it? Cammie owed Dee for this. Big-time. And at the right time and place, Dee was going to be very pleasantly surprised.

The Headline Was a Screamer

"**W**ow."

Sam turned the last page of the script and closed it. Wonder of wonders, she had found a screenplay that she actually liked. A comedy called *Ass Man*, it was about a Hollywood actor who had struggled for years before getting cast in a commercial for a hemorrhoid cream that America fell in love with—the commercial, not the cream. The gig turned out to be the guy's big break, and he went on to ridiculous fame and fortune.

The script skewered Hollywood, the movie business, and the world of advertising in equal measure, while the hero was a well-drawn, multidimensional, interesting character. It was also insanely funny, which wasn't surprising, since the screenwriter had worked on the TV show *Arrested Development* before that show had died a premature death. She didn't know whether this was the right screenplay for her father's production company, but she was prepared to do something shocking: write a nice coverage. In fact, she wanted to direct it. The producers would want to change the title, of course. She'd fight to keep it. It would be a hell of a battle, even though she'd probably lose.

"So how's the one you're reading?" she asked Anna.

Anna made a face. "*'Have You Ever Heard the German Band'*? About an old man who refuses to believe that World War II is over."

"Dreadful, huh?"

"You can't imagine. My lead character just did a three-page monologue in a bunker he dug behind a Starbucks in Albuquerque about his relationship with his dead schnauzer."

"Who wrote it?" Sam joked. "Norman Shnorman?"

It was Tuesday afternoon, and the two of them were up in Sam's room, getting caught up on a huge backlog of screenplays. Tomorrow—the day of the fashion show—would be busy, and Sam hoped to pitch in out of loyalty to her friends. But today was a good day to chill out, read, and write coverages.

Even her father had taken the day off, since there were no *Ben-Hur* scenes involving him and he'd just worked sixteen days straight. She had seen him briefly at breakfast, looking more tired than she could ever remember. He'd eaten a brioche, drunk some orange juice, and gone straight back to bed. All the while, Poppy doted on him like she was a servant girl and he was the lord of the manor. It made Sam sick, knowing what she knew about Poppy and that Poppy could have gotten what was rightly coming to her.

What was weird was that, even though it was over,

she couldn't bring herself to talk about the aborted Parker/ Poppy project with anyone. Not Anna, not Cammie, not even Eduardo.

Anna had been sprawled across the bottom of her king-size copper-frame bed with the custom-made Hypnos mattress and box spring (manufactured by the same company that made all the bedding for the British royal family) since just after lunch, as they plowed through scripts and wrote coverages on their respective laptops. Sam had been leaning against her Martex Brentwood Gold pillows, trying to focus on her reading but feeling totally distracted.

Five different times she'd started to tell Anna about how she had plotted to take Poppy down. Five different times she couldn't get the first word out of her mouth.

"You need to read the one I just finished. *Ass Man.* It'll restore your faith in screenwriting."

There was a knock on her closed bedroom door.

"Yeah?" she called, expecting one of the maids. "Come in!"

It wasn't one of the maids. It was Jackson. He was wearing a red silk robe and white pajama pants and looked like he'd just come from the shower. Under his right arm, he carried several movie scripts of his own.

"Hey, now that's what I like to see. Two smart girls writing coverage. Can I tell Beau in the kitchen to send anything up for you?"

"We're good," Sam nudged her chin toward the scripts he carried. "Whatcha been reading?"

He pulled over one of the Cojines! Cojines! multi-functional square hassock-pillows that Sam had recently purchased for her room and plopped down on it.

"Funny you should ask. Sam, you wrote the coverage for this thing by Norman Shnorman? *Burnt Toast?*" He flipped to the first page and read aloud. "'Norman Shnorman deserves to be amongst the pantheon of top film industry writers for life.'"

Sam gulped. How had her father gotten this coverage already? Anna had just fudged it a few days ago.

"I just read the whole screenplay. It's definitely . . . one-of-a-kind," Jackson acknowledged.

"That's exactly what I—"

"Execrable shit. Should be used for toilet training small pets. You know who Norman Shnorman is, don't you? In real life?"

"Isn't he Andrea Jacobson's son?" Sam ventured.

"Yep. And he needs to find a new career. Maybe as a sanitation engineer. Of course, being who he is, he'll probably end up becoming a development executive. What's with this glowing coverage, Sam? And don't bullshit me. The script doesn't deserve it."

"Dad, I—"

She was shocked when Anna jumped in on her behalf. "It's my fault, Mr. Sharpe. Sam wrote something like that. But I changed the coverage."

"You *what?*" Jackson looked pissed.

"Changed it. Sam wrote the original, saying that the screenplay was really awful. But I went into your office at the studio late one night and changed it. Once Sam told me who had written the screenplay, I thought it was the right thing to do."

Anna's tone was even, and Sam realized her friend was prepared to fall on a sword so that she, Sam, would remain blameless.

Jackson looked puzzled. "Why do you think it was the right thing to do, Anna?"

"Because I was concerned that it would get back to his mother and reflect badly on your production company."

Sam noted that Anna had been careful not to say "reflect badly on Sam."

"This was all your idea, Anna?" Jackson asked.

She nodded. "Yes. A hundred percent."

He eyed Sam. "You backing up that story? Where were you when this happened?"

"Not there." Sam knew she was being evasive.

Jackson sighed but didn't press. "With your boyfriend, probably. And you let *Anna* here do your dirty work for you."

"Sam didn't. I wanted to do it. If she'd known, she would have stopped me, I'm sure." Once again, Anna to the rescue.

The story seemed to satisfy Jackson. He rose, then tore Sam/Anna's coverage off the front page of the script and ripped it to shreds, letting the confetti fall on Sam's white silk-upholstered Kravet bedspread. "Just this once, I'm going to write coverage of a screenplay. And when I'm done, I want both of you to read it, because you'll each learn something useful that you might use in the future. It'll be an exercise in neutrality. Five pages long, and by the end, Andrea Jacobson won't be able to tell whether I liked it or hated it. Which is absolutely on purpose."

No wonder her father was so successful and made so few enemies in the business.

"Jackson?"

He turned toward the door where his personal assistant, Kiki, now stood, nervously shifting her weight from one foot to the other. A diminutive woman with a pixie haircut, Kiki seemed to be somewhere between glum and horrified.

No, Sam corrected, she looked scared to death. What the hell?

"What's the matter, Kiki? Did you just read *Burnt Toast*, too?"

Kiki seemed to gather her courage as she took a periodical out of her black Kate Spade shoulder bag. "Did anyone call from the *Galaxy*?"

"That rag? No. Why?"

"They just messengered over an early edition of what's pubbing tomorrow."

He laughed. "What is it? Did they Photoshop a picture of me kissing Tom Hanks at the toga party? Or put my head on someone else's body and say I needed to spend more time in the gym?"

What little color had been in Kiki's face drained away. "I think you'd better take a look at this."

Then she did a very un-Kiki-like thing: she dropped the copy of *Galaxy* on the floor and fled.

Jackson sat back down on the square cushion. "Get that for me, Sam."

Sam did. Once she saw the front page of the *Galaxy*, she did a reasonable imitation of Kiki, her face going white. The headline was a screamer:

ACTION JACKSON'S WIFE FINDS ACTION OF OWN! EXCLUSIVE *GALAXY* PIX!

The two front-page photographs on which the headline had been superimposed were utterly damning. One was Poppy at the toga party, passionately kissing her yoga instructor, Bodhi. Despite its poor quality—a cell phone camera had clearly taken it— there was no doubt as to the identity of the subjects or the location.

The other picture had been taken in front of the Vagabond Inn, at the far reaches of Ventura Boulevard at the butt end of the San Fernando Valley. This time Bodhi's hand was clearly on Poppy's right breast, and they were sucking face. Much clearer, this photo was of professional quality.

"What is it, Sam?" Jackson's voice was calm.

Shit. These were completely different photos, taken by someone else. Even though they were about to do to her father and Poppy exactly what Sam had wanted to do with her own pictures, she still felt like throwing up.

"Sam? Bring me the damn *Galaxy*. Please."

She shuffled across the hardwood floor, handed the tabloid over, and sat on her bed next to Anna. Then she went to work chewing her Nails by Margie magenta manicure, as her father looked at the front page and then turned to the centerfold spread. There were more photographs there, equally damning. She had to read upside down, but she got the gist of the article: Bodhi was a yoga teacher who liked to step out, though he preached abstinence as the key to long life and happiness. One of the other guests at the toga party had been having an affair with him, too. When she saw Poppy and Bodhi kissing, she'd snapped the cell phone picture. Then she'd sent it to the *Galaxy*, which had put a tail on the yoga teacher. The photographer had caught Bodhi and Poppy at the Vagabond Inn and had even followed them to room 301.

The rest was history. In black, and white, and color.

Jackson came to the end of the story and then started again at the beginning. His face was inscrutable. Finally, he closed the magazine, took his BlackBerry out of the pocket of his dressing gown, and pressed a number into speed dial. When he spoke, his voice was as smooth and melodious as in an appearance on Leno.

"Poppy? . . . Yeah, I know you're downstairs. Can

you come up to Sam's room . . . ? No, leave the baby, I'll see her later. I'll be waiting for you, sweetheart."

He disconnected the call and slipped his phone back into his pocket.

Sam thought about summoning all of the maids in the house and putting them on standby outside her room. That would be prudent. Because the shit that was her stepmother was about to hit the fan.

Guilt Jerk

Sushi & Kushi IMAI was located in a strip mall on Wilshire near San Vicente Boulevard in Beverly Hills. It was utterly unpretentious, with a red lacquered interior, but every single seat at the tables and booths was full during the dinner rush, as well as at the seven-seat sushi bar. As Dee waited for a table there with Jack, she heard him explain how his boss at Fox had not only recommended this particular restaurant but had personally put in a call to the head sushi chef on their behalf.

Within minutes, they were whisked past the waiting throng that spilled out the front door, to a secluded table in the far reaches of the restaurant that had mysteriously opened up.

"I heard the sushi-kushi combination is the way to go." Jack reached across the small wooden table and took her hand. "*Kushi* means 'happiness' in Hindi. So it seems appropriate. Not that I have any idea why a sushi place would be talking about kushi."

"Me neither. That's really sweet. But didn't you once tell me that you hate sushi because fish poo in the water?"

"I did. But people change, Dee. Sometimes, anyway. If they find someone worth changing for.

"Hey, I was thinking maybe we could go away next weekend," Jack proposed, after they'd ordered the house special sushi-kushi, a pot of green tea, and some sake. "Up the coast, maybe. Santa Barbara or Carpinteria. I've never been, but I hear it's fantastic. What do you think?"

Dee groaned inwardly. She was already heading in that direction, but for a far different reason. Aaron was going to be released from Ojai on Saturday. He'd sent her approved e-mail—outbound e-mails from Ojai were all censored—mentioning that fact. Dee had volunteered to come up and meet him. She didn't want to tell Jack, though. It would probably hurt his feelings.

"But . . . you always work on the weekends," she pointed out.

"Only because my priorities have been fucked up."

A sweet-faced waitress brought their tea, poured some into tiny white cups, and departed. As she sipped, Dee tried to figure out just what it was she wanted to say to Jack. How had things changed so much? Where was the guy who wasn't looking for a serious relationship, who wanted to take over Twentieth Century–Fox and then possibly the world? That was the guy she'd fallen for. But to be fair, hadn't she changed a lot, too?

Dee sighed. Why was being mentally healthy so much more complicated than being nuts?

"That was quite the sigh," Jack noted. "Something up?"

She couldn't very well deny it.

"I love you."

No, wait. That wasn't how she had intended to start this conversation.

"And I love you too, Dee. Now and forever. Man. I've never said that to another girl in my life. I always thought it would make me feel suffocated. But instead, now I know what all those lame love songs are talking about."

She tried to smile. This was terrible. This conversation had already veered in a completely wrong direction. Okay, what had they told her at Ojai? You were allowed to call do-over, as long as you did it right away. As long as you told the truth.

"Jack, I can't go away with you this weekend because I'm picking Aaron up at Ojai. He's being released."

She blurted it out and received a full-on scowl from Jack in return.

"Aaron? That asshole."

"He's not an asshole. He's very sensitive and deep and sweet—"

Jack looked incredulous. "No way are you breaking up with me to be with that loser."

"First of all, you don't even know him. Second of all, I wasn't planning to break up with you. But there's no reason for you to be mean to me. The right thing to do would have been to ask me if you could come along, instead of getting all negative. I'm sure Aaron could use the support, after what he's been though." Dee felt herself bristle.

The waitress brought them their sushi. It sat in front of them, about as lifeless on its gold-and-tan platter as their conversation seemed to be.

"Okay, let me rephrase that." His voice was tense. "The guy is an alcoholic. Right or wrong?"

"Right."

"And the guy did drugs. Right or wrong?"

"Right."

"Probably while his parents were going crazy about it. Right or wrong?"

"Right," she admitted. "Both right. But he admitted himself to Ojai. He's been clean and sober for weeks."

Jack picked up a piece of shrimp kushi—shrimp that had been skewered on a stick, and then roasted— bit it into it, and chewed thoughtfully. "This is good. Anyway, I grew up with an alcoholic, also known as my old man. Just when you think they've changed . . . bingo, they break your heart. When push comes to shove, they will always love the bottle more than they love you."

"But I can help him," Dee maintained.

He nodded slowly. "That's what you want? Someone broken you can fix?"

Dee bit her lower lip. She hadn't looked at it like that. Was that what she wanted? In the past, she had always been the broken one. "I don't know. He's my friend, though."

"Can I ask you something?"

"Sure."

He pointed the empty kushi skewer at her. "Answer this without making a scene. Please. I won't make a scene either. Are you fooling around with this jerk you barely know?"

"For one thing, when you're at Ojai, you're not allowed to have sex—"

"Yeah, like no one ever broke that rule," Jack scoffed.

"I don't even know if I want him . . . like that. I mean, when I'm with you, usually I'm thinking about the next time I can get your clothes off. I don't feel that way with Aaron. Not at all. But because we were at Ojai together . . . "

God. How could she put this so it wouldn't hurt his feelings?

"Because we were both at Ojai, there's a special kind of connection."

There. That was honest. Even so, it didn't get the reaction she had hoped for. Instead of understanding, Jack laughed cynically.

"This is rich. It's like payback for every girl I ever put moves on when I was only into her for the night. So I'm, what, your boy toy?"

Damn, why was this going so badly? Why was he being so negative?

"I just want to be Aaron's friend."

He shrugged, but his face was hard. "I don't tell you who your friends can be, Dee."

"I know. But I feel like we . . . like maybe you and I are going too fast, and . . . it's kind of confusing." Dee winced. She hated, hated, *hated* hurting him.

"Is this the 'I need space' talk? Because I hear what that really means is 'I'm not into you anymore.' So if that's it, just fucking say it. I'm a big boy. I can take it."

"No, no, that's not it!" She felt a lump in her throat. She was just not used to doing this. "I really just mean that I need . . . space."

"Ha. I called it."

"But not that kind of space. More like, I don't want to plan the future or talk about marriage or babies or things like that. I'm so sorry if I'm hurting your feelings."

For a long moment, Jack was silent. He poured himself some tea. Then he warmed hers up, too.

"That kind of space, huh? I can handle it."

She smiled. "Yes."

"No more talk about the Jersey Shore. Scout's honor." He held up three fingers like a Boy Scout.

"Exactly."

"So we're still good?"

Dee nodded. She was pretty sure she meant what she said, but not positive. At least she'd told him what was on her mind.

He took her hand again from across the table. "Okay, then. First, we eat. Really eat. Then, when we leave here, we go back to my guesthouse, and I give you the best massage of your life. And after that . . . we'll talk about what's for dessert."

Dee felt the tension ooze out of her body. She was relieved enough to spear a delectable slice of ahi with her chopsticks. "Can't wait."

"Let me tell you, Dee. I don't know if you'll ever experience it, but karmic payback? It's a bitch."

"I'm really interested in karma. But what are you talking about?"

He grinned the grin that she loved so much. "Trust me. You don't really want to know."

"So let me understand this." Eduardo literally scratched his head. "Poppy is gone. Your father kicked her out after he saw the *Galaxy*."

"Yes, she's gone. Ding-dong, the witch is gone. That's the good part."

"But she left the baby behind?" He sounded incredulous. "I can't imagine any mother leaving her child behind."

"Well, start imagining," Sam said bluntly.

It was a serene night and they were in a serene place, the outdoor café at the W Hotel practically around the corner from UCLA. Sam couldn't help but feel extremely pleased about the departure of Poppy Sinclair Sharpe from her father's Bel-Air estate, to be followed as soon as possible—one could only hope—by the departure of the name Sharpe from that same Poppy Sinclair. It was almost enough to make one believe that the H in the HOLLYWOOD sign stood for "Higher Power," and that said Higher Power had booted Poppy out on her cheating ass.

The Backyard at the W had recently become one of Sam's favorite destinations. With its canopied white tenting and white umbrellas, beautiful brown wooden furnishings, and secluded location behind the hotel that shielded it from the vehicular noise of the nearby 405 freeway, the Backyard was one of those few Los Angeles spots that had not yet been overrun by tourists. When Sam had called Eduardo in the aftermath of the Blowout in Bel-Air (as she termed it), she'd been in an ebullient mood. Mostly. In any case, she was upbeat enough to propose taking him to dinner at the Backyard. She told him she had news for him. Big news. The biggest possible news.

"You got a movie to direct?" he'd asked.

"Not that big. But almost."

Now here they were, sitting at Sam's favorite table closest to the pool, enjoying the Backyard's signature cucumber martinis, a romaine-lettuce-and-sliced-Portobello-mushroom salad for Sam, a cheeseburger on pita bread with a side of couscous for Eduardo, and a platter of chilled oysters on the half shell for both of them.

She felt so damn happy. Just looking at Eduardo across the table from her was thrilling enough. He was dressed in his typical style, in dark summer-weight gray linen trousers and a white cotton dress shirt so well tailored that it had to have been handmade in London or Hong Kong. His shoes were black Bruno Maglis, and he had on a simple, masculine Peruvian Indian necklace made of bamboo and hemp.

It had been a pleasure to recount the story. Mostly. How quickly she'd gotten over the nausea she felt when she first saw the *Galaxy*. How Poppy had blanched so much when Jackson showed her the tabloid that Sam swore the color drained even from her hair. How Poppy, faced with the evidence in front of her, didn't deny having the affair with Bodhi, but blamed it on Jackson's absence. How her father had launched into a staccato monologue that could have been written by David Mamet, recounting the course of their relationship, the many ways in which he'd compromised what he personally wanted in order to make her happy, and slamming the perfidy of the mother of his new infant daughter. How Poppy had dissolved in tears and rushed away. And then, how Jackson had retreated to his downstairs office to call his publicist and draft a statement that would be issued to the press in the morning.

Eduardo took a thoughtful sip of his martini. "How do you feel now?"

"Better than I have all year. Since they got married, anyway."

He pursed his lips. "That's sad, in a way."

"Please, he only married her because she was pregnant. My father is an old-fashioned guy."

The waitress—an Italian girl with a riot of dark curly hair springing free from the bun she clearly had been told to wear to keep her hair out of the food—brought over a fresh basket of homemade bread. Eduardo waited for her to depart before he continued.

"Your happiness is so tied up in what your father does or doesn't do. You just finished high school. You could have moved out of that house anytime you wanted. Certainly since we came back from Peru. And yet you've stayed there and let yourself be irritated by her. Of course, that irritant is now gone, but what's going to happen with the next young actress your father meets? You told me he has a pattern of this."

Sam hadn't expected this response. She hadn't even considered that this would be his response. She actually hadn't thought about it at all. What was harsh about it was that Eduardo was speaking the truth. She *could* have gotten the hell out of there, if she'd really wanted to.

He smiled. "Perhaps you ought to think about contacting a real estate agent. There are some wonderful condominiums not far from me."

"Okay, you have a point," she conceded. "However, it's my home. She was using my father. So it seems to me the one who should leave is her." Sam felt positively smug. "And she did."

"Your father will be very sad. Have you thought about that?"

Not enough, maybe. She finished her martini. There was something else she wanted to talk to him about. It would require fortification, alcohol calories be damned.

"There's something else I need to tell you."

Shit. *Why* did she need to tell him? That was the question. She wasn't responsible for the photos in the *Galaxy*. It would be so easy to keep what she and

Parker had done a secret; Eduardo would never find out. Parker would never tell. So what was with this, this *compulsion* to tell him? It could ruin everything. Yet she plunged ahead toward the abyss. "There were other pictures taken. Of Poppy."

"Of course there were. The tabloids don't print them all."

"That's not what I meant." She couldn't bring herself to meet his soulful dark eyes.

"Okay, then. So what *do* you mean?"

"I was involved."

Eduardo seemed to take in the implications of this. "Sam, you mean *you* are responsible for the photos in the *Galaxy*?"

"No, not those. Others."

"Explain."

She did, starting with her suspicions of Poppy and Bodhi at the Peruvian meal Eduardo had cooked the day when that designer, Gisella, had come over, right through what she'd helped instigate between Parker and Poppy at the Ritz-Carlton in Pasadena.

"There was a PI in the Lobby Lounge," she continued hoarsely. "The same detective who found out where my mother was living in North Carolina. She was dressed like an old woman. She took pictures of Poppy kissing this guy I hired. Right there in the lounge." No way was she going to admit it was Parker. Eduardo knew him. He knew Eduardo. She had to leave Parker out of this.

"You still have those photographs," Eduardo surmised.

"No."

"No?" He raised his eyebrows.

"I destroyed them. Actually, she destroyed them for
me. I couldn't go through with it."

His eyebrows stayed high. "Why not?"

Why not, indeed? She didn't know. There'd been a
dozen times when she'd been ready to leak the envelope
to the *Galaxy*. It was stamped and ready in her night-
stand. No return address. No way to trace it to her. Yet
she hadn't done it. The question was: Why not?

"I don't know."

He smiled. "'How beautiful it is to do nothing, and
then rest afterward.'"

"What's that?"

"An old Spanish proverb. It sounds better in the
native tongue, but it means the same thing. I'm proud
of you. You did the right thing."

"By having those pictures taken?"

"No." He broke off a piece of one of the rolls, but-
tered it, and handed it to her across the table. "By
destroying them. Bravo. And then Poppy got caught
anyway. I don't believe much in karma, but this could
make me change my mind."

She cocked her head slightly sideways. "Wait. You're
not mad at me?"

"For what? Doing the right thing? Let's eat. I have a
surprise for you, which you'll have to see after dinner."

"A surprise?" Sam said coquettishly. "I like surprises."

Eduardo grinned and then extracted a key card from his wallet. "Penthouse. How hungry are you, really? Or perhaps the better question is: What are you hungry for?"

Desperate for Champagne

Lizbette had an arm around Champagne's naturally well-defined shoulder as they strolled through the fashion and costumes gallery at the LACMA, which Anna considered to be a very good sign. She and Cammie were following a discreet distance behind, doing everything they could to make it look like they were taking in the exhibit instead of straining to catch every word that the Greek princess was saying to their young friend—and now, Cammie's protégé.

Anna watched them stop in front of a mannequin in a Plexiglas cube. The mannequin was garbed in a stunning olive green silk jacket, very fitted, with a flounced peplum and matching skirt. Lizbette pointed at the outfit and explained how it was designed in 1945 and that the color corresponded to what American soldiers were wearing in the war at the time. Champagne nodded, rapt with attention.

Anna checked her watch. Four-thirty. They'd been walking through the museum for close to an hour. She knew they'd have to wrap this up reasonably soon if they were to make it back to the Lichtenstein gallery to prep for the fashion show.

She and Cammie—all the girls in the show, in fact—had been at the museum since nine that morning for last-minute fittings and to clean, arrange, and decorate, along with a small army of New Visions participants and adult volunteers. Mrs. Vanderleer miraculously granted everyone a couple of hours of freedom between three and five, on the proviso that they were not to leave the museum.

Luckily, Lizbette had agreed to come to LACMA to meet Champagne. As usual, the princess was dressed immaculately, in a spectacular gray Fendi minidress, black Donna Karan tights, Christian Louboutin wedges with tiger stripes, and an incredible custom-made tiger-striped belt. Cammie had on a beautiful vintage pale pink shirt and skirt with inverted pleats, while Anna had chosen a simple black eyelet starlet dress by Burberry. They'd only told Champagne about Lizbette's visit fifteen or twenty minutes before the princess's arrival, and their instincts had been right. Champagne had been surprised, but there hadn't been enough time for her to get truly nervous. That she was wearing her black Bebe outfit from the Beverly Center made her feel more confident.

"What should I do? What should I say?" she'd asked Anna right before Lizbette arrived.

"Be yourself," Anna advised.

Finally, Lizbette turned back to Cammie and Anna

and gave a slight nod of her head. Then she turned back to Champagne.

"Champagne, could you excuse us for a few moments? Perhaps you'd like to go into the next gallery and look at the designers from the 1950s. Givenchy, Dior, Charles James? You may recognize the names." Champagne took the hint and walked away, leaving Anna and Cammie with the cosmetics magnate.

"Champagne is a lovely girl, Anna," Lizbette declared, once the girl was gone. "Truly stunning. A face that's one in a million."

"We think so, too." Cammie matched her enthusiasm.

"I'm thrilled that Anna sent me her photos and set up this go-see. You have an excellent eye for beauty and talent, Cammie."

Anna felt Cammie give her arm a little squeeze. She hadn't anticipated that Lizbette would make her decision right here in the museum. Yet it seemed like that was exactly what was happening. Champagne would be beyond excited. Her life was about to change completely. How ironic that Anna and Cammie getting arrested and being assigned this particular community service could turn out so positively. Within a year, Champagne's face would be in all the magazines, and probably on—

"I love her. Absolutely love her," Lizbette declared. "She's beautiful, she's charming, she's innocent, and there are so many positives about her. But I can't use her. She's just not quite what I'm looking for."

What?

"What?" Cammie asked incredulously.

"It's very difficult to make these decisions. A choice made from the gut, oftentimes. Champagne will not be the face of my new cosmetics line, but I do envision a brilliant career for her and encourage you wholeheartedly in your efforts. Thank you for having me come to meet her. It was well worth it. I look forward to the show."

Anna hadn't been much in favor of this whole modeling thing for Champagne, thinking that there were better things for a girl as smart as her to do with her life. But now that they had come so close, she found herself terribly disappointed.

"You knew from the minute we met you that you were going to turn her down, but you didn't say a word." Cammie didn't raise her voice, but Anna could tell she was furious.

"Cammie, please. There's a way to do this kind of thing. It is not the kind of thing one blurts out." Lizbette tried to defuse the tension.

"Oh, really?" Cammie interrupted. "Well, maybe 'one' doesn't know what the hell one is talking about. If you can't see that Champagne is the face of the twenty-first century, it's because your vision is stuck in the twentieth century. You are going to come begging to me—begging!—in a few years, desperate for Champagne to do a commercial for you. And you know what I'm going to tell you? I don't work with uncreative anachronisms and neither does my model. So call PacWest, and realize you're only getting second best."

Lizbette was obviously stunned but didn't say a word. She simply turned and walked away. As for Cammie, Anna couldn't believe it. She was actually *smiling*.

"Do you know what you just did?"

"Absolutely."

"She's going to hate you. And you didn't do me or my family any favors, either."

Cammie shook her head. "You have *so* much to learn, Anna. She'll respect me for fighting for my client. If I don't completely believe in Champagne, then why should she?"

This was unbelievable. Impossible. How could Cammie even think in this direction, let alone curse out the CEO of one of the biggest cosmetics firms in the world?

That's exactly what Anna asked her.

"It's simple, Anna. I am who I am, and where I am is where I came from. When she was talking, it was like I had a fucking *revelation*."

"Well, maybe you could fill me in."

Anna was already thinking about how she'd apologize later to Lizbette, at the fashion show. Or how she would explain when her mother called—which she inevitably would—to tell her that Lizbette had been treated horridly by a friend of her rude, ingrate daughter.

"Okay, first of all, you worry too much."

Cammie motioned Anna to one of the wooden benches at the center of the gallery. "Second of all, you don't know what fun it can be to say exactly what's on your mind, instead of always fudging it."

Anna shook her head as they sat there together. "That's not a sane way to approach the world."

"Maybe. Maybe it's genetic." Cammie brushed her hair off her face. "My mom was so fucked up she killed herself. Who the hell knows?"

"I'm sorry. I didn't mean—"

"Yes, you did, so stop apologizing. For the last few weeks, I've been thinking how much I'm like my mom, which, I guess, means maybe I've got her good traits *and* her bad traits. But when that idiot Lizbette was talking, I remembered that I am also my father's daughter. *Big*-time. I just did what he would have done, and said what he would have said."

"I just—it goes against everything I was raised to believe."

"But you need to ask yourself: What do *you* believe? Who do *you* want to be?"

Anna didn't have an answer; at least not a handy one that she could package into some nice sentiment.

"I appreciate the help you gave me with Champagne. I really do. But my father didn't get to be who he was by holding hands and singing 'Kumbayah.' He did it by being himself. I say, learn from the best." Cammie nodded, as if approving her own words. "Want to help me break the news to Champagne?"

"Honestly? No. But I'll do it anyway."

"Know what? Don't do me any favors."

Cammie stood. Then, just as the princess had done moments before, she turned on her black Charles David heels and walked away.

Umm . . . What Goes Under This?

"Mr. Rittenhouse?"

There was a half hour until the show was to begin; Cammie had just spotted her favorite designer of the evening over by the backstage refreshment table. He was wearing a black tuxedo that was surely of his own design, with a purple polka-dotted bow tie and matching cummerbund, plus a thin black man-bag that was obviously more accessory than useful.

The designer turned around and offered Cammie a friendly grin. "Yes? That's me."

"I'm Cammie Sheppard. One of the organizers tonight." Cammie exaggerated only a little. "And one of the models. I just wanted to introduce myself."

Rittenhouse offered a hand as manicured as any Cammie had ever seen. Fortunately, he eschewed clear nail polish—a fashion disaster on any man. "It's a pleasure to meet you. How did you recognize me?"

"I've seen your photograph. I just wanted to say, I think you're showing the best clothes of any designer in the show. In fact, it's not even close."

"I'm flattered," Rittenhouse said. "Very flattered, in fact."

"No need to be. I'm sure you must already know it. But it's not egotism if it's true," Cammie assured him.

The designer laughed. "I guess not. Will you be wearing any of my clothes?"

Cammie shook her head. "No. But a—a girl I know will."

Whoa. She'd almost said, "a friend of mine." That would have been overstating the case just a little bit.

"Pity. Well, perhaps someday you will."

"I hope so."

Cammie swallowed, and glanced across the backstage area. Champagne was fifty feet away, over by the clothes racks. Now was the time. She'd had a setback with Lizbette. No doubt about that, no need to call it anything other than what it was. Yet her father had told her many times—if you get turned down on a project, make another phone call right away. It's the only way for an agent to keep any dignity, because agents get turned down all the time.

Well, she was Champagne's agent now. And this was the equivalent of making a phone call.

"Mr. Rittenhouse, I was wondering . . . if you would consider a model I represent, to do some work for you, in the future."

Rittenhouse raised his eyebrows. "Who?"

Cammie pointed quickly toward Champagne. "Her."

Rittenhouse frowned. "She's beautiful. But so short."

Cammie was prepared for this. "She's five-foot seven. She'd be perfect if you ever decided to do a petite line. You could call it . . . Martinette! That would be—"

"No. No petite line," Rittenhouse declared, in a way that closed the subject. "I'm still trying to establish myself in couture." He looked at his watch. "If you'll excuse me, I need to meet some friends who are waiting for me. Have fun tonight, Cammie. Thank you for the kind words."

As Rittenhouse moved off, Cammie sagged a little inside. It had been the longest of long shots. She hadn't really expected Rittenhouse to say yes.

"Fifteen minutes, everyone! This is your fifteen-minute call!"

Virginia Vanderleer bustled around the fashion show's crowded backstage area in the museum gallery, making sure everyone knew how close they were to showtime. She'd given up on the ladies-who-lunch theme and donned a black taffeta Ralph Lauren skirt and gold brocade jacket.

The past three hours had been intensely hectic. So hectic, in fact, that Anna hadn't had much time to think about Caine, who she hadn't talked to at all since their encounter at the Firehouse.

She hadn't called him, he hadn't called her. Now he was standing in front of her, and they got through a quick hello before two of Mrs. Vanderleer's assistants

arrived. Caine had been hustled off to the guys' changing area for some quick last-minute work on one of his
outfits, while Anna was brought to the hair and makeup
arena.

There, she'd been done in the same radical sixties
look as at Raymond's salon, except that her stylist
here—a plump, frizzy-haired, exceptionally enthusiastic
older woman named Nicole—had actually drawn exaggerated lower lashes on the skin below her eyes, then
showed her a photo of a skinny sixties fashion icon
named Twiggy who had made the look popular. Close
to the mirror, the inked eyelashes looked appalling, but
from a distance of ten feet or so they gave her an
appealing, wide-eyed look.

From styling, a dresser helped her into her first
show outfit, by an up-and-coming Italian designer
with the unlikely name of Guglielmo DiGiacomo.
There were black leather pants, very wide at the
bottom—evidently called "elephant bells"—with black
velvet lace-up granny boots (although the nearly four-
inch heel on them definitely did not scream "granny")
and a very fitted red paisley jacket with a Nehru
collar.

Her second outfit would be by Martin Rittenhouse,
a very short black satin dress tucked under the bust.
Anna much preferred it to the DiGiacomo, though the
Italian designer was far better known.

"Ten minutes! Ten minutes, everybody!" Mrs. Vanderleer was now running around like the town crier.

Anna's stomach did a somersault. She was equal parts excited and nervous. On the heels of Mrs. Vanderleer's announcement, the backstage stress level rose another notch—people were hollering, shouting, and bitching at each other. Anna opted for a quick pit stop in the ladies' room. What could be worse than being caught on the runway with a desperate need to go?

Falling on her face. That could be worse.

Fortunately, the backstage area of the gallery had its own small restroom, so she hurried into one of the stalls and peeled out of her bellbottoms. When she was done, as she was washing her hands, she was surprised to see Champagne dart into the next stall. Anna could have sworn that Champagne was wearing the short black Rittenhouse dress that was supposed to be her own second outfit.

When Anna came out of the restroom, there was another surprise. Caine was just outside the door, wearing a black Lycra T-shirt under a Hugo Boss black jacket with a silk screen of a large skull on the back, and black jeans so tight that Anna wondered if they posed a threat to his reproductive future. So tight, it was difficult for her to keep her eyes on his face.

"How are you?" She winced inwardly because she sounded way too much like her mother—pleasant, cool, removed.

"Extremely uncomfortable, actually," he admitted. "The jeans are a killer."

"So . . . you didn't mention that you'd be here."

"I'm kind of a last-minute replacement. You think I should have called you." He gave her a half-smile.

"It would have been nice. But . . . I thought a lot about what you said the other night."

This wasn't easy. Certainly her mother would have pretended that nothing had happened, that she hadn't actually seen the guy with whom she was involved at a place called the Firehouse wearing jeans, suspenders, and nothing else.

"And?" Caine asked.

She looked at the wall clock. Five minutes to show-time. She couldn't draw this out. "I decided you were right. You had no responsibility to tell me about your part-time job. I don't own you." She shrugged. "I don't even know you that well," she admitted.

He gave her a very direct look. "Do you want to?"

"Really know you? I do," she replied.

Caine smiled. "Good. You understand that this is no reflection on our relationship."

"I do." The problem was hers, not Caine's.

"Well, great—"

"Showtime!" Cammie hurried over to them. Her first runway outfit was a bottle green minidress with green fishnet hose, and brilliant orange satin shoes with a green platform and heel. She looked Anna up and down. "I will only say this once. You look hot."

"I'll second that," Caine said, giving Anna a sexy half-smile. He turned and nodded at Cammie. "You too."

"Thanks, Tattoo Boy," Cammie purred. "I barely recognized you with your shirt on."

"How's Champagne doing?" Anna ventured.

"Depressed. Can you blame her?"

"Showtime! Showtime!" Mrs. Vanderleer was in shout mode again, waving her well-toned arms for all the models to line up—guys to one side, girls to the other.

"After the show?" Caine asked Anna, as Cammie moved off.

"I'd like that."

She took her place with the other girls near the extension of the catwalk that penetrated from the audience side of the gallery under the red curtain and into the backstage area. Mrs. Vanderleer had placed assistants on both sides to send the models out when they were called. To make things go more smoothly, two big-screen closed-circuit TV monitors had been erected so everyone could see what was happening on the other side of the curtain. Right now, they showed a thick crowd of people trying to find their seats. Anna felt herself hoping that her father was out there. She rather doubted he would be, though, since he'd been more stoned than Gibraltar when he'd mentioned going.

"Hi." Champagne stepped over to her. Anna saw she wasn't wearing the black satin dress at all. Instead, she had on aquamarine velvet knickers and a skinny ribbed poor-boy T-shirt under a short purple leather motorcycle-style jacket, with a newsboy cap perched at a rakish angle on her head. She looked absolutely stunning.

"Hey. How are you holding up?"

The younger girl managed a sad smile. "It doesn't pay to get excited about things. You just get your heart broken."

"I know you're disappointed," Anna commiserated. "But it's not the end. It's just one job."

"I really thought she liked me."

Cammie eased over to them. "She did like you, Champagne. She just made an incredibly stupid decision."

Champagne smiled sadly again. "Cammie's a lot madder than I am. It was a great opportunity. I should thank you too, Anna."

"You are very welcome." Once again, Anna thought how much she liked this plucky girl.

"Showtime! Showtime! Twenty seconds to showtime!" Mrs. Vanderleer crossed the line from overdrive to hyperdrive. Then her prerecorded voice came over the public address system. "Ladies and gentlemen, please welcome our mistress of ceremonies for tonight's very special fashion show, the star of the hit TV drama *Hermosa Beach*, Ms. Pegasus Patton!"

The audience applauded. The hostess for the evening would be the lead young actress from the hit TV series packaged by Cammie's father. Anna had met her, when she'd briefly worked as an intern for Clark. Pegasus, who played a lovely girl named Alexandra, was in reality a very unpleasant human being. But she was also one of the hottest young actresses in town. Sam had told Anna that Pegasus would be wearing a gown made by a Peruvian acquaintance of Eduardo's, a designer named Gisella Santa Maria. It was black, strapless, and richly embroidered—Anna thought it was gorgeous.

Evidently, Gisella had been unhappy at first that the only representation of her work would be on the MC. When she realized that Pegasus would be photographed in the gown, and that the photos would end up in *In Style*, and girls and women all across the country would be clamoring for Gisella Santa Maria couture, she'd happily agreed.

Pegasus started her preshow spiel. "Thank you so much! I'm so happy to be here this evening, to help raise money for the New Visions foundation, which helps at-risk kids. The children are our future! Do it for the children!"

Cammie sidled over to Anna and mock-stuck a finger down her throat as if to say, *Pegasus makes me gag.*

Anna bit back a laugh—Pegasus was far from her favorite person. "Probably she's just nervous," she whispered to Cammie.

Cammie rolled her eyes.

Pegasus prattled on. When she was finally done, the show began.

Early Beatles music blared through the sound system, to go with the sixties theme, and the show began, with Pegasus reading the name of the designer and a description of each outfit off small cards. The guys went first, so Anna took a moment to check out the crowd on the monitors. She saw the young district attorney who'd brought Cammie and her to New Visions in the front row—he was with a drop-dead gorgeous redhead wearing black Armani. There were a few semi-stars of stage, TV, and screen near the catwalk. Behind them was Sam, with Eduardo on one side of her and Parker on the other. And a row behind them, sat Dee, Jack . . . and Ben.

Anna felt a little bolt of electricity in her stomach. She hadn't invited Ben, hadn't known he'd be here. Yet—

"Ladies, get ready! Ladies, ready!"

Mrs. Vanderleer was backstage again and ushered them into place. Anna saw that Caine was now on the catwalk. When he reached the T, he took off his black jacket and slung it over one shoulder so the tattoos on his muscular arms showed. The camera panned the crowd; Anna could see Dee whisper something to Jack, while Ben's jaw was set in a hard line.

With the first pass of guys concluded, Pegasus announced the female models. Cammie burst through the red curtains like a sexy surprise package and did the model strut—one foot lifted high to come down directly in front of the other foot—as if she'd been doing it her entire life. At the end of the runway, she did a three-sixty turn, whipping her hair over one shoulder. Raymond's people had added some clip-in green hair extensions here and there, which oddly enough looked great against the strawberry blond curls. Parker put two fingers in his mouth and whistled; Sam and Dee were grinning. But the mine-doesn't-stink model look never left Cammie's face.

Daisy went out next, in a psychedelic blue, green, and red flower skirt, with a bright red baggy-sleeve top. Then Mai, wearing a sleeveless drop-waist pink-and-white polka-dotted dress, and a matching hat. Anna got ready and her heart thudded as Pegasus introduced her outfit. She had never had any desire at all to model. The idea of being stared at or examined felt oddly invasive; as if all the people looking at her could see not only her flesh, but her thoughts, too.

So it wasn't with a sense of fun that she heard the music switch to something by the Yardbirds, and she took her first steps onto the runway. She knew she wasn't supposed to actually look at the audience, but she couldn't help but glance down at Ben, Dee, and Jack. Dee applauded. Jack gave a big thumbs-up. Ben? He was absolutely inscrutable.

She kept her eyes dead ahead as she made her turn at the T and headed back upstage. And then, thank God, she was behind the curtain again. One down, one to go. She hustled over to the costume rack and looked for the black Martin Rittenhouse dress, but it wasn't there.

She looked again and then checked the other racks. Nothing. She checked out the other models to see if maybe someone had put it on by mistake. The last thing she did was look for Champagne, since she'd thought maybe she'd seen her wearing the Rittenhouse in the bathroom before the show started. Champagne had already been dressed in a hot pink vintage peasant blouse and elephant bell jeans, and said she had no idea where the dress was.

"Anna? Why haven't you changed?" Mrs. Vanderleer hurried over, her tone of voice akin to that of someone asking why Anna had just made a cat call at the president. "Where's your second outfit? Put it on. Put it on!"

"I can't find it!"

"Well, you have to find it. It's everyone's favorite in the entire show."

"I looked for it on my rack, and on the other clothing racks—"

Mrs. Vanderleer didn't wait for the rest of her answer. She grabbed two of the backstage assistants and told them they had exactly two minutes to produce the Rittenhouse dress. "Anna, get undressed so you'll be ready when we find it."

Anna scurried back to the changing area and handed the black leather pants and the jacket to yet another assistant, then pulled on the white silk blouse she'd worn to the fashion show so that she wasn't just standing around in her Jolie white silk lace bra and bikini panties. She looked up at the monitors. They had started the second shift of guy models and she was still standing there half-naked.

Two minutes turned into three, and three into five.

Mrs. Vanderleer hurried back to her. She thrust something at Anna. "This is the backup emergency outfit. Put it on."

Anna took a look at what she'd just been handed. It was two pieces. One was a dress of white chiffon, very short and totally see-through. The other was what looked like a matching wedding veil. "Um, excuse me, but . . . what goes under this?"

"You."

"I can't wear this with nothing underneath!"

"It's the alternate Rittenhouse outfit, that's all I can tell you. And you're supposed to be the grand finale of the show."

"Wait, wait! This goes under it." One of the assistants, a petite redhead, rushed over to them with a matching white lace corset.

Anna stared at the ensemble. "You're kidding."

"You can do it. I'm counting on you." Mrs. Vanderleer turned to the assistant, her hands practically in a begging gesture. "Help her. That's why you volunteered."

Don't think about it, Anna told herself. *For once, just do it.*

She pulled her silk shirt over her head, turned toward a clothing rack for at least a semblance of privacy, and poured herself into the corset, leaving on her own panties. Over the top went the gossamer dress, and then one of the assistants fastened the veil to Anna's hair, anchoring it with bobby pins. All the while, Mrs. Vanderleer was urging them on.

"Hurry, hurry! You're next!"

And then Anna was through the red curtain and on the catwalk. The audience gasped over the music—the Rolling Stones' "Satisfaction." Was it a good gasp or a bad gasp? She had no idea. But two things she did know. First, that her mother would rather eat glass than step onto a catwalk in what Anna was wearing at that moment. Second, that Caine regularly worked wearing a whole lot less than this, and he was probably watching her right now on the monitor.

Those two thoughts propelled Anna forward. She actually found herself strutting to Mick Jagger. A smile curled on her lips. "You go, Anna! Do it for Norman Shnorman!" Sam yelled through cupped hands.

The audience started clapping to the beat. Anna had no idea what possessed her to do what she did next, when he reached the T. She yanked off the veil and whipped it into the audience. It definitely wasn't a moment sanctioned by the *This Is How We Do Things* Big Book (East Coast WASP edition); the clapping and whistling that greeted her spontaneous act was that much sweeter because of it.

Shoplifters' Olympics

"**O**kay. We've got a little problem here. If I don't get some answers very quickly, it could turn into a big problem in about five minutes."

Assistant District Attorney Levitan stood together with Mrs. Vanderleer, Mrs. Chesterfield, and the designer Martin Rittenhouse in front of the five New Visions girls, Anna, and Cammie. They were all assembled on the edge of the catwalk backstage. The fashion show had ended with its gala curtain call about five minutes before; even now, the post-show din was nearly overwhelming—the shouts and cries of friends greeting each other punctuating a sixties dance mix.

Instead, once Mr. Levitan had been informed by Mrs. Vanderleer that the Rittenhouse dress destined for Anna had turned up missing, he'd conducted the world's quickest backstage investigation—one that now centered on the New Visions girls.

The Rittenhouse dress that had disappeared during the New Visions girls' visit to the Rittenhouse workshop had never been found. Now, the same designer had been victimized again. No way was the DA going to take this lightly. No way he should, Cammie thought. But the way he was focusing his investigation on the New Visions girls was pissing her off. She'd watched him and a few of the museum's security people do a perfunctory questioning of the male models, stylists, dressers, and other personnel who'd been backstage before or during the show. Then these people had been dismissed, and Levitan had zeroed in on who he obviously thought were his prime suspects.

Now the district attorney paced back in front of them like he might in front of a jury. Cammie and Anna sat in the middle, with Champagne to Cammie's left and everyone else to Cammie's right. She was directly atop the crack where two pieces of the prefab catwalk had been pushed together.

"You might wonder why everyone has been released and you're still here," Levitan declared. "It's because when you hear hoofbeats coming your way, you think horses, not zebras."

"What does that mean?" Daisy asked. Cammie could tell she really didn't understand.

"It means that you girls—not you, Anna or Cammie, but you other girls—have the most to gain by liberating a dress that doesn't belong to you. That's why you're here. And that's why I'd like whoever did this to speak up."

The group was silent. Cammie could feel the girls' embarrassment. She had a gut feeling that none of them was responsible, no matter what had happened at Rittenhouse's workshop.

"Excuse me, Andrew," Mrs. Vanderleer broke in. "I know these girls. I'd be very surprised if any of them took this dress. The only girl I don't really know all that well is Champagne."

"Fine. Let's focus on her. Did any of you see Champagne doing anything suspicious?" Levitan looked from person to person, until Mai raised her hand.

"Yes?"

Mai pointed right at Champagne. "Her. Before the show, I saw her try on the black dress."

Cammie saw Mrs. Vanderleer and Mrs. Chesterfield trade knowing looks. She felt like slapping them across their supercilious faces.

"Yes. I did try it on," Champagne admitted immediately. "Right before the show. It's a beautiful dress. But I did not take it! I just wanted to see what it looked like. I put it on and went to the bathroom. And then I put it right back on Anna's rack."

"Anyone else see Champagne here wearing Mr. Rittenhouse's dress?" Levitan queried.

Cammie saw Anna slowly raise her hand.

What?

"I did," Anna said. "About ten minutes before the show. But trying on a dress does *not* mean she stole it. And I think it's unfair to accuse someone with absolutely no proof. Sir," she added, scrupulously polite.

"I did not take that dress," Champagne repeated. It sounded to Cammie like she was ready to cry.

Mr. Rittenhouse stepped forward. "I hope you understand the seriousness of this. That dress is as much a work of art as the *Mona Lisa*. I toiled for days designing it. Just like that other dress that disappeared. How do I know you didn't take that one, too?"

Mrs. Chesterfield nodded and entwined her narrow fingers, staring pointedly at Champagne. "Oh, dear. This is very upsetting."

Go choke on your pearls, Cammie thought.

"Martin?" Mrs. Vanderleer gave him a cool look.

"Yes?"

"If you would kindly allow Mr. Levitan to investigate. Mr. Levitan?"

"Yes?"

"If you would kindly move this along. Either one of these girls has the dress or she doesn't. If one does, make the arrest and let the others join what is a wonderful party on the other side of the curtain. If none of them has it, look elsewhere and let the rest of us go have a cocktail."

Levitan's response was to keep up his questions, despite the fact that he was getting no useful information from anyone. Then he put Champagne under an intense cross-examination. Champagne got more and more flustered, and finally Cammie could take no more. She jumped to her feet so quickly she pushed apart the two halves of the catwalk, so there were a few inches of bare space between them.

"Mr. Levitan, give it a rest. You're railroading my client!"

Levitan gave Cammie a scathing glance. "Your client? What are you talking about? This isn't one of your father's shows, and you're not some hotshot defense lawyer."

Cammie felt the bile rise in her throat. "I still represent her."

"For what, may I ask? Shoplifters' Olympics?"

"*Modeling.* I'm Champagne's modeling agent."

"Sit down, Miss Sheppard."

"I don't want to sit down." Cammie was so pissed at that moment that she was ready to go to jail for Champagne if she had to.

"Miss Sheppard? Take three deep breaths. Then *sit down.*"

Cammie saw Anna motion with her hand: *Sit. Don't be stupid.*

Fine. She wouldn't be stupid. She turned around and started back to the catwalk, mostly because she was afraid of what she might say to Levitan. As she did, she saw Rittenhouse flash her a patronizing look. What a jerk. With that ridiculous overstuffed man-bag . . .

Hold on.

She stopped in her tracks and zeroed in on the man-bag. When she'd seen him with it before the show, the bag had been as thin and neat as an empty envelope. Now it was actually bulging. And no metrosexual worth his styling pomade would ever overstuff a slim leather bag unless . . . Could it possibly be . . . ?

"Mr. Levitan?" she asked sweetly.

The DA blew an exasperated breath between his lips. "*Yes?* I asked you to sit down."

"I'm going to. Right now." Cammie returned to her place on the catwalk. Then she looked at the DA again. "Could you ask Mr. Rittenhouse to please open his bag. Please?"

"Whatever for?" Levitan demanded.

Cammie fixed her eyes on the designer. She saw fear in them.

"Because I think that's where you'll find the missing dress."

"That's the stupidest thing I've ever heard!" Rittten-house blustered. "I didn't steal my own dress!"

Levitan frowned. "Mr. Rittenhouse is one of our designers. I think it's highly unlikely that—"

Cammie got some help from an unexpected source. "I don't see you making any other progress, Andrew," Mrs. Vanderleer proclaimed. "And if Martin has nothing to hide, he has nothing to worry about." The event organizer marched over to Rittenhouse. "Your satchel, Martin. Open it."

"Don't humiliate me like this, please," he begged.

"Now." Her voice was steel.

Rittenhouse handed over the bag. Mrs. Vanderleer opened it. Inside, somewhat crumpled but still easily identified, was the missing black dress. "I can explain! I can explain!" he pleaded.

Cammie looked at him with murder in her eye.

"Explain what? You son of a bitch. You loser son of a bitch."

Levitan pointed at Rittenhouse. "You. You stay." Then he pointed at Cammie. "You, stay too. All the rest of you?" His eyes swept over the New Visions girls. "You did a wonderful job tonight. You have a lot to be proud of. Champagne, I owe you one. Now go have fun. Mrs. Vanderleer, you should go join your own party, too. I know how to deal with scum like this guy."

Mrs. Vanderleer shook her head. "I want to hear Martin's explanation. If he has one. And I want him to apologize to Champagne. Champagne, please stay."

Cammie watched as Anna and the New Visions girls stepped away. Now, only she and Champagne remained.

"I can explain!" Martin exclaimed, once most everyone was gone.

"You said that before," Mrs. Vanderleer recalled. "So here's your chance. Make it convincing."

For a moment, it seemed to Cammie like he was going to spin out some big excuse-filled yarn. Instead, the designer just seemed to crumple.

"Publicity," he muttered, so softly that Cammie could barely hear.

"Publicity? Publicity!" Levitan thundered.

"Yeah. I thought I would get it when the dress disappeared at my workshop. When that didn't happen, I thought if there was *another* robbery here, it'd be all over the *Times* in the morning."

Cammie seethed. What an asshole. What was he

going to do, wait until they broke down the catwalk and then retrieve his gear and the dress? And still blame it on Champagne? What a lot of nerve. Champagne could have been arrested, but he obviously didn't give a shit.

"You could have ruined one of these girls' lives," Cammie said through gritted teeth.

"But I wasn't going to try to press charges!" he insisted, sputtering. "I was . . ."

Cammie didn't need to hear the rest of it. "Going to use your 'generosity' in not pressing charges to milk even *more* publicity out of this situation? Make yourself look like a real hero?" she finished for him.

Rittenhouse looked down, silent.

"Mr. Levitan? You could arrest this bottom feeder."

"I could."

"But I've got another idea," Cammie went on. She did have another idea. An incredibly great idea, of which both her father and mother would have been proud.

She looked directly at Rittenhouse. "Tell me right now that you'll use Champagne here as a model in all the showings that you'll be doing over the next two years. Tell me right here, right now, in front of everyone."

"I can't do that! She's too short!" Rittenhouse exclaimed.

"Of course you can," Cammie cajoled. "Because you're also going to be featuring a new petite line called

Martinette. If you do, I'm going to recommend to the district attorney and to Champagne that we forget this sordid little incident. To Mrs. Vanderleer, too. And don't worry, they'll listen to me. As you're witnessing now, I can be very persuasive."

Martin didn't hesitate. "Done."

"I'll hold you to it, too, Martin. Or you'll never show clothes in this town again," Mrs. Vanderleer told him. "Now, an apology to Champagne."

The designer apologized to Champagne. Champagne accepted the apology. Then she hugged Cammie in a way that Cammie remembered once hugging her own mother. It felt sincere. And real. It felt absolutely great.

As Mrs. Vanderleer put her arm around Champagne to lead her to the party, the district attorney asked Cammie to stick around for a minute.

"I need to thank you," he told her.

She smiled sweetly. No need to rub it in. "Truth, justice, and the American way. Just don't jump to conclusions again."

"This'll help remind me not to," Levitan admitted. "I'm just lucky you were around to figure it out. Maybe you've got a future in law enforcement."

Cammie guffawed. "I don't think so. I don't do blue uniforms. Not my color."

The DA offered her his hand. She shook it and smiled sweetly again. It never hurt to have a district attorney on your side. Never, ever.

Double Dating

Cammie took in the reflection of her mother's pale pink blouse and skirt in the backstage mirror before heading out to join the after party. She ran her fingers over the smooth, silky material and tried to remember. The feel of her mother's well-manicured hands, her mom stroking her hair, reading her *Where the Wild Things Are, Winnie the Pooh, Charlotte's Web*, until she fell asleep. The same mom who managed to hide a depression so severe that she finally couldn't continue her way in the world.

Did anyone ever know anyone, really? Or was it that everyone had two sides, different faces seen by different people at different times?

Through the red velvet curtain, she heard the Supremes wailing, "Stop in the Name of Love," and a DJ urging everyone to dance. She knew what was happening on the other side. People were eating. Drinking. Dancing. Flirting. Getting their tax-deductible money's worth. Neither her father nor her self-involved step-mother had shown any interest in attending, but her friends were out there. Her new client, Champagne. And Ben.

She'd left him an oh-so-casual message, reminding him about the fashion show. Had he come for Anna, or because of the invitation she'd offered? What would Adam think when he heard that Ben was here? Or about their almost-encounter at Trieste?

Cammie knew just what she had to do.

She left the fashion show backstage area, but went in the other direction instead of joining the party, into an empty adjoining gallery that held half a dozen enormous abstract expressionist canvases by Clyfford Still. She took out her cell and pressed speed dial. He answered on the third ring.

"Hello?"

"I'm wearing my mother's clothes."

"I've been thinking about you. What did you say about your mother?"

"Never mind. So, I haven't heard from you in a while."

"I know. I miss you like crazy."

Adam sounded different somehow.

"That's so sweet. Are you coming home this weekend? That was your plan, right? Before all that silly nonsense you told me, about loving the Midwest and thinking about the University of Michigan, and all that."

"I'm not sure when I'm coming home, exactly. I really still need to figure some things out."

"Maybe I can help you with that." She shook out her Raymondized curls and moved the silver Razr closer to her lips. "It's Wednesday night. If you're not home by Sunday at midnight—Los Angeles time, that gives you a few extra hours—we're over. Four days, Adam. Four days."

She waited while an elderly security guard in a gray uniform padded across the empty gallery, his footfalls echoing against the walls. All the while, Adam was silent. Then, he managed a single, strangled word.

"*What?*"

"Over and done and it's been fun."

"You can't possibly mean that. Because I need some time to think . . . you'd *break up with me?*"

Cammie shrugged, even though she knew he couldn't see it. "I guess I needed less time to think than you did."

"That's not love, Cam. Please. Try to look at it from my point of view. I love this place, Cammie. The way you love L.A."

She could feel herself soften, feel something turning inside her heart. No. She was as much her father as she was her mother. Yes, there was a time for kindness. But also, yes, there was a time to be an asshole.

"Adam, I am telling you this sincerely. Come back. I'm here and I miss you. I want you. But if being in Michigan is more important to you than being with me, then . . . oh well. So I hope to see you soon. I'll be waiting for you. Don't call me. Just make it happen. Sunday night. Midnight. 'Bye."

She snapped her phone shut before she could lose her nerve.

* * *

"I love the gown Pegasus wore." The district attorney's aggressively thin wife, with aggressively implanted breasts and a too-long nose, was gushing to Gisella. "Could I get your card?"

Sam was happy for Gisella's success. She seemed like a lovely woman, and there was no question about her talent quotient. But success wasn't really what was on her radar as she stood with the Peruvian designer and Eduardo. Gisella wore a red-and-black embroidered gown of her own design, with a black off-the-shoulder sweater and long, dangling red earrings. The dress left no doubt: Gisella had the most spectacular behind in Southern California. Sam compared it to her own, in True Religion dark wash jeans and a pink Sweet Pea mesh T-shirt that crisscrossed under the bust. Gisella's butt was by Michelangelo. Hers was by Land Rover.

Gisella had a better body. Gisella was artistically talented. Gisella spoke Eduardo's language. Worse than that, after the DA's wife moved off, Gisella kept finding reasons to touch Eduardo during conversation that flitted from Spanish to English and back again.

Gisella and Eduardo were *still* yammering in Spanish. Sam looked around. There was Parker, over by the bar. He motioned to her.

She excused herself. The DJ was playing the Beatles' "Here, There and Everywhere." She met Parker in the middle of the small, crowded parquet dance floor that had replaced the runway and gave him a warm hug.

"I owe you another one, Sam," he murmured, and mussed her hair up in back.

She had to admit it felt great to be in his arms, knowing that he had to be the best-looking guy at the party. He wore dark black pressed trousers and a white button-down cotton shirt with the sleeves rolled up—nothing special, but she felt the stares of other girls, and even of other guys. It happened no matter where Parker went.

"You owe me nothing." She beamed at him.

"I do. For what you decided to do with those pics of me and Poppy."

"And then the gods of Hollywood intervened on my side."

"I guess they did. Your dad kicked her out, huh?"

"He did. And the funny thing is, I'm glad she left the baby behind."

Parker wrinkled his forehead. "You hate that baby!"

"Past tense. Hated. Not anymore. One day, Ruby Hummingbird is going to look at me as her savior. Of course, she and I are going to have to do something about that ridiculous name. What do you think of the name Summer?"

"If you're suggesting it, I like it."

Sam laughed. "Smart, Parker. Very smart."

The song ended; he thanked her again for giving a power boost to his budding career and for telling the PI to destroy the damning photographs. Then he went off to flirt with Daisy, whose eyes got huge when she saw him approach.

"Hey." Sam felt a tap on her shoulder and turned around. The night improved drastically in that split second. It got better when Eduardo kissed her cheek. "I am going to take you back to my place and then buy you breakfast in the morning."

Sam got shivers down her spine. Then she shook her head ruefully. Her competition was zeroing in on them like some kind of perfect-butted humanoid cruise missile. "Oh Eduardo, you must come to lunch with me this week!"

Sam was thrilled to feel Eduardo slip a proprietary arm around her shoulder. "My schedule is very busy this week. But if Sam and I are free, perhaps we could join you. And now . . . Sam, wasn't there something else we were going to do tonight? The *thing*?"

Sam nearly laughed aloud. Eduardo had just cracked an inside joke from one of the funniest old movies in history, *Annie Hall*.

"Oh yes, the thing."

"Yes, the thing." He winked.

"How could I have forgotten the thing?"

They said good night to a thoroughly baffled Gisella and soon were outside the museum in the cool night air, walking to the parking structure. The air smelled like orange blossoms.

"It's gorgeous."

"You're gorgeous," Eduardo corrected.

Sam forgot about Gisella. This was what happiness was.

* * *

"You looked so hot in that bridal thingie!" Dee gushed to Anna, waving around a glassful of iced tea. "Was it fun to be up there knowing everyone wanted to ravish you?"

Anna blushed the same color as the pale pink wraparound silk shirt she was wearing with her favorite faded jeans. "Gee, I didn't exactly think of it like that. But it's certainly good to know. Where's Jack?"

As Dee waved vaguely toward the rear of the gallery, her green Stella McCartney slip dress pulled tight against her petite, curvy body.

"Back there, with Parker. I think."

"Let's . . ." Anna's voice trailed off as she spotted Caine across the room, chatting with Bryson and Champagne. "Will you excuse me for a while?"

Dee smiled knowingly as she followed Anna's eyes with her own. "Which guy?"

"'Bye, Dee. Have fun tonight."

Anna excused herself again and edged through the crowd to Caine, Champagne, and Bryson. The guys were each in city fire department T-shirts and jeans, while Champagne wore the Bebe outfit that Cammie and Anna had bought for her at the Beverly Center.

"Hey," Caine greeted her enthusiastically. "That was kind of fun, huh?"

"Yeah, actually it was," she agreed.

"So what's this I hear about your friend Cammie turning my cousin into a model?" Bryson asked. The beer he was holding was nearly empty; he gave it to a passing waiter.

"She did it. She's my hero!" Champagne exclaimed.

Anna didn't get it. The last she'd heard, Lizbette had turned her down.

"You haven't heard," Champagne realized aloud.

"Heard what?"

"That I'm going to be Martin Rittenhouse's feature model for his new petite line called Martinette!"

"Cammie arranged this?" Anna was stupefied. Since when?

"Ask her yourself."

"I will. But I'm not surprised. Cammie Sheppard always gets what Cammie Sheppard wants."

Champagne was practically vibrating with joy. "I'm learning that. But I wanted to thank you as well. Two weeks ago, you'd never heard of me, and you went out of your way to try to help me. You're an amazing person, Anna."

"I'll second that," Caine agreed, and looked at her expectantly.

"You're so welcome, Champagne. And good luck. I really do think you're going to have an amazing career. And no one deserves it more than you." Now Anna turned to Caine. "Could you meet me in the Warhol gallery in about ten minutes? I'd really like to talk to you. Just go through that door at the far end of this room, and you can't miss it."

Caine nodded. "Definitely."

"Great." She couldn't help smiling, though her stomach was doing flip-flops as she anticipated the conversation. "See you then and there. Excuse me."

She circulated through the crowd for a minute or two, looking for . . . and there he was. Not far from the DJ booth, Ben was chatting with an actress from a CW teen drama who'd recently departed from the show in a bus plunge. He excused himself from the actress and crossed the crowded gallery toward her. He wore black jeans, a Trieste T-shirt, and a well-cut black Italian sport coat. Not very sixties, but very hot.

"Sorry to interrupt," she told him. "Can you do me a favor?"

"Sure, Anna." As always, her name in his voice made her knees weak.

"I just wondered if you could meet me in the Andy Warhol room. In about five minutes?"

She found him there when she arrived, staring at a huge triptych of Marilyn Monroe.

"Andy Warhol made a fortune." Ben hitched a thumb toward the painting. "Do you get that? Because it's lost on me."

"It's lost on me, too. John Singer Sargent is more my speed," she admitted, sneaking a glance at the door. Where was Caine? "So, how're things at Trieste?"

"The Monday night thing is great. You really need to come check it out. I love it. I feel like it's mine, you know? I'm in charge. And that feels good." He smiled warmly at her. "Did you hear Sam shout when you were on the runway? You were hot up there. No. Post-hot."

"Anna?"

She turned—Caine had stepped into the room. The frown he sported had to be inspired by the third person in the room. "Why do I feel like I just walked into a really, really bad play?"

"You two know each other. You met at the movies. At the ArcLight," she reminded them. Where had she ever gotten such an idiotic idea as to bring these two together?

"I remember," Ben responded coolly.

Caine assessed her as coolly. "What's up?"

Anna took a deep breath. She would not, would not lose her nerve. "Thank you both for coming."

No! What kind of thing was that to say? Where did she think she was, at a cotillion? She started again.

"I hope you both will hear me out. Ben, we met on a plane and things got intense between us very fast. Too fast, maybe. I . . . I wanted too much, expected too much, and that wasn't fair, to either one of us. Caine, Ben and I were having problems. You and I met and liked each other. And somehow I went from there to . . . to some kind of feeling that we were in a relationship. But as you pointed out to me, we aren't."

Caine nodded and waited for her to continue.

"I think because Ben and I got involved so fast, I sort of expected the same thing to happen with us. But I was wrong. I'm not sure it's even what I want."

She opened her burnished chestnut leather Coach

shoulder bag and took out a folded sheet of paper. As the guys looked on in confusion she unfolded it and read aloud. "'Date. Noun. A social appointment or occasion, arranged beforehand with another person.'"

Ben scratched his chin. "You want to . . . *date*?"

"Yes."

"Both of us," Caine declared, as if guessing Anna's intent.

"Both of you. I know you think that dating is kind of an antiquated notion, Caine. So you might not be interested. But I don't think I'm ready to tie myself down to anyone. So I want to date both of you. If you would each like to date me. If not, I can accept that."

"We *share* you?" Ben's tone was withering.

"Oh no, not at all. There won't be any . . . you know."

Caine actually laughed. "How does that work?"

Good question. She had no idea. "I've never been in this situation before."

Caine nodded slowly. "So you're saying . . . you're free to do what you want. And we're free to do what we want?"

"That's it," Anna said. "No more of me feeling like I have a right to know what either of you are doing when you're not with me. No more rushing to make something into the kind of relationship that takes time to build. So, that's my proposal."

"Well, hell, I'm in," Caine replied easily. "We'll just take it slow and see where it goes. I don't know about Romeo over here." He glanced at Ben, kissed Anna on the cheek very close to her lips, said he'd be in touch, and walked out.

"I fucking hate that guy," Ben said staring after him.

Anna resisted the impulse to respond.

"What, you really expect me to say yes to that? Dating? After what we've been to each other, you think that'll work?" He seemed incredulous.

"It would be so easy for me to fall right back into your arms. Maybe I'm crazy not do to do it. But if we get back to that place again, I want it to be because we both thought about it and took it slowly, and didn't lose ourselves along the way." He hated Caine? She hated the way he was looking at her. "I wouldn't blame you if you told me to go to hell."

He leaned over and gave her the softest, sweetest kiss in the world. It felt like . . . coming home. But she wasn't going to be lured into that place where she gave away her heart so quickly. This time, for a while at least, her heart would belong to her.

"We'll play it your way," he whispered in her ear. "Because I can't lose you."

Anna returned to the party in hopes of finding Mrs. Vanderleer, to thank her. The show had raised six figures in one night for an important cause. Lots of people were dancing, but since Caine and Ben had both left, she decided to get a drink and watch. When she got to the bar, there was Mr. Levitan. When he saw her, he grinned wildly. "Anna Percy. The poster girl for community service."

"I wouldn't go that far," she told him.

"Why not? You helped put on a great event, and your friend Cammie solved the crime of the century. Or at least the night." He turned to the bartender. "Two olives in those martinis, please."

"I'm glad everything turned out okay."

"Me too." The DA dropped his voice. "And by the way, you can tell Mr. Sheppard that we've got a watch on Gibson Wills. Word on the PCH is he has a bit of a taste for driving under the influence."

The shaven-headed bartender pushed the martinis across the bar to the DA, who thanked him and dropped a fiver into the tip basket. "So have a good time tonight, Anna. And thanks again."

The DA took his drinks and drifted into the crowd. Anna had just ordered herself a Flirtini when she felt a tap on her shoulder.

"Just the girl I was looking for." Cammie smiled. She was holding some sort of green concoction. "Having fun?"

"Yeah. You?"

"Absolutely."

"What you did for Champagne. Twice. That's amazing."

Cammie nodded sagely. "I have only begun."

"That's great."

The bartender gave Anna her drink.

"To my news!" Cammie raised her glass.

"Absolutely. I'll definitely drink to Champagne," Anna agreed.

"Who's talking about Champagne? I have other news. I called Adam tonight in Michigan. I told him if his ass isn't back to Los Angeles in exactly four days, I'm breaking up with him. I mean, enough is enough of this back-to-nature shit."

"Why would you do that?" Anna was shocked. "Adam adores you. And you adore him. At least I thought you did."

"Well, we'll see if he adores me enough, won't we?"

What could Anna say? Adam was one of the greatest guys on the planet. She would never understand Cammie.

"One other thing," she added. "If I do break up with Adam, I'm going after Ben. I thought it was only fair for you to know."

Anna's mouth fell open. "You're . . . but . . . "

Cammie smiled. "You're stuttering."

Anna took a deep breath. She was surprised. No, shocked. "He's not a prize, Cammie."

Cammie's eyes went to half-mast. "Wanna bet? You want to jack Ben Birnbaum around, more power to you. Because you will jack him right back into my arms. Well, lovely chatting and all that shit. It's been an interesting two weeks. I don't know about you, but I'm kinda glad I got arrested."

She headed off into the crowd. Anna felt her heartbeat quicken.

God, Ben and Cammie, that would hurt. She had to acknowledge that. But if that was what he wanted, then . . . that was what he wanted. Six months ago, if someone had told her that she'd be in this situation, she would have thrown herself into Ben's arms rather than risk losing him. Not anymore. Love was something that happened slowly, because you gave it time to grow. It couldn't come from fear or even from seduction. It came because you felt whole enough and strong enough all on your own to let another person in. It sounded cheesy. It was an utter cliché. But it was also true.

Bryson bellied up to the bar and ordered a Heineken. "Having fun?"

"Actually, yes." She had no romantic interest in Bryson—juggling two guys was all she could handle, nor was she the kind of girl to flirt simply for the sake of flirting. But she was on the road to being fine all on her own, which meant she could have guy friends and embark once again on the solo adventure she had intended when she came to California.

"So, Bryson," she ventured with a smile. "Tell me about yourself."

He did and she listened.

When Anna left the party all by herself a half-hour later, she inhaled the orange-blossom-scented, balmy night air and gazed up at the starry night. She didn't know what would happen with Ben and Caine. Nothing about her situation was sure or safe or easy.

But instead of thinking it to death, she whirled around like a little kid, all feeling, all possibility, on the edge of whatever would come next.

THE FIRST ADULT NOVEL BY ZOEY DEAN,
AUTHOR OF THE BESTSELLING **A-LIST** SERIES

When recent Yale grad Megan Smith is fired from her assistant job at the trashy tabloid *Scoop*, she takes a position that's a little more suited to her skill-set: tutoring seventeen-year-old identical twins Rose and Sage Baker of Palm Beach, Florida—yes *the* infamous Baker heiresses. Unfortunately for Megan, the Baker twins aren't about to bend their social schedules to learn basic algebra. And they certainly aren't going to sit down for a study session with Megan, who associates the words "Seven" with *math* and "Diesel" with *fuel*. Megan quickly discovers that if she's going to get the $75,000 bonus she's been promised if—and *only* if—the girls are admitted to Duke University, she'll have to know her Pucci from her Prada to get in good with her very special students. And if she can look the part, maybe—just maybe—she can teach them something along the way.

How to Teach Filthy Rich Girls
Coming in paperback August 2007
www.howtoteachfilthyrichgirls.com

WARNER BOOKS